EBURY PRESS

STRICTLY AT WORK

Sudha Nair became India's first-ever winner of the Amazon KDP Pen to Publish contest in 2017 with her debut novel, *The Wedding Tamasha*. This novel, about love, family, values and traditions, was the culmination of a lifelong dream of hers to connect with people through the power of the written word. Since then, Sudha has written eleven bestselling books and was even a judge for the 2019 KDP Pen to Publish contest.

Having lived in India and the US, this former techie, wife and mother of two now calls Bangalore her home. Her passion is to create an immersive experience for her readers, with the relatable characters in her stories, and hopefully inspire the next generation of writers.

Sudha can be found at:

WEBSITE: sudhanair.com
EMAIL: sudha@sudhanair.com
FACEBOOK: facebook.com/SudhaNairAuthor
INSTAGRAM: instagram.com/sudhagn

STRICTLY AT WORK

SUDHA NAIR

EBURY
PRESS

An imprint of Penguin Random House

EBURY PRESS

USA | Canada | UK | Ireland | Australia
New Zealand | India | South Africa | China

Ebury Press is part of the Penguin Random House group of companies
whose addresses can be found at global.penguinrandomhouse.com

Published by Penguin Random House India Pvt. Ltd
4th Floor, Capital Tower 1, MG Road,
Gurugram 122 002, Haryana, India

Penguin
Random House
India

First published in Ebury Press by Penguin Random House India 2021

ISBN 9780143452546

Typeset in Adobe Caslon Pro by Manipal Technologies Limited, Manipal
Printed at Replika Press Pvt. Ltd, India

www.penguin.co.in

To those seeking the courage to be with their person and to all the missed connections

ONE

Anything that could go wrong would go wrong.

Anyone who'd heard of Murphy's Law could tell that Simi's morning was a perfect example of anything that could go wrong would go wrong. Her toast got burnt, five cabs cancelled on her until she found one to take her to work, and as soon as she got out of the door to get into the cab, it began to drizzle.

Simi worked at Murano, a furniture manufacturing company. It had decided to move its marketing team to a new co-working space in Whitefield due to space constraints in its current office. Simi was so excited for her first day at the new office that she'd decided to be there earlier than usual.

She tut-tutted as the rain fell harder. Why did it rain at the most inconvenient times in Bangalore? She'd forgotten her umbrella at home as usual. As her cab stopped right outside the gates of a large building, she hesitated to step out, wondering if she could make a dash to the entrance without getting drenched.

'Madam, destination has arrived,' the cabbie announced, irritated that she hadn't even opened the door yet. Obviously, she was making him late for his next ride. She remained seated and watched the downpour through the foggy window, the excitement of her first day slowly slipping away. 'Madam,' the cabbie repeated, impatiently.

With a groan, she opened the door and stepped out. The entrance to the building was less than a metre away. She looked to her left and right and made a dash for it.

Only, she hadn't seen the muddy patch on the road right in front of the magnificent steel and glass building with a huge sign that read BizWorks.

Her sandal landed in the patch of slime and squelched. She looked down in horror. It was stuck in thick gooey muck.

Yuck!

The rain showed no signs of letting up. Water dripped off the bag she held over her head like an umbrella as she looked around for help, but there was no one.

What a disastrous start!

With some difficulty, she managed to pull her sandal free and hobbled to the entrance quickly, her hair and churidar wet by the time she made it inside.

She pushed the giant, squeaky-clean glass door, and it swung open. She stepped in and stopped in her tracks as she took in the swanky office space—a bright reception area to the left and turnstiles just beyond.

The receptionist sat behind a huge marble desk. Walking up to her, Simi said, 'Hi, I work for Murano. We're moving in here today.'

The receptionist smiled at her. 'Hi. Sure. I'll get you an ID.'

Soon, she was scanning her new ID at the turnstile. The elevators beyond it would take her to the first floor, where Murano had one corner to the right of the elevator lobby.

But first, she found a bathroom and used paper towels to dry her hair and clean up her shoe. Just getting the ID card and cleaning up took up half an hour.

But, at least she was here.

She headed over to the section marked out for Murano.

This place was nothing like her old stuffy office. It was a posh space with polished wooden floors, plush couches, conference rooms, rows of gleaming desks and chairs, a large coffee area, the works.

She blew out a soft whistle, her head spinning with delight, as she pulled out her phone and dialled her colleague, Deepa. 'Where are you, girl? This place is fricking amazing!'

Deepa lived even further away from Whitefield, and she sounded pissed. 'I'm going to get out of the cab and manage the traffic myself,' she said, growling into the phone. 'How did you get there so early?'

The place was empty, except for a man standing in the coffee area to the right, huddled over his phone, sipping a hot drink.

'I don't know,' she whispered to Deepa, not wanting the man to hear her, now that she realized the place was not all empty. 'The cabbie seemed to know a shortcut.'

Deepa puffed out a breath at the other end. 'Now you get to see the office before I do!'

'I'll look for good desks,' Simi promised, hanging up on Deepa before she could go on a tirade of complaints.

Simi found two perfect desks facing a large window for her and Deepa, and sat down at one of them.

She hadn't been able to finish the important presentation for this morning. Instead of working on it last night, she'd pushed aside work to indulge in one of her guilty pleasures—watching *DDLJ*. Her brother, Ayush, and she loved watching it over and over again— he was a huge SRK fan, and she loved the way it ended. She could never tire of watching the film—the epitome of love stories to her. Anyhow, she might have finished the presentation if she hadn't got late, on top of everything else this morning.

Panicking about the presentation, she opened up her bag, pulled out her laptop and set it on the table. She blinked at the unlit screen for a few seconds, wondering what had happened to her laptop before realization hit. It was out of charge. She'd forgotten to plug it in again! When would she stop being so forgetful?

Rummaging in her bag, she pulled out her charger and plugged it into her laptop. A minute later, she frowned.

Her laptop refused to wake up. The charger wasn't working! *Hell!* How did that happen, today of all days?

She redialled Deepa.

'What?'

'Do you have your charger with you?'

Simi heard a rustle as Deepa looked in her bag. 'I do.'

'My charger is not working! When will you get here?'

'Another hour at least.'

Oh no! Simi groaned, slapping her forehead. 'Murphy's Law . . . ' she muttered to herself.

Getting up from her seat, she went searching for help.

* * *

Ranvir groaned. *'This is what happens when you don't check your emails right before you go to bed and first thing in the morning,'* he berated himself.

At least twenty new emails had showed up in his inbox in the last eight hours.

Goddammit!

Ever since he had started his new job at Fintura six months ago as a financial analyst, his mornings and nights had merged into one, to the point that he'd decided to switch off his phone after 10 p.m. and only check it after he reached work.

Fintura was a promising fintech start-up that was building a new app to connect small traders to large banks for loans. He had to crunch numbers, check out the market, and demand and prepare for the soon-to-be-launched app, which had almost doubled his work.

Previously he'd worked at Dorlays Bank where his days were structured, his routines set, and his life not so busy. But still, he enjoyed this job more than the previous one.

Here, his involvement was crucial to the company, his role vital in setting up the app requirements, detailing its financial features, and enabling ease of use and simplicity for their clients. It was the kind of job that challenged him and gave him an immense feeling of satisfaction and recognition.

As he reached for his cup of hot espresso, he opened his emails and started tackling them one by one.

This was the most peaceful time in the morning when he was the only one in the co-working space. The place would be teeming with people a little later, so he always made it a point to arrive early to get work done.

He was peering into his phone screen at the latest spec requirement when a tap on his shoulder made him look up.

'Excuse me!' A woman resembling a drenched mouse, her hair plastered to her ears, her churidar clinging to her legs, smiled at him.

He swivelled his chair, straightened his spine and turned to face her. 'Yes?'

'I . . . I was wondering if you have a working laptop charger?'

He blinked.

What sort of question was that? Did people carry non-working chargers? A smile tugged at his lips. He fought the urge to pull her leg, to tease her. But something about the innocent question and the hopeful look in her eyes made him decide against it.

After all, he didn't know her.

He settled for 'Yes.'

Her hazel brown eyes brightened with hope. 'It's my first day and no one's here yet. Can I borrow it for an hour, if you're not using it now? Please?'

'Sure. Yes.' He pulled out his charger from his bag, and she reached forward to take it, but her elbow struck his cup, knocking over his coffee and splashing the black, hot liquid all over the counter.

'Oh!' she cried, jumping backwards to avoid getting any coffee on herself, just as the heel of her sandal caught against the edge of the desk, and she lost her balance.

It all happened so quickly. Her arms flailed as she fell backwards. He jumped up from his chair to grab her. The next thing he knew, she was in his arms, pressed against his chest, her arms around him, her eyes squeezed shut.

He stood dazed for a few moments, feeling the thud of her heart against his chest. Slowly gathering his bearings, he drew his hands off her waist. 'You okay?'

She let go of him, her cheeks flushed, her gaze lowered. 'I don't know how that happened.'

The coffee dripped to the floor. He shrugged. 'It's okay.'

She looked troubled. 'I've caused such a mess.'

He felt that smile tug at his lips again as he handed her the charger. 'Nothing a few paper towels can't fix.'

She looked relieved as she took the charger. She motioned towards her office. 'I hope it's fine if I give it back later? Will you be here all day?' Her eyebrows were furrowed like question marks.

He caught himself staring at them and looked away. 'No problem, I have a spare one at my desk. I'm here around the same time most mornings.'

'Thanks, and sorry I spilt your coffee. I'm Simi, by the way.' She smiled for the first time, her whole face lighting up.

His gaze snagged on the small dimple that appeared on her cheek, and he swallowed the odd sensation in his throat. 'No problem. I drink a lot of coffee.' He extended his hand. 'Ranvir.'

She shook it. 'Thanks, Ranvir.' Still smiling, she turned around and headed to the office across his, disappearing into the labyrinth of desks and cubicles.

After a moment, Ranvir turned around and let out a whoosh.

I drink a lot of coffee?

What in the world had made him say a weird thing like that!

TWO

Simi walked back to her desk, the charger clutched tightly in her hand and the image of her saviour swimming vividly in front of her eyes.

His playful, teasing gaze danced in front of her eyes; the faint whiff of his cologne lingered on her; his deep, throaty voice rumbled in her thoughts. It was a wonder she hadn't swooned in his arms.

She squeezed her eyes shut and let out a deep breath, trying to bring her focus back to her ruined morning.

It was just a charger, and he was just a stranger who'd helped her in her time of need.

And she'd proven how clumsy she was on her very first meet. Typical Simi-style!

A glass or cup filled with anything was a disaster where she was concerned. She should have been careful.

'More careful!' she reminded herself

She plugged the charger into the socket, pushed aside her truant thoughts, and got to work.

She'd made some headway through her presentation when her arch-enemy, Champak, made his grand entry—the strap of his satchel bag taut across his chest, his round glasses slipping off his nose, his sharp, hawk eyes darting around to take in everything.

Champak, the all-knowing, overachieving, obsequious, boss's chamcha, was taken aback by the sight of Simi at work.

'You're here already!' he exclaimed. He made a dash to claim the seat opposite Simi, to her inward groan.

'Why do you have to sit here?' Simi frowned. 'There are so many other seats.'

'It's motivating if we can see each other.' His fake smile grated on her nerves. 'Healthy competition, you know . . . '

In their old office, Champak had sat a few cubicles away from Simi, but even then, he had constantly kept an eye on her and anyone who came into her cubicle. He knew everything—how late she came in, how long she took for lunch, how early she left.

He bragged about his skills, always trying to ingratiate himself with the boss and bag the best campaigns.

Now, he was right in her face. There was practically no escape!

Deepa waltzed in right after him.

'Hey!' Deepa twirled around and took in the new place, looking just as much in awe of it as Simi had been. 'This is wonderful!'

'You're late,' Champak exclaimed.

'You?' She groaned. 'Couldn't you find another place to sit?'

If Simi called Champak a prick, Deepa called him a flirt. Deepa was the designer on the team, and Champak was always at her desk with some changes or the other.

'What better place to see you all the time.' He grinned at Deepa. He thought he was flirting with her, but on the contrary, he was irritating the heck out of her.

Deepa rolled her eyes. 'More like see and hear us all the time,' she muttered under her breath.

He was such a pest!

'Now we can't even talk in peace,' Deepa whispered to Simi.

Deepa was right.

But that didn't stop their whispered raptures about their window seats and proximity to the break room and restrooms.

'Girls, does either of you have a red gel pen?' Champak asked, setting up his laptop, a notebook beside it, and three coloured markers neatly arranged on the side.

Ugh! He was so irritating! The git!

Both of them ignored him and got to work.

Simi continued to work on her presentation slides, thanking her stars for the charger or she wouldn't have been able to do anything until now. At 10 a.m., they all got up and headed to one of the small conference rooms for the meeting.

She gave her presentation on the new social media campaign for the Pumpkin chair. Champak interrupted her on almost every slide with questions and suggestions for improvement.

'I think green will look better for that message,' or 'A stronger punchline would make a better impact!'

She tried to keep her cool and not get pulled into the black hole of his questions.

Every time Champak opened his mouth, she felt a tightness in her belly, as if he was going to expose a mistake that she'd inadvertently made and make her look like a fool in front of everyone. Sometimes their boss, Nandan, picked up on Champak's suggestions, but today, it looked like even he wasn't in the mood for interruptions.

'Let her complete her presentation, Champak!' Nandan said finally.

That made Champak shut up through the rest of the slides.

When they were finally done, Simi and Deepa made for the bathroom for a break. It seemed to be the one place where Champak couldn't eavesdrop on them.

Champak eyed them suspiciously as they got up from their desks.

'The dude doesn't even need to use the bathroom!' Deepa hissed into Simi's ears.

Simi nodded in agreement. 'How can he stay glued to his seat the whole day?'

'Maybe he uses diapers so he can take a leak right in his seat,' Deepa sputtered and then sniggered. Simi couldn't help but follow suit, tears rolling from her eyes despite a hand firmly clasped over her mouth to hide her laughter.

Champak gave them a glare as if he knew they were talking about him.

Simi squeezed Deepa's hand to make her stop laughing, and the two carried on to the bathroom with straight faces, laughing loudly once they were inside.

Deepa dabbed at her tears with a paper towel. 'Gosh, I hope I haven't ruined my eyeliner!' she said, still giggling.

The first thing that had struck Simi the first time she'd met Deepa were her eyes. From the dazzling shimmer of eyeshadow over her lids to the shiny blue-coloured wings she sported, Deepa had seemed enigmatic. Somewhat dispassionately aloof and unfriendly even.

Simi had recently joined the office, and she'd never thought Deepa would make conversation with her. But, when the aromas from the home-cooked dabba sent by Simi's mother lured Deepa to her desk one afternoon, and every afternoon after that, Simi made a friend.

Deepa lived in a PG in JP Nagar and had sustained on dosas and bisi bele rice for lunch from street motels, until Simi's mother started packing two dabbas for lunch. Deepa soon became a permanent resident at Simi's desk during lunch hour. She transformed into a bubbly friend, and Simi turned into a keen and awestruck listener of her dating adventures.

Deepa was washing her hands when she turned to Simi and said, her eyes twinkling with excitement, 'Guess what! Pratik has a surprise for me this weekend!'

Just then Simi's phone rang. She groaned. 'It's Champak.' They'd been out of his sight for just five minutes.

She ignored it, switching off the ringer so it was quiet once again and got back to Deepa, eager to hear the latest. 'Really? Is *he* going to propose?'

Deepa's eyes got instantly dreamy. Simi could imagine all the happily-ever-afters swirling around inside Deepa's head. She always lived inside an idyllic world of romance and drama.

'Well!' Deepa threw a surreptitious glance over her shoulder as if Champak might be hiding in one of the stalls. 'I think he is!' She jumped with excitement again. 'He didn't want to tell me about the surprise, but I made him. He—'

Simi threw the paper towel in the dustbin and turned around to listen to the whole story when her phone rang again.

Startled, Simi accidentally clicked on the accept button.

It was Champak again. 'I want to discuss the meeting minutes. You think you can get out of the bathroom sometime soon?' he snapped with complete disregard for their personal space, not to mention the fact that he was interrupting a very interesting turn in the conversation. It seemed like Champak was testing her patience today.

'Champak, I'm in the bathroom!' Simi glowered into the phone and cut the call. Deepa threw her hands up in frustration.

For all the fantasies Simi had harboured about this new co-working office, none had involved an overbearing co-worker being so in her face every single moment of their work life.

She tried to push aside her anger and focus on Deepa's love life. Deepa had dated some pretty interesting men—a broke guitar player who serenaded her with songs until she got tired of it because he turned every conversation into a song, an English teacher who spewed verse in the throes of love-making but was a commitment-phobe, and others. For all Deepa's daydreams about the perfect date and love life, she had some pretty terrible stories about men with commitment issues. There had been men who only wanted a good time, and whenever she wanted to take their relationship forward, they would break things off. Until a few months ago, when she'd met Pratik—the hero of her latest love story—on an online matrimonial site for divorcees.

That one had stumped Simi. Why look for a man on a matrimonial website for divorcees?

'They're the only ones who're ready for commitment,' Deepa had said.

Deepa's family, her mother and six sisters, lived in a village up north. To them, it didn't matter who Deepa married as long as she found her own man.

'But why start with a man who's already failed his first commitment?' Simi had argued.

'Exactly! Because a divorce will give him more clarity,' Deepa had argued back.

And it looked like she had been right.

'So Pratik wants me to meet his parents,' Deepa said.

'You're going to Delhi?' Simi interrupted. A part of her wished Deepa would never marry a man who did not live in Bangalore. What would she do without her best friend at work?

'No, only on Zoom, silly!' Deepa smiled. 'I'll go over to Pratik's place and talk to his parents on the call. Then, I'm sure he'll propose,' she yelped with delight. 'My search will be over.' Her smile suggested it wasn't so much the search for an end as the thrill of the adventure.

Simi's heart swelled at the mere thought of adventure as well. There were two things that Simi hoped for in a blooming love story—one, for the hero to sweep the girl off her feet, and two, for there to be no villains lurking in the background.

Simi didn't know what being in love felt like. She watched every single romcom movie and cried sweet tears at the happily-ever-after endings. She longed for a soulmate and dreamed of it. Although it hadn't happened to her yet, she believed in it with all her heart and soul. If Deepa was happy and convinced she had found the love of her life, Simi hoped and prayed that Deepa's love story would have a happy ending.

'Come, want to check out the new office now?' Deepa said, holding her hand, and walking her out of the bathroom.

They slipped out of the office area, while Champak was busy on a phone call with someone.

'Why do we have to behave like he's our boss?' Simi said, as they headed first to check out the break room.

'Exactly!' Deepa concurred with a laugh. 'His meeting minutes can wait.'

They crossed the small lounge area, which had large sofas, pretty bookshelves across the walls and racks holding a few board games.

The tiny break room was right next to the coffee area where she'd met Ranvir this morning. White-washed walls, a ceiling-to-floor pantry cupboard and a small kitchenette greeted them. There was space for a table and three chairs.

Deepa walked over to the counter to check out the variety of flavoured teas on the rack. They had the option of jasmine, ginger, tulsi, chamomile and honey-lemon. There was a coffee machine, a microwave and a mini fridge filled with some tetra juice packs and flavoured milk.

'We can make noodles here if we want to,' Simi exclaimed, eyeing the pans, plates and cutlery in the mini cabinets and drawers, and a small sink at the end of the counter for washing up.

There was another large office space, just like theirs, on the other side of the coffee area.

'Let's explore more,' Deepa exclaimed. They took the elevator down to the ground floor.

The whole space was built in a circular fashion around a cool, central open courtyard with a few trees and benches, stepped seating area, lots of open space and a huge projector screen at the front.

As they walked around, a garden café caught Simi's eye. They stopped and entered. The gorgeous café had pastel walls covered with cartoon murals, and a large skylight in the ceiling that brought in natural light and protection from rain. A few chairs and round tables were scattered around the bright area where you could sit and order a sandwich and coffee while working. It looked like they had entered wonderland.

A few people were already seated at some of the tables, headphones on.

Deepa oohed and aahed, noticing everything with sharp designer's eyes—her eye for colours and details that made her invaluable to the design team. 'They've blended in the pastels so well!' she exclaimed.

Eager to explore more, Simi and Deepa wandered towards the other side of the courtyard, which led to the food court.

Even from a few metres away, they could hear the bustle of the food court and smell the lip-smacking aromas emanating from there. While it was still not lunch time, the place was teeming with people eating, chatting and laughing.

'Does any work get done here at all?' Deepa wondered aloud.

'Oh! This place is heaven,' Simi said, inhaling the aroma of fresh donuts and coffee.

They walked through rows and rows of tables and hit the end of the food court where she could count at least fifteen different stalls.

'I think we better get out of here before we get too hungry,' Simi suggested as her stomach made slight rumbling sounds.

'Yes, we have lots more to see,' Deepa said, eyeing Pizza Corner and Chinese Dragon. 'I think we should definitely check out the food court in detail.'

Simi agreed. She'd have to tell her mother to not pack lunch until she finished sampling all the food.

As they exited the food court, Deepa pointed to a sign to their left. 'Did you see that?'

HAPPY HOURS BAR & GRILL, the board said. Muffled beats of music thumped through the thick oak doors of the bar. There was indoor and outdoor seating.

'We're going to have a lot of happy hours in there,' Deepa said, laughing as they turned the other way, circling back towards the elevators. That side of the floor was lined with stores.

They walked by a small pharmacy and a hair salon.

'Look! A bookstore!' Simi's eyes widened with delight at the quaint little store run by an old woman, who was sitting at the counter. She smiled and waved at them as they peeked inside through the glass walls.

'I'm definitely coming back,' Simi said, squeezing Deepa's hand.

'Now, this is my true calling,' Deepa said, eyeing the yoga studio next to it. 'If only I could afford it!'

'They might have a special package for people working here,' Simi offered helpfully.

The childcare *crèche* next to it was almost empty. Probably because it was a Friday. The two girls inside were setting up the large play mats and cleaning up the jungle gym and the trampoline.

When Simi's phone rang for the third time, they decided to cut short their office tour.

'I'm glad I finished my presentation despite the dead charger,' Simi said as they headed back to their office.

'I completely forgot about that. How did you finally manage without one?'

'A guy I met lent me his.'

'A cute guy?'

Simi nodded. 'Yeah, he was cute!'

Deepa was all ears. 'Tell me everything. Where did you find him?'

There was nothing to tell. She'd spilled his coffee and fallen into his arms—the two most incongruous things she could think of for her first introduction.

'Which company does he work for?' Deepa's eyes danced with excitement.

'I don't know.'

Deepa's eyes shone as she waited for Simi to tell her more. So, Simi told her everything.

How she'd walked out of the office and seen him sitting there with his coffee. How she'd knocked his coffee over and how he'd smiled and told her he'd take care of it.

Deepa smiled goofily. 'How cute!'

Simi blushed. She'd wondered, as they'd explored the new office, if they'd run into the cute guy again but was a bit disappointed when they hadn't.

The first thing she did when she returned to her seat was to place a request for a new charger.

THREE

Loud music thrummed through the floor as Ranvir opened the door to his house late that evening.

'Happy birthday!' his friends squealed and shouted as he made his way inside, taking in the maze of drunk, swaying and dancing bodies.

Right at the centre of a tight circle of friends clinking their wine glasses stood his girlfriend, Parul. She looked stunning in a figure-hugging, shimmering black gown, her hair coiffed up prettily, her thick kohl-lined eyes sparkling with joy.

Even in a room full of pretty, sexy people, she managed to stand out. She always did. Even in college, where they'd met, she had been different from the others. To this day, he did not know why she had chosen him among all the good-looking boys in their class who had wanted to date her.

'Hey, you!' she said, parting her way through her friends and reaching him in two steps. She hugged him, holding her glass away to avoid a spill, and lay a perky kiss on his lips. 'Happy birthday to the birthday boy,' she shouted over her shoulder, raising her glass in the air.

'To the birthday boy!' the gang chorused.

Parul turned back to Ranvir, a happy glaze in her eyes, one he'd seen rarely recently. Parties brought out the goddess in her. She loved people and a chance to show off the home that she and Ranvir lived in.

A couple of strobe lights and the stereo system with surround sound had set the tone for the party. The light bounced off the crystal glasses and ash trays on the gleaming glass dining table. The entire room, and the rest of the house, was all leather, glass and metal, with an eclectic and modern mix of paintings on the walls.

The décor was a complete reflection of Parul's taste, and Ranvir often felt like a stranger in his own home. Had it been up to him, he'd have had low-level cushion seating and flowy cotton curtains and bamboo lamps.

Parul had downed a few glasses, so she was a bit tipsy when she leaned closer to him and pouted. 'Why are you so late?'

'Didn't I tell you I didn't want a party?' Ranvir said, struggling to keep the irritation out of his voice. They'd argued about it two weeks ago, but she'd gone ahead and planned a party anyway.

Her response was a long face. As if to remind him of what she'd said, 'You don't want anything these days!' According to her, he'd become boring, frustrated and unexciting. The last holiday they'd taken to Pondicherry last year seemed like eons ago. And Ranvir couldn't completely disagree with her either. The old him would have come home early and taken her out to dinner. Or gone to a pub, had a few drinks and danced. The new him couldn't be bothered, even if it was his birthday. He was so hopelessly tired after a long day. His limbs ached. He couldn't wait to fall into bed and crash.

But here he was, standing amidst a group of people, many of whom he hadn't seen in at least a year.

He ran a hand through his hair as Parul tried to save the mood and pasted a goofy smile on her face before she looped her arm through his. 'Come, let's cut the cake and then I have an announcement to make.'

She weaved her way through the bodies, tugging him along. A beautiful three-tiered cake sat on the dining table. The only problem was that it was decorated with strawberries. He was allergic to strawberries.

'You never told me that in nearly five years, jaan!' she said, frowning, when he told her he couldn't eat it.

Almost five years. That's how long they'd been living together right after college. When they were doing their MBA—he in finance and she in tourism—they'd found a nice little apartment and lied to the landlords that they were married. Luckily the old, sweet couple had not asked to see their documents.

It was fun to be in the same college and at home together. She was good company during the long, boring weekends, when all they'd do was finish up projects and catch a late-night movie in the theatre every Saturday night.

They split the housework. He cooked and did the dishes. She took care of the groceries and the laundry. It was all so novel when they started living like a couple.

Slowly, the newness and fun had dimmed. Now, they mostly took care of their own dishes and laundry. They ate cereal for breakfast and ordered in all the other meals.

Their friends gathered around him and sang happy birthday. Parul made a big show of cutting the cake and bringing it to his lips so somebody could take pics. He could not even take a bite.

She kissed him on the cheek and left him to mingle with people he hadn't seen in ages, while she sashayed to the mini bar counter near the stereo player to refresh her drink. 'Do you want a drink?' she called over her shoulder.

He shook his head. 'No, I'm fine.' He'd had too much coffee all day and the mix of liquids wouldn't agree with his system. Besides, it would only give him a bad hangover in the morning. He didn't want that as a memory of his birthday—the one he'd forgotten about in the first place.

His old college friend, Sandy, pulled him aside. 'Still going strong, I see.' He winked and ran his hand through his thinning hair. 'I'm quite surprised to see you two still together.'

'Take a hike, bro!'

'Seriously, macha! I never thought you'd last!'

Even he hadn't thought his relationship with Parul would last. Their being together had started as a dare. There had been many guys who had wanted to date her in college. Zubin was her boyfriend until she'd caught him cheating with one of the freshers.

Ranvir had been sitting on the last bench of an empty classroom that morning, going through his Risk Management notes before the next class. He preferred an empty classroom to the library, where students kept walking in and out, distracting him.

Parul strode into the classroom thinking it was empty, plonked on the front bench in a corner, and burst into tears. While he could have just ignored it and let her cry, her hiccups grew louder until he couldn't focus on Risk Management any longer. He finally stood up and went to her.

'What's the matter?'

Her tap dried up instantly. 'Nothing,' she said, her chin tilted upwards, guilty of being caught in a vulnerable state.

He should have left her alone, but he'd stayed. Something about the kohl smudged all around her eyes made him stay right where he was.

He knew who she was—Zubin's girlfriend, an identity that had robbed her of her individuality—but he'd never spoken to her before or seen her like this.

She turned out impeccably dressed to college every day in bodycon dresses with short jackets, and short skirts with ankle-length boots. All the boys in college would ogle at her.

Nobody had seen her with snot over her cheeks, smudged eyes, and limp hair framing her face. He felt sad for her.

He was about to leave her alone, but she grabbed his arm, making him stop in his tracks. 'Will you just . . . ' She paused to blow her nose. 'Will you just hold my hand and come outside with me?'

He would later realize that she was hedging her bets with a nerd like him. Not a good-looking nerd, but just a nerd.

'Please,' she pleaded.

His head moved of its own accord, nodding in response to her plea.

They walked out together, her hand in the crook of his elbow. He had no clue what she had in mind. But they took two rounds back and forth along the corridor. From the corner of his eye, he saw Zubin watching them, mouth agape.

He thought his role in the whole charade was minimal, just a special appearance, but apparently not.

The very next day, she sought him out in the empty classroom again, and after that, the classroom became like the very library he'd avoided.

She invited her friends to join, she had impromptu parties in there, she and her friends played music and danced on the benches.

One thing led to another until she asked him to be her boyfriend, and just like all the other times when she'd asked him for things—his notes, or his time, or more parades along the corridor for Zubin's sake—he accepted.

Sandy clicked his fingers in front of Ranvir's face. 'Parul is the catch of the century.'

Ranvir glared at Sandy. 'Stop eyeing my girlfriend.'

'Che, Che . . . ' Sandy dismissed his concern. 'She's too much for the likes of me. Look at her shake, macha!'

Ranvir punched his shoulder. 'Watch your tongue, bro! You're talking about my girlfriend.'

Sandy laughed. 'Kidding, macha!'

FOUR

Simi had a skip in her step as she got off the auto and paid the driver. It helped that the fares were fixed, and she did not have to haggle with an Ola auto.

It was late. Deepa had wanted to go shopping for a nice outfit for her Zoom call with her prospective in-laws. Simi wondered how Deepa had space in her PG to house all her clothes.

The day had turned out to be lovely despite the crazy start. She'd bumped into a cute guy, heard Deepa's uplifting news and gone shopping. Three fabulous things that made her heart sing.

She cut across the neat front lawn towards her apartment elevator.

There was already a crowd standing in front of it, which was going up at a snail's pace. Simi inched closer to the door, vying for a prime spot which would enable her to make a dash into it when it came.

A young boy smiled at Simi just then, tugging at her dupatta so she'd notice him. He was holding a squeezy ball in his hand. He giggled with delight every time he squeezed it and it gave off a horn-like sound. She smiled back at him. He kept doing it again and again until the man standing beside him gave him a tap on his shoulder, shushing him the next time he squeezed the ball. The boy made a face and stopped reluctantly.

Simi's patience was wearing thin. Where was the lift when you needed it? It took so long to go up all the fifteen floors and come down. She could have been home a long time ago.

The crowd around the lift was bigger now. It was so congested that an old man was practically leaning his walking stick against her, its knob poking the small of her back.

'Ow!' she yelped as the knob pressed further into her back.

She looked over her shoulder, pleading with the old man to take away his walking stick. He obliged.

Her phone rang. It was her mother. 'Simi, where are you?'

'Waiting near the elevator. Coming soon,' she said. It was already past dinner time, and her stomach was rumbling.

She eyed the lift like a hawk as it made its descent, slowly counting down from nine, eight, seven . . . The crowd gathered around her was getting impatient. A child wailed somewhere to her left. Missing the lift meant they would have to wait a long time for it to come back.

'Do you have to be late the day I want you to come early?' her mother pressed.

Before she could reply, the lift opened with a ding. The crowd charged towards it like a pack of hungry wolves falling upon their prey. She was pushed and swept in, going along with the mighty flow like a wave in the ocean.

'The elevator is here,' she squeaked before her phone got disconnected and she was squeezed out of breath.

The lift door shut and it creaked as it journeyed upwards. It had barely climbed a couple of floors, when a sharp cracking sound swept through the bottom of the lift. The next moment, the lights inside went off and the body of the lift shuddered and came to a grinding halt. A collective groan went through the tiny space. They were stuck now that there was a power cut.

It took Simi a few moments to get used to the darkness. The lift was crowded as hell. A child started to wail. And then she began to panic. She felt suffocated.

People began banging on the doors. Their cell phones had no signal.

Minutes passed.

Simi began hyperventilating and drawing in large gulps of air to get more oxygen into her asthmatic lungs.

Horror stories of people stuck in lifts and dying of carbon dioxide inhalation came to her mind. She had never been stuck in a lift before! Would help come on time?

Claustrophobia hit her, a wave of nausea causing her to squeeze her eyes shut. She was gasping for breath. She was dying . . . *Oh God! Oh God!* she prayed.

The child screeched and threw a tantrum, jumping around, causing the elevator to squeak and shake.

Oh God! No! Please!

Unable to take it any more, Simi gathered the last of her breath in her lungs, and banging her fists on the door, began to scream. She did not care that the child was screaming along with her and that the people were shouting for the two to stop. She did not care that everybody had started yelling and screaming now. She screamed and screamed and screamed . . . and couldn't stop.

* * *

By the time Simi reached home, she was shaken. The old man with the walking stick had come to their rescue by wedging the thin sharp end of his stick through the door to let in some air.

Simi's screaming, accompanied by the terrified wailing of the child, had brought the guard to the scene in minutes. A few other people had pitched in and forcefully pushed open the door, widening the gap until it was enough for them to pull themselves up to the floor above. Thankfully, the lift had stopped at a place that was close to one of the floors. Simi had been the first to tumble out with relief.

Thank God she lived on the fifth floor and had to climb up only three floors more to her house.

Her mother, Gauri, was at the door, ushering her in urgently.

'Ma, I almost died in the lift but what a day I had!' Simi started, eager to tell her about the wonderful day. 'The office is so beautiful and Deepa and—'

With a finger on her lips, Gauri shushed her. 'We'll talk about that later,' she hissed. 'First, come in and see who has come. They've been waiting for so long. Why are you late when you should have come on time?'

'But Deepa wanted—' Simi froze in surprise at the sight that met her eyes.

On the couch were Babita Aunty, Dheeraj Uncle, Kalki and Karan—smiling.

'Hi, beta!' Babita rose from the couch and walked over to Simi, embracing her in a tight hug. 'Remember me?'

Dheeraj Uncle and her father, Venkat, used to work together at the same bank. The families used to meet every year at the bank annual gatherings. Though it had been a few years since Simi and Ayush had stopped accompanying them.

Simi smiled awkwardly. 'Yes, Aunty.'

Babita beamed. 'And Karan?'

Karan?

The first time Simi had met Karan, he was about ten. The bank had organized a lunch party for all its employees. Karan had come with his parents, holding on to a lollipop that he sucked on continuously from the time he came until he sat down for lunch. Simi was seven then. His parents had coaxed him to give her the other lollipop he had, but he'd shaken his head vehemently and refused.

Yeah, this was the same Karan.

Simi's smile faded slightly. 'Yes, Aunty.'

'That's what I thought. These kids have grown up so much since,' Dheeraj said cheerfully, clapping Venkat hard on the shoulder.

Venkat was pushed sideways at the impact. He straightened up before saying, 'Of course!'

Karan's sister, Kalki piped in. 'And me?' She was about nineteen, gaunt and fair with short blunt-cut hair that bobbed around her shoulders. Her braces gleamed when she smiled.

'Yes!' Simi smiled back.

Kalki's face brightened. She turned towards Babita. 'Ma, can I go to Ayush's room and check out his video games?'

It was then that Simi noticed Ayush standing in a corner, his arms crossed over his chest, looking annoyed. He'd never liked Kalki, although she'd always adored him. She'd always run after him when they'd been little.

'Please?' Kalki pleaded, rising from the couch and looking at Ayush expectantly.

'Fine, go!' Dheeraj said impatiently.

Kalki beamed with excitement and turned to Ayush, who unenthusiastically led her to his room.

Simi bit back a smile.

Dheeraj turned to Venkat. 'Karan and Simi also haven't met in a while. They can talk too if they like.'

'It's fine,' both Karan and she said in unison, shaking their heads at the same time.

Venkat waved to Simi. 'It's all right, beta. You both can go to the balcony. Show him the view.'

There was no view to show, but Simi had no choice. She gestured to Karan.

He rose from the couch and followed her.

They stood against the railing for a bit. Their balcony faced a children's park. It was empty at this hour.

Karan said, 'Not a bad view! Though it must be pretty noisy during the day.'

'It is.'

'You still play badminton? Remember the time you had that silly band around your wrist? What was it called?'

It was a memory from a bank gathering a few years ago. She remembered it was when she was first learning to crochet. She'd made a tiny band, almost like a bangle. She had worn it while playing badminton. All the children were divided into teams, and Karan and she were paired against two others.

At match point, her racket got stuck on her crochet band and she missed the shot. They lost that match, and Karan was mad.

'Crochet,' she said, referring to the band.

He laughed. 'What a grandmotherly hobby! You still do that stuff?'

She did. In fact, she loved crochet. 'Yes, I still crochet.'

He laughed again. 'I can't believe it! You're strange, Simi.'

'Thank you,' she replied, her words laced generously with sarcasm. 'You were no less weird.'

'Weird? Me?'

'You only ate out of a white plate. You carried a rubber band and a stone in your pocket. You called it your secret weapon against thieves and—'

'That was childhood stuff. I don't do that any more.' He turned to her, frowning, and gave her the once-over. 'I see you've changed too. You don't have oil in your hair,' he said, grinning.

She crossed her arms over her chest and frowned.

The last time they'd met, he was in college, smartly dressed, his hair styled with gel. She'd been admiring him when he had passed a derogatory remark about the oil in her hair. 'Doesn't it stink?' he'd asked.

She'd called him snooty.

He'd called her 'shabby' which wasn't true, although she'd never cared to dress up much—wearing a simple churidar kurta most of the time.

He looked down at her smugly. He was wearing a fine, cream-coloured shirt and trousers that fit perfectly.

'I think they're calling us in,' she lied, straightening her kurta and patting her hair self-consciously. If all they were doing was remembering all the things she'd long forgotten and did not wish to remember, she'd rather not stand here making small talk.

Karan turned around and looked through the glass door. 'Really? I didn't hear them.'

'Really.' She strode back to the living room without giving him a chance to argue. He followed.

'Had a nice chat?' Dheeraj asked expectantly.

Karan nodded. 'Yes, Papa.'

Nice chat? Whatever that meant! Simi did an inward eye roll.

'They are still such good friends, no?' Babita sounded upbeat.

Simi did another eye roll. If only the parents knew what they were talking about outside and how she didn't really want to talk to him again.

'I saw Simi when she was just a *baccha*. How much she's grown!' Babita went on.

Dheeraj cleared his throat. 'Venky, actually, I have a proposal. I hope you don't mind.'

Venkat straightened in his chair. 'Of course not, Dheeraj! What proposal?'

'We've been looking for a girl for Karan for long, but he doesn't like anyone.' He paused and smiled. 'So, we were thinking about Simi for Karan? What do you think?'

Venkat's mouth fell open. Gauri's eyes lit up with joy.

Simi looked from her father to her mother, shocked at the proposal. What were they talking about?

'I . . . I don't know what to say, Dheeraj,' Venkat mumbled, his eyes turning moist.

Dheeraj clapped Venkat's shoulder. 'See, we've been friends. The kids' marriage will take our friendship to the next level.' A wide smile blossomed on his face.

Simi couldn't believe her ears.

She thought Karan would refuse. Surely, he did not like her or want to marry her? They had nothing in common.

'I'll . . . I want to wait until my promotion,' Karan stuttered as vaguely as possible. He seemed as taken aback as she was, although it wasn't comforting in the least.

'Yes, that's the idea. Karan's promotion is coming up,' Dheeraj said. 'No hurry. Let them get to know each other, haan?'

'But, Papa—' Simi started saying.

Waving his hand, Venkat cut her off and turned to Dheeraj. 'We're not in a big hurry to get Simi married either.'

'Let the children decide.' Babita gave Simi a wink and turned back to her parents. 'I think they like each other. They've known each other for years!'

Years! The word rang ominously in Simi's ears.

Gauri went to the kitchen to bring something sweet to celebrate the good news.

Gah! What was wrong with everyone?

Karan was a sort of constant, like the friend the teacher asks you to sit next to on the first day of school who becomes more like the scenery than an exciting part of your life.

There was nothing to decide. They did not like each other. She certainly did not like him. She did not want to marry him!

But her dumbstruck silence had been taken to mean yes.

Or so it seemed, because nobody had let her finish her sentence.

'Venky,' Dheeraj said. 'We're celebrating our anniversary in two weeks. All of you must come home.'

'And, Simi, could you call me in a few days, beta? I want to talk to you,' Babita said.

Simi looked at her in surprise. 'Me?'

'Yes,' Babita said, smiling.

Venkat and Gauri congratulated the couple.

Gauri distributed the sweets, everyone ate, and laughed and chatted some more.

Karan's family left, leaving Simi staring in their wake, wondering what the heck had just happened to her dreamy and peaceful life.

Surely, this was a dream? No, a nightmare!

FIVE

Someone turned up the volume and the dance scene perked up. Sandy wasn't wrong. There was something sensuous about the way Parul danced. All eyes were on her tonight.

Her gaze connected with Ranvir's, and she gestured to him to join her.

Ranvir was tired after the long day, but he trudged towards her.

Soon, he was by her side, shuffling his feet while she shimmied and jiggled to the raging beats. Just as the tempo built and people started banging their heads and pumping their fists, Parul left his side, walked up to the stereo and turned the music off.

A sudden silence descended on the room, followed by a wave of 'What!' and 'Oh no!'

Parul picked up a glass from the table and clinked it with a spoon. 'Guys, I have an announcement to make!'

The crowd grew quiet.

'I know most of you know this, but Ranvir and I are soon going to be celebrating five years together.'

Claps and cheers resounded across the room.

Parul smiled wider, her misty eyes glittering. 'We're planning an anniversary trip to . . . ' She paused and took her own time laying out the punchline. 'Paris!'

The friends went berserk. 'Woohoo!' someone shouted.

'Yes!!! To Paris!' another shout came, followed by more clinking of glasses.

Ranvir went still. He hadn't seen this coming. Paris? When? Why hadn't she mentioned anything to him?

A sudden shattering sound broke the merriment, a glass crashing to the floor. A moment later, a girl screamed. 'My foot is bleeding.'

Chaos erupted. Another scream. Someone else had got hurt. Somebody was rushed to the bathroom. Suddenly, the music came on again and Ranvir watched in utter shock as confusion abounded.

Parul's face turned white. 'Who switched on the music? Switch it off!' she yelled.

Ranvir pulled Parul aside and made her sit on the couch. 'You sit. I'll take care of it.'

He was glad for the disruption. The party had turned too raucous, and he wanted it to end. He switched off the music and announced that the party was over. People looked around in confusion, everyone a bit high and slow to understand. First, he made sure that the people who had got hurt were okay and got a couple of the more sober people to bandage their cuts. Then he started handing his friends their belongings, so they got the message. Some people were harder to convince and lingered over goodbyes.

Finally, when he had ushered nearly all the guests out, he swept the glass shards off the floor, took the leftovers back to the kitchen, and washed the pile of dirty dishes and used wine glasses.

Another college friend of his and Parul's, Shyla, had volunteered to stay back and help. He had been reluctant, wanting her to leave too, but she had insisted. But now he was glad for the help as it was a lot of work.

When they were all done, Shyla wiped her hands on a towel and sighed with relief. 'I hate parties.'

'Thanks for staying back to help. I don't think Parul is in any state to do anything,' he said, hoping Shyla would not want to hang around and chat. He was exhausted.

As they walked towards the door, she turned around to face him and poked his chest lightly. 'Have I told you that you're a great guy?' Her eyes were glazed over. 'I've . . . I've always fancied you.'

He stepped back, away from Shyla's hand, which was now trying to land on his chest and inching towards the buttons on his shirt. 'No, please, Shyla. I don't think you'll want to remember what you just said tomorrow.'

She bristled slightly then relaxed her features. 'I wasn't hitting on you.'

He rubbed a hand over his face. 'Shyla, I think you should go. Thank you for coming and helping with everything.'

'Right!' She laughed. 'Of course, no problem. If you need me . . . '

'Yeah, thanks again!'

Shutting the door behind her, he let out a long, tired breath and raked his hands through his hair. What a mess! He was lucky he didn't have to deal with people like Sandy and Shyla every day.

Parul was no longer on the couch. Ranvir went to the bedroom to check on her.

She was splayed on the bed with her head between her hands.

He went closer. 'Parul.'

She stirred and dropped her hands to her sides. 'I'm tired. Did everybody leave?'

'Why did you have to do all this?' he asked calmly. 'Birthdays can be quiet celebrations too.'

'Yeah, but you always come home so late.'

'We needn't have celebrated at all.'

'That's not fair.' She turned over to the side. 'How is it fair that all our friends celebrate their birthdays every single year?'

He helped her out of her heels.

Parul fisted his collar and yanked him close. 'I want us to go to Paris for our anniversary.'

He leaned over to pull up a blanket over her. 'I told you it's impossible to take off. Work's busy.'

'You always do this to me!' she yelled. 'You never have any time for us, for me, for anything. You've become such a—' She picked a pillow and threw it on the floor.

'Parul, I—'

'Ughhhh!' she screamed, crushing her head against her pillow. 'I'm tired of your excuses! I'm tired of you!'

Ranvir picked the pillow and walked back to the living room, letting her blow off steam.

He was tired. Period. Tired of everything.

There was nothing he could do to make her feel better. There was nothing he could say. They were back to the thing they had been fighting about since he'd left the bank. Tonight was no different. Tonight, he was back on the couch.

He'd hoped to come home to a peaceful dinner and a restful night's sleep.

He plonked down on the couch to clear his head. Today had been a busy day. He'd planned to go through the spreadsheets after dinner. When he rummaged in his bag for the charger, he remembered that the one he carried in his laptop bag was with the woman he'd met at the office that morning.

Her drenched outfit and hazel brown eyes flashed in front of his eyes.

I was wondering if you have a working laptop charger?

He shook his head. She had his charger and he'd forgotten his spare one at work. That meant he couldn't finish his work either.

Something had been bothering him since he'd walked in that evening. He now realized what it was.

He needed to do this, although it was almost midnight.

Putting his laptop away, he picked up the house keys, locked the door softly behind him, and left.

SIX

Settled on the sofa beside her mother, glued to the Travel Network episode on Europe, Simi tucked hungrily into the aviyal and rice her mother had made for dinner.

Karan and family had long left. Her mother had stuck some brownie dough in the oven and settled in front of the TV as if nothing had happened.

As if Simi's world had not come crashing down around her!

She'd complained to her parents about the proposal, but to no avail. Her mother thought they were lucky to find someone they knew.

Her father had gone to his room to watch the second TV in the house.

The aroma of brownies baking in the oven and the sound of the TV had managed to calm Simi's nerves.

'How beautiful the styles of these buildings are,' Gauri said, of the architectural splendour of Prague.

Her mother was fond of baking and watching shows about travelling. Usually, she managed to do both together.

Which was, set up a few buns or a cake or brownies in the oven, and then flop in front of the TV to relish her armchair travel. The house almost always smelled of oranges or vanilla or cinnamon on most evenings.

It helped that they had two TVs; her father loved to watch sports on the one in the bedroom.

Gauri and Venkat kept out of each other's way. So, when Gauri travelled vicariously, she had the rule of the living room kingdom. Meanwhile, Venkat enjoyed the privacy of his room.

'Ma, what was that about Karan's mother wanting to speak to me?' Simi asked, as she wolfed down the aviyal-rice.

Gauri looked away from the TV for a second, gave Simi a disdainful look and lightly tapped her leg reproachfully. 'Eat slowly.'

Simi finished eating, taking her time over the food, while her mother watched the show. She then washed her plate in the kitchen sink. After she had settled back on the couch, she poked her mother to demand her attention.

'What? Wait . . . ' her mother said, palm raised, eager not to miss the description of the wonderful castle pictures on the screen. 'What a beauty!'

'Ma!' Simi prodded her mother again. 'Why does Karan's mother want to speak to me?'

'Something about their wedding anniversary. I don't know. Ask your father. He probably knows.'

Simi tsk-tsked. She just could not get her mother to tell her anything in the middle of the programme. But it sounded strange. Now, what would Karan's mother want to speak to Simi about?

'Do I have to call her?'

'What's the harm in calling her?' Gauri said dismissing her again, in her usual calm and soothing voice. 'She's going to be your mother-in-law one day—'

'Ma!' Simi scowled in protest and pulled her knees up to her chest.

Gauri chucked Simi under the chin and smiled indulgently. 'At least they're a family we know. You don't have to marry a stranger. I hardly knew your father!'

'Hey, cry baby! Heard that you got stuck in the elevator.' Ayush ambled back into the living room just then.

'*Hey, cry baby!*' she mimicked him. 'What would you know about my tyrannized lungs in that old rickety elevator? I don't know when that thing is going to die!' She shuddered at the memory.

'You should use the stairs next time.' Ayush snickered with amusement, all six feet two inches of him looming in front of the couch in a couple of long strides. He was lanky, with scant hair on his face. The hair on his head was shaggy and unkempt. He claimed that it was the style mark of a studious, languishing-in-a-mountain-of-books type of engineering student, though all he really did all day was watch movies and play video games. His smile was beatific, just like her mother's. To the world, he was a quiet, introverted boy, but with her, he was a real brat. 'Glad to see you got out of the elevator in one piece, oily head!' he said, teasing her.

She ran a hand over her soft, shampooed hair self-consciously, and glared at him.

Simi had stopped oiling her hair the day Karan had teased her about it, but Ayush still loved to call her 'oily head' since then.

Ayush ruffled Simi's hair playfully, making her madder. Because he was so tall, Simi couldn't do the same to his hair, but she gave him a fitting retort nevertheless. 'Look at you, shaggy head!'

'Anniversary celebrations!' he said, his eyes glinting with mirth. He wiggled his eyebrows comically and sputtered with laughter.

For the first time since the 'proposal' incident, Simi felt mirth bubble up inside her too.

'You think they're going to do the second vows or something?' He couldn't contain his laughter now.

'*Second vows?*' Simi joined him, and they both held on to their stomachs and hollered with laughter.

Gauri paused the TV and glared at them. 'Can you children let me watch this in peace? Simi, why are you laughing at them? You're going to marry into that house.'

'Stop it, Ma.'

'Haha . . .' Ayush mock-laughed and disappeared back into his room.

Simi decided to check on her father to see if he knew what Karan's mother wanted with her!

Venkat was lounging on his favourite easy chair in the bedroom, his long limbs stretched in front of him. He was watching a Formula One race.

'Papa!' Simi came up behind him and threw her arms around his neck.

Venkat choked at the tight squeeze. 'Oof, Simi.'

She came and stood in front of the TV, blocking his view.

'Move!' he yelled. 'I can't see!'

'First, tell me why I have to speak to Karan's mother.'

'Because she wants to speak to her daughter-in-law,' her father rattled off, shooing her away from the front of the TV.

She scowled. 'I'm not her daughter-in-law! But what's it about?'

'Must be something she wants to tell you,' he said offhandedly.

'That's what I want to know!' Simi said, literally in his face now. 'What does she want to tell me?'

'I don't know!'

'What if I don't want to call her?'

'Okay, you can do whatever you want. But can you get away from the TV, please? I recorded this to watch it in peace.'

'I don't want to marry Karan.'

Her father paused the TV and looked at her. 'Don't want to marry Karan? Why?'

Because I don't love him.

Because I don't want to marry someone I don't love.

'When your mother met me for the first time, she didn't want to marry me either.' Her father chuckled.

Simi went around and sat by his feet, and hugged his legs. She adored her father. He would make her run alongside him on his morning jogs when she was just two years old. At four, he threw her into the pool and asked her to swim. By six, she was taking singing lessons, and he wouldn't let her go to bed until she had practised her songs every day. He made sure she enrolled in every debate, elocution and annual competition in school. She'd thrived under his love and guidance. He'd done the same for Ayush, but the opposite had happened. While Simi had grown into a happy teenager, Ayush had withdrawn into a shell.

Her father's soft grey eyes bore into her. 'What happened now? Did Karan say something?'

It wasn't what Karan had said or done, she wanted to tell her father. It was just him. She did not feel for him what she must feel for the man she was going to marry.

'When your mother and I met for the first time, I called her Gomati instead of Gauri. Somehow, I got her name mixed up.' He tittered with glee. He loved telling this story. It got a lot of laughs at get-togethers.

Simi smiled, even though she'd heard it before.

'Gauri was mad at me but she didn't say anything then. It was just once that I had made a mistake, mind you! We hardly met two times before the wedding. But look at how happy we are now.' Venkat skimmed the top of her head lovingly. 'Karan is a good boy.' He smiled. 'Hmmm?'

'But we have absolutely nothing in common. And I don't know him, and I don't feel . . . Papa, I—' The words stuck in her throat just wouldn't come out.

I don't love him!

Was there a man out there she'd meet and fall in love with? Or was it all a useless dream?

'You should get to know each other,' her father said, jumping at the opportunity to set things right immediately. A wonderstruck look shone in his eyes.

Simi slapped her head and groaned. 'No, Papa! I don't like him!'

He gazed at her lovingly. 'How can you like him when you don't know him enough? What you know of him is from when he was much younger. Such a nice proposal may not come again, beta. Better a known family than an unknown family, no? Besides, there is no hurry. And Karan is such a respectful and wonderful young man.'

Karan?

Stubborn, grumpy, obnoxious Karan?

Her parents loved him because he was so sweet to them. What were the odds that she could refuse him?

Venkat patted her head. 'I'm getting old, beta—' His voice broke suddenly and he cleared his throat.

She inched closer to him and wound her hands around his knees, a heaviness squeezing her chest.

Ever since his heart attack last year, he often worried about not living long enough, not seeing his children settled in their jobs and marriages.

'Once you get married and Ayush gets a job, I can retire in peace.'

The odds against Karan looked pretty slim. She didn't have a secret boyfriend or somebody she liked. If not Karan, she was doomed to go through matrimonial sites. Her options were limited. A known devil or an unknown one?

She said nothing.

Venkat tipped her chin and peered into her eyes. 'But, you're right! You and Karan have to get to know each other. And I'm going to take care of that pronto.'

She had no idea what her father had in mind. But the last thing she really wanted to do was to get to know Karan any more than she already did.

Ugh! What had she got herself into?

SEVEN

Ranvir parked his car by the side of the street and walked up to the small house. He opened the latch on the gate and let himself in. The neighbourhood was quiet and peaceful. Most of the lights on the street were switched off. Through the window, he could make out a small light on as he made his way up the two steps to the main door. He wasn't able to tell if anyone was awake because he knew that tiny light would stay on the whole night. That was how it had been for as long back as he remembered.

The key to the front door was hidden beneath the rug as usual. He picked it up and unlocked the door. A birthday cake sat on the dining table.

Ranvir looked around sheepishly. He hadn't planned on coming but now he was glad he did.

'Over here,' his father's voice called from the backyard. 'Get the cake and join me.'

Ranvir stepped into the kitchen for two plates and a knife. Just for the heck of it, he rummaged in the drawers to look for a candle and a matchbox. Then armed with everything, he made his way to the backyard.

As the lamp in the backyard fell on the square game board in front of his father, he was hit by a wave of nostalgia. His mother would sit across him, and they would play most evenings after dinner.

Ranvir had come home for summer holidays when his father, Lalit, told him his mother had cancer. Ranvir had been in boarding school since eighth grade after his mother had decided to join his father in Kuwait. Lalit was an electrical engineer. But that last year of high school, he had quit his job and returned to India for good.

Ranvir did not want to return to school after the summer, but his mother would not hear of it. 'I'll get better,' she said.

But she didn't. She already had stage 3 cancer when they found out. She passed away six months later. His newly married elder sister, Tina, his father and he became the small family she left behind.

And now his father had stayed up for Ranvir, playing alone in the middle of the night.

'You thought I'd forget?' His father chuckled, folding up the game board so that Ranvir could put down the cake on the table.

Ranvir set the plates on the small round table in front of them and took a seat beside his father. He sank into the chair and gazed at the pitch-dark open space beyond. 'I'd forgotten it was my birthday. Why didn't you call and tell me you bought cake?'

His father made a gruff sound. 'When do you ever come when I call?'

Touché! He was used to his father's soft jibes. Smiling, he eased further into his chair and felt his body relax. Fireflies lit up the branches in front of them. This was his favourite place in the whole world, especially at night.

When his sister and he were younger, they used to catch the fireflies in glass bottles and watch them glow. Then, they'd release them. He wondered if she'd forgotten that it was his birthday.

He turned to his father. 'I thought you'd be asleep so late.'

'I'm glad you took a chance on me, and I did not disappoint.'

'You never disappoint, Papa!' he said, chuckling.

'I'm not getting younger. You shouldn't have kept me waiting.'

His father had learnt to cook for himself after his mother's death. In the last nine years, he'd become a decent cook. He would invite him and Parul over on weekends, especially on birthdays, but Parul had come only once.

Ranvir would often make some excuse or the other or come by himself, usually with groceries to stock his father's fridge. Lalit did not need Ranvir to shop for him, but Ranvir liked to do it. He'd have dinner with his father too, if it was not too late. They would talk about Ranvir's work or about his sister or about his father's friends.

One time, Lalit had said, 'Parag's daughter is getting a divorce. Did I tell you? The couple had no sex in their marriage.'

Ranvir had shrugged, wondering if Parag's daughter had told them openly about why her marriage had failed or if it was something they'd concluded.

Sometimes, Ranvir had the feeling his father wanted to know how Parul and he were doing, if they were happy, if they intended to get married, and so on. He wished his father would ask him about his relationship, offer advice, but he did none of those. He was a hands-off parent. Ma would have been so different.

She'd barge into Ranvir's room whenever she felt like asking him something, or she'd bang on his door if he took too long in the shower, or she'd scold him for staying out late. But not his dad. Lalit was the best father a son could ask for. He never interfered. He'd made peace with Ranvir's live-in relationship. Very unlike what his mother would have done, had she been alive. Ranvir would probably still be living at home if his mother were here.

'Had dinner?' his father asked.

'Yeah, but I didn't eat any cake.'

His father chuckled. 'Why? You didn't like the flavour?'

Ranvir laughed. Nobody knew him better.

'No, it had strawberries.'

His father guffawed heartily until tears rolled down his eyes.

It made him miss his mother more.

'Now, pick up that phone and call Tina,' his father said, wiping his eyes. 'She said to call her no matter how late you got. Let's get your birthday rolling.'

Only then did it hit him hard. His father and sister had wanted to surprise him on his birthday and celebrate it with him. His work and the party at home had made him forget even that.

He picked up the phone and dialled Tina, starting a video call.

After a few rings, her face showed up on the screen. It looked like she was sitting in the dark.

'Why did you get so late?' Tina hissed.

'Where are you?' Ranvir hissed back. 'Hope I did not wake up Jas?' Jas was her husband.

'I slept on the couch waiting for your call. Let's cut the cake.'

Ranvir lit the single candle.

As his father and sister sang happy birthday, their sharp contrasting voices cutting through the silence of the night, the fireflies danced around the trees. Ranvir blew out the candle and cut the cake. He held up a slice, pointing to the screen at Tina.

'Mmmm . . . ' she said, taking a mock bite. 'Happy birthday to my twenty-seven-year-old baby brother!'

'Happy birthday to my big boy,' his father announced, lifting up his slice and biting into it. 'It was Tina's idea to get coffee caramel. God knows why you need so much coffee, even in your cake.'

The image of the girl who'd spilled his coffee that morning sprang to his mind again.

Ranvir smiled cheekily, his heart feeling light and happy. 'Thank you for the birthday wishes. I love coffee!'

It was so nice to celebrate his birthday this way at home. It made him wish the day would never end.

EIGHT

Mondays were busy and hectic as hell. To top it off, it had rained again this morning. Why did it have to rain just as she was leaving her house to get to work? Simi reached BizWorks late, dumped her bag on one of the desks and rushed to find their meeting room.

Simi was bummed when Champak bagged the radio campaign for their latest Custard settee. He'd jumped at the opportunity because she was late, and then gloated about it all throughout the meeting.

Deepa looked drawn and morose all morning too, and Simi couldn't wait for a bathroom break to find out what was bothering her. She wanted to escape Champak's scrutinizing glare. He always managed to find a seat right next to theirs. It felt like being in a classroom with the teacher breathing down their necks.

'What's wrong?' Simi nudged Deepa when they finally managed to get away. 'You don't look so well.'

'Nothing,' came the pat reply but Deepa's lightly kohl-lined eyes were starting to blink rapidly already, and Simi knew something had to be wrong.

Just last Friday, Deepa had been so excited about meeting Pratik's parents on a video call. By the look on Deepa's face, the meeting had not gone well.

'Did you like your future in-laws? How did it go?'

Deepa's face fell. Her lips trembled. It looked as if she was going to cry. 'Not so well. Pratik and I are no longer together. I broke things off with him.' The words tumbled out in a rush.

'What?'

Deepa pinched the bridge of her nose and nodded. 'Yeah.'

'What did his parents say?' Simi pressed on.

Tears sprang to Deepa's eyes. 'Guess what? I wished them and called them uncle and aunty. Then all of a sudden, his dad said, you should know how to address your elders. If you don't, you should ask your parents.' A big tear rolled down Deepa's cheek. 'I thought things were going so well.'

Simi's eyes widened. 'What was wrong with you calling them uncle and aunty?'

Deepa jabbed at her tears now falling rapidly down her cheeks. 'Heck, I don't know!'

'What did you do then?'

Deepa sniffled. 'What could I do? I was so stumped for words. I just managed with some courteous haanjis and yeses and so on. The chat was completely one-sided.'

'Well, did Pratik say anything to their comment?'

'Pratik said nothing. He just stared dumbly at the screen and let them rant at me for no fault of mine. He didn't even take my side.'

'Maybe he was just as stunned as you were.'

'Made me wonder if I really know him that well. And if he loves me.'

'Awww! Of course, he's into you,' Simi gave her best friend a tight hug, feeling ever so disappointed in Pratik. How could he have let his parents behave like this?

'I don't think it'll work out between us . . . ' Deepa was sobbing now.

Simi patted her back softly to shush her. 'It will work out.'

Her eyeliner was smudged, her pretty eyes were a mess. Deepa blew her nose on a paper towel, making her nose redder than before. 'They made it very clear they wanted me to move to Delhi after the wedding because his entire family is there. They told me what Pratik liked and disliked, and so on. Not once did they want to get to know me.'

Simi did not know how to console her friend. Maybe it was no wonder that Pratik's ex-wife had left him. 'I'm not sure I can live with overbearing in-laws either,' Simi mused out loud, shuddering at the very thought.

Deepa washed and wiped her face, her sobs petering down to hiccups now. 'It's kismet! I just haven't found *the one*.'

Simi was heartbroken for her friend. She could not find it in herself to disagree with her.

Deepa was always dating men and breaking up with them. It was such a shame with Pratik. He'd seemed so promising. Unlike the other guys Deepa had liked earlier,

Pratik had seemed perfect for her. He'd been openly affectionate, treated her with respect, and taken her out on great dates. It had even made Simi envious.

To think that Pratik and Deepa's blooming love had been crushed by his villainous parents!

But, being the optimist she was, she was sure that Pratik would work it out. All Deepa and Pratik had to do was be positive and have patience.

Positivity and patience were the solutions to all problems in life. They could move mountains, if need be.

Brightened by the thought, Simi tugged at Deepa's hand and beamed. 'I think the best antidote to a broken heart, besides ice cream, is a brew of hot tulsi chai.'

Deepa looked at her through watery eyes and smiled back wryly. 'I love you for being my friend.'

'Come, let's have some chai,' Simi said, linking her arm through Deepa's elbow as the two headed towards the break room.

* * *

Ranvir and his colleague, Abhi, were in the break room on their tea and coffee break.

'There's this girl I met online whom I want to meet but first she wants to know if I want a serious relationship!' Abhi said.

Ranvir turned to Abhi at the question, amused, while the machine dispensed coffee into his cup. 'Good question. Do you?'

'I don't know if this is a trick question. I mean, don't I have to meet her first to know if I want a serious relationship? What if I just want to meet her and then find out?' Abhi put his cup under the spout after Ranvir was done. He yelped as some of the hot liquid fell on his fingers. 'Ow!'

'Are you okay?' Ranvir asked as Abhi winced and thrust his hand under the cold water tap.

'Yeah!' Abhi said, blowing on his hand and shoving it under the tap alternatively. 'Just a slight scald.'

'Should watch the water instead of thinking about girls. Women are complicated!'

Abhi gave Ranvir a sheepish grin. 'Tell me about it! If a guy only wants to chat, the girl wants to meet, and if a guy wants to meet, the girl only wants to chat.'

Ranvir took a deep, long sip of his favourite black coffee, half his mind on how good this coffee tasted, so much better than what they had served at the previous office.

Abhi waved his hand in front of Ranvir's face and tsk-tsked. 'Earth to Ranvir.'

Ranvir took another long sip. 'Go on . . . '

Abhi frowned at Ranvir's indifference. 'I'm in need of solid relationship advice and the only guy who is in a relationship can't give me any. What sort of a friend are you?'

Ranvir smiled at Abhi, wondering why his friend thought he was the one who could dish out advice of any kind. 'No advice from me. Sorry! I suck at anything besides financial advice.'

'Oh, come on! You sound like a ninety-year-old.'

'I feel like one,' Ranvir said, putting his hand on his neck, which was stiff from the hours he'd spent over the weekend going over numbers and graphs.

Abhi ignored him and rummaged among the tea sachets. 'They're out of my favourite tea!' he exclaimed and pulled out each and every sachet to check. Finally, having found what he was looking for, he took it out and looked at it longingly. 'I'll tell them to restock. So, what do you think? Should I meet the girl or not?'

'What do you want to do? Chat or meet?'

'I'm not sure,' Abhi said, looking troubled. I don't know what it is,' he explained, 'They love what I write online. They go ga-ga over my shayari and sweet nothings over chat but the moment I ask to meet me, they ghost me.' Abhi turned to Ranvir suddenly, mid-explanation. 'So, while I want to take it from chat to meet, I'm worried it will end. So, should I say I want a serious relationship if I want to meet her or will that drive her away?'

Ranvir shook his head. 'This seems way too complicated for me.'

Abhi's phone rang right then, and he swore as he looked at the number. 'I'm late for the ad hoc meeting,' he said, rushing to the door. 'I don't know how I forgot! See you later, bro! I still want to know what you think about this girl.'

Ranvir smiled as Abhi rushed off. He picked up his coffee and headed back to his desk.

* * *

'What a cute room this is,' Simi said, entering the quiet break room with Deepa.

Deepa rubbed her forehead. 'I have a headache.'

'Let's look for some tulsi tea bags.' Simi saw none in the tray but strangely there was one on the counter.

She asked Deepa to sit down and set about getting some hot water for the tea.

A young guy walked in then. He was wearing black-rimmed glasses which were the same colour as his thick, curly hair.

Just as Simi turned around to pick up the tea bag for the water, he walked to the counter and picked it up.

'Hey!' she said. 'That's mine!'

He smiled sweetly. 'Sorry, but not sorry, it's mine!'

Simi put her hands on her hips and stared at him. 'What? I was just getting that for my tea.'

'I was too. I forgot it here and I came back to get it.'

'You did not!'

'I did too!'

Deepa got up from her seat and came up to them. 'Hey, give it back!'

'What if I don't?' he argued.

She snatched it from his hand before he could realize what she'd done.

'Hey, that's not fair!' he yelled. 'I got it before you did. And I have a meeting I have to get to. I can't sit through a meeting without my tea.'

Deepa gave him a tight sympathetic smile. 'So sorry, amigo! I can't give you my tea!'

'That's my tea!'

'Is that so?' she said.

Simi couldn't believe they were fighting over a tea bag. Just then, the guy reached behind Deepa and took it from her hand.

'Hey!' Simi yelled, trying to put an end to this ridiculous squabble.

The guy was holding the tea bag high above his head. Deepa tried to get hold of it but ended up pushing him. The guy staggered backwards and just as Simi moved out of the way to avoid him, her hand struck the cup of hot water on the counter and it crashed to the floor.

A deafening silence followed and both pairs of eyes turned to her.

'I'm so sorry.' Simi slapped her hands to her mouth in horror. 'It was an accident!'

'Here!' the guy said nicely, holding the tea bag out towards Deepa. 'Take your tea!'

Deepa snatched the tea bag and tore it accidentally. The tea leaves fell to the floor.

Deepa's face turned red. 'Happy?' Her eyes flashed anger at the guy.

The guy looked surprised. 'That wasn't my fault.'

'Guys, this is an office, not a school playground, for God's sake!' Simi snapped.

The guy raised his hands. 'So sorry for the trouble.' The next moment, he turned around and walked out.

'Ugh!' Deepa said, letting out with a deep huff.

She was still mad, while Simi managed to clean up the mess as best as she could and made a lemon tea for her.

That would have to do for now. They'd wasted so much time already.

'I thought there'd be cute and sweet guys here!' Deepa said, lifting her eyes to the sky. 'Not the types that fight over the last tea bag!'

This reminded Simi of her own guy trouble that had begun on Friday. By the time she finished telling Deepa about what had happened, it was Deepa who was feeling sorry for her.

'Technically, Karan didn't say yes. He only pushed for time,' she told Deepa. 'The thing is, there is no spark between us whatsoever.'

'Oh, poor you,' Deepa said, giving her a hug, forgetting about Pratik momentarily and consoling her.

Simi had no idea what sense to make of the sudden proposal. She wanted no part in it. She just wished she could wiggle out of it and go back to her normal, carefree life.

In just one weekend, it was Simi who was practically betrothed and Deepa who was probably single.

It was unbelievable.

But at least they could comfort each other.

* * *

Lunch time rolled around. Deepa was back to speaking in monosyllables and looking gloomy.

The food court was packed. Simi eyed the various food stations. The Chinese Dragon called out to her. She was craving some noodles, but there was a huge line at the counter. Finally, they decided to get chicken wraps from their favourite wrap station.

Deepa had just placed the order for a chilli chicken wrap for herself and a chicken tikka wrap for Simi, and was waiting for it, when the guy from the break room came up to them.

Deepa turned red with anger at the sight of him. 'Are you following us?'

'Hello to you too!' he said simply. 'I'm Abhi and you are?'

'Ma'am, chilli chicken is over,' the man at the counter called out. 'Can I get you something else?'

Deepa turned to Abhi instead of replying to him. 'How is it that I never get what I want when you're around?'

A smile tugged at Abhi's mouth. He shrugged. 'I didn't know I had magical powers like that.'

'Smart!' Deepa retorted, oozing vitriol.

Somehow, Simi couldn't stop herself from smiling. She'd never seen Deepa go at a stranger like that.

The seller turned to Abhi just then and handed him his wrap. 'Chilli chicken, sir.'

'Wait a sec,' Deepa said, hands on her hips. 'You just told me you're out of chilli chicken. Then how does he get one?'

'Fast selling, madam! Last one.' The seller's eyes darted between his two customers, trying to make peace. 'Sir ordered before you.'

Abhi grinned. 'You heard what he said . . . '

Deepa threw her hands up in exasperation.

'Calm down, Deepa! Let's not make a scene,' Simi hissed in her ear.

Before the argument could go any further, Abhi offered his chilli chicken wrap to Deepa. 'Here, take mine. I order it every day.'

Deepa scoffed. 'I don't want your charity. You can have it.'

Abhi looked like he'd been slapped.

Simi felt sorry for the poor guy. He was trying to make up for earlier but Deepa wouldn't budge.

'Please take mine,' Abhi insisted again.

'I said no!' Deepa said, shaking her head hard. Finally, Abhi took his wrap and left.

'That was mean!' Simi said.

Deepa lifted her chin defiantly. 'I'm not taking seconds. Especially not from him.'

Deepa seemed to be having a day of tantrums.

Giving up, Simi shook her head and let her be.

* * *

Ranvir got out of the meeting and headed straight to the Subway counter. Picking up a coffee to go along with it, he made his way to his usual sitting place at the far end of the food court. Abhi was already seated at their usual table, a spread laid out in front of him.

'This is lavish, man!' Ranvir said, eyeing the tall glass of juice, a plate of noodles and the wrap Abhi was biting into. 'Special day?'

'Something like that!' Abhi said, his eyes downcast. 'So, how did the investor meeting go?'

'Fine.' Ranvir eased into the chair across from him. 'Have to work out new numbers by the end of the week.'

'Mmmm . . . ' Abhi said, slurping his fruit juice. 'Good luck with that! I have some reports to work on too.'

Ranvir unwrapped his sandwich as Abhi finished his wrap and pulled the plate of noodles towards him. 'So, what's special today? Why the sudden craving for all this oily, bad-for-the-heart stuff?'

'I've fallen in love, macha!' Abhi said, causing Ranvir's jaw to slacken in disbelief. 'My heart is craving for everything that's bad for it cos it's bad news anyway.'

Ranvir did a double take. 'First of all, what are you talking about? Falling in love? With whom? The online date?'

'No. Someone I met in person.'

'Already?'

'Thank God she didn't reject me over chat!'

'What's the bad news?'

'She hates me already.'

'Oh! Already? What did you do?' He regretted it when he saw Abhi's face fall.

Abhi looked heartbroken. 'I went back to the break room to collect my tea bag . . . '

Ranvir nodded as he took a bite of the sandwich.

'Well, there were two girls there and one of them was about to use it to make tea for her friend. I told her it was mine but the friend butted in and told me it was hers. The friend and I fought over it and it tore. I swear I meant to give it to her. But it tore.'

'That was unfortunate,' Ranvir said, a grin forming on his face. He couldn't help it.

'That was not the end of it, macha! I saw her again just now. I was getting my usual chilli chicken wrap and she wanted the same thing. But it was sold out and she didn't get hers.'

'How is it that you both wanted the same thing again?'

'That's what I'm telling you, macha! It's the strangest connection I've ever seen.' He shook his head as if he couldn't believe it himself. 'Anyway, stop interrupting! So, the idiot wrap guy said chilli chicken was already over. Then, she got angry with me as if I was taking away whatever she wanted. So, I offered her mine. But she refused to take it. It felt as if she was refusing my heart!'

Ranvir couldn't contain a soft chuckle.

'I tell you, her eyes! I fell flat for her eyes.' Abhi closed his eyes and took in a deep breath.

Ranvir rubbed his neck in agony. 'Oh no! Don't start with poetry.'

Abhi slipped into a poem nevertheless, dreamy-eyed, his hands up in the air, the fork still held in one. 'It was over a sachet of tea that she broke my heart . . . It was true love for me from the start . . . '

Ranvir chuckled heartily. 'Super! So how does this new love story end?'

'It hasn't even begun, macha! *Abhi toh picture baaki hai* . . . ' His rant stopped mid-sentence and he froze. Then, he looked at Ranvir and began hyperventilating. 'There she is, macha! She's coming this way . . . '

Ranvir turned around but he couldn't see anyone. 'Where?'

'Don't look . . . ' Abhi hissed. 'I'm going to ask her to sit here.' He grabbed Ranvir's hand, shaking his sandwich and making some of the filling spill on to his plate. 'Whatever it is, please support me, macha. Okay, cool, cool . . . . Here she comes!'

Ranvir was itching to turn around but he focused on his sandwich.

Abhi slid a hand over his face as if to compose himself. A few moments later, he looked ahead, and there was a sparkle in his eyes. It was obvious that whoever she was, had arrived. 'Hi!' he said.

Except, it was someone Ranvir hadn't expected.

His breath hitched the moment he raised his head to have a look at who it was, his eyes falling on the familiar face he'd seen last Friday.

Her hair was tied up in a ponytail and long earrings dangled from her ears. She'd turned into a different person altogether from the shaking, rain-drenched woman he'd lent his charger to.

Ranvir straightened in his seat unconsciously, putting his sandwich back on the plate, trying very hard not to stare.

Simi stopped mid-stride when she saw him and smiled.

It was the very same dimpled smile that had flashed in his mind over the weekend every time he'd looked for the charger in his bag and found it missing.

'Hi,' Simi said, the first to break the sudden silent spell at their table.

Was this who Abhi had fallen for?

NINE

'Hi!' Ranvir said.

'Please sit. This is my friend Ranvir. I'm Abhi, as you know.' Abhi jumped into introductions without further ado.

Simi smiled. 'I'm Simi, and this is my friend Deepa.'

That was when Ranvir saw the woman behind Simi.

'I know Ranvir,' Simi said. 'He lent me his charger on my first day at BizWorks.'

'Oh, you know Ranvir?' Abhi said.

'You're the cute guy who lent Simi the laptop charger?' Deepa followed.

'What are you saying?' Simi said, her cheeks turning red.

Cute guy, huh? Ranvir chuckled.

Simi shook her head and gave Ranvir an awkward smile. 'Don't pay any attention to her.' She put her tray on the table and sat beside Ranvir, leaving the seat next to Abhi for Deepa.

Deepa looked at the empty seat, scowled and sat down.

Abhi turned to Simi. 'Small world! We meet again. So, where do you work?'

'Murano. It's a furniture company.'

'Ooh, I've been looking for a new couch. Maybe you guys can guide me a bit.'

Simi chuckled. 'We're the marketing department. But we can always get someone in the sales department to help you out.'

'I see,' Abhi said, with a dejected look.

'Where do you work?' Simi asked him, while Ranvir noticed that Deepa was giving Abhi a glowering scowl.

'We both work at Fintura. I'm in accounts. Ranvir is in the strategy team. In fact, this is our only office. And we have a lot of meetings all day. I have a lot of tea during those meetings, and tulsi is my favourite—'

'Excuse me!' Deepa said, rising from her seat suddenly. 'I'm going to get some salt.'

Abhi's face paled as she left. 'I think I'll go find some ketchup.' He got up and followed her.

Ranvir found himself alone at the table with Simi. 'I wonder what's got into Abhi today. He isn't usually this weird.'

'Deepa isn't usually like this either,' she said. 'She's just having a bad day. Abhi tore her tulsi teabag in the break room earlier. And then the wrap place ran out of her favourite wrap.'

So, the idiot liked Deepa, not Simi. Everything made perfect sense now. Ranvir peered at Simi as he bit into his sandwich and chewed. 'Oh, so that's what Abhi was talking about.'

'What was he talking about?' Simi asked, unwrapping her roll and taking a bite.

'That he'd met someone today, they'd got into a fight, and he'd fallen in love with her.'

She stopped mid-bite, looking shocked.

'It's hard to believe a fight led to falling in love . . . Usually a smile leads to it . . . ' The words were out of his mouth before he could stop them.

Suddenly, she choked and spluttered.

Stop! He literally stuffed the sandwich into his mouth to stop the nonsensical blabber. What terrible small talk he was making.

Before he knew it, she was having a coughing fit, tears rolling from her eyes.

'You okay?'

'Water,' she gasped and extended her hand.

Something made him grab her hand at that very moment. If he had been a second late, the glass might have been knocked over, meeting the same fate as the coffee cup.

* * *

Simi didn't know how it happened. One moment Ranvir was talking about Abhi and Deepa falling in love and the next she was choking.

She had not even seen the glass of water on the table right next to her hand.

All she knew was that her heart was hammering at the way he was looking at her.

Ranvir's hand had come out of nowhere.

As if he'd known she was about to drop the glass.

The very next moment, his hand closed over hers.

She gasped as a wave of awareness coursed up her arm. The coughing stopped on its own.

'I got you!' he said.

Warmth crept up her neck.

'You're a good striker.' He looked amused. 'Played a lot of TT?'

Badminton, actually. She was suddenly annoyed, despite his cute smile, because he was laughing at her.

'No!' She flicked him a haughty glance just as Deepa and Abhi returned to the table. Both were scowling now.

What was wrong with them?

Simi was about to raise the glass for a sip of water when she felt a tug. She looked down and realized something.

Ranvir was still holding her hand.

Ranvir stared down at their hands, realizing the fact himself. He looked back up to meet her gaze and let go of her hand guiltily.

* * *

'You should watch liquids around her,' Deepa said to Ranvir, as Simi took a long sip of water.

Abhi was slumped in his chair, looking forlorn, until he began talking again.

When Abhi talked, nobody could stop him. It seemed like he was determined to impress Deepa, which didn't seem to be working despite his best effort to tell them all about the food counters and what was the best thing to try at each of them, how the Supremo coffee was cheaper than the Nescafe, and how the yoga studio conducted classes thrice a week.

Deepa focused on the food in front of her, ignoring him.

Ranvir could do nothing except sit back and enjoy the show.

Finally, Simi and Deepa were done eating, and rose to leave.

'I still have your charger. At . . . at my desk, I mean,' Simi stuttered. 'Sorry, the replacement is going to take longer.'

'Don't worry!' Ranvir said. 'I can wait.'

She looked relieved.

'It was Ranvir's birthday last Friday,' Abhi said suddenly.

Ranvir was confused. Why was Abhi bringing up his birthday?

Simi's face lit up. 'The day we met?'

Ranvir nodded. 'Yes.'

She offered a handshake. 'Belated happy birthday!'

Her hand was so small and soft against his large palm. 'Thank you!' he said and was pleased to see two red dots of colour rise to her cheeks. He released her hand, and she withdrew it hastily.

'Happy birthday!' Deepa chimed in.

'We're having a small party at The Happy Hour,' Abhi said, much to Ranvir's surprise. 'Ranvir thought we should invite you too. Right, Ranvir?'

The Happy Hour? Birthday party?

Was Abhi out of his mind?

Abhi forced a tight smile, silently willing Ranvir to go along with his plan.

'Yes. Yes,' Ranvir said. 'They have the best grills. Please come. It'll be a few friends. That's all. Small and simple.'

'I wish I could come but I have a lot of work to finish,' Simi said. 'I don't think I can make it.'

'Yes, you can. What time?' Deepa said out of the blue.

'6?' Abhi jumped in, his eyes sparkling brightly.

Ranvir nodded. 'Yeah, 6 should be good.'

Ranvir waited until Deepa and Simi had left. 'Birthday party, bro? Have you gone nuts?'

'Didn't you see how angry Deepa was with me? I was trying so hard to get another chance to meet her.'

'You really are insane!'

He grinned. 'I wouldn't have been able to set up this date if I hadn't remembered your birthday.'

'So, this is a date?' Ranvir said, smiling. He liked how ingenious his friend was when it came to date ideas.

'Yeah, my first date with Deepa.'

'You don't waste any time, do you?' Ranvir asked, still teasing his friend.

'It can get so boring when you live alone like me. How long can one keep up the online dating with strangers which leads nowhere?'

'Deepa isn't a stranger?' Ranvir asked innocently.

Abhi just glared at him in response.

'Anyway, I can't even imagine a party. I have tons of reports to work on.'

Abhi scratched the back of his head. 'Said the first thing that came to mind. There was no other way to meet Deepa again.'

'Besides, who'll come for a party on a Monday?'

'I'll manage to get a few peeps, macha! I need to see Deepa again.'

'You know nothing about her,' Ranvir tried to reason.

'How will I know anything if I don't even get a chance? It's as if she hates me for no reason.'

Ranvir smirked and shook his head. 'You and your crazy ideas!'

* * *

'What was that?' Simi asked Deepa as they walked back to the office. 'First, you don't like Abhi. Now you want to go to the party?'

Deepa looked guilty. 'It's not his party. It's Ranvir's.' She stopped and turned to Simi, giving her a pointed look. 'How sad that you don't want to celebrate the birthday of the guy who helped you with your dead charger.'

'That's not what I meant.'

'Sorry for wanting a bit of happiness after my terrible weekend,' Deepa went on, sarcasm lacing her words. 'I know Abhi and I fought over that stupid teabag, but I can't hold it against him forever. Besides, who says no to a party and making new friends.'

Valid points; especially, if it helped Deepa get over her break-up with Pratik.

'Okay, you're right!' Simi said. 'A party is just what you need. But I really can't go. Champak has taken the Custard settee a tad too seriously. He won't stop discussing it, and my meeting might go beyond 6 p.m.'

Deepa pursed her lips and gave Simi an irritated look. 'It's after work. It's a birthday party! Birthday parties don't come every day. So, quit worrying about Champak and let's have some fun.'

There was no point arguing with Deepa when she wanted to have fun.

TEN

The Happy Hour was a cosy, dimly lit place with solid, wooden tables and benches. Lanterns were hung from several corners to make it a look like a dhaba. But the semi-enclosed booths, and a DJ bopping to tracks he was expertly mixing added a modern touch.

Music thrummed through the floor as Simi and Deepa made their way in, not really able to see much until Simi's eyes finally got used to the dim lighting. She found herself tapping her feet already.

This wasn't such a bad idea after all.

Most of the place was full. It seemed like a great hangout for office goers.

A large table had been set up in a corner where Ranvir, Abhi and some of their friends had gathered.

Abhi waved to them and got up from his seat to welcome them.

He asked Simi and Deepa about their choice of drinks.

Simi wanted a margarita. Deepa wasn't sure, so Abhi took her to the bar counter, while Simi wound her way towards the table where Ranvir was sitting.

Ranvir smiled and waved to the empty seat next to him.

Simi indicated to the bar, shouting over the din. 'Abhi's gone to get Deepa a drink.'

'It's okay. He'll find another place,' Ranvir shouted back.

Three people had to move from their seats so Simi could get in. The air around Ranvir felt charged.

'How was your day?' Ranvir said, leaning in to make sure she could hear him.

'Good!'

The office crowd was rowdy. Their shouts and laughter barely made it above the sound of the reverberating beats. Simi felt herself relax and slip into a party mood.

For once, she put aside her worries about her pending work and just decided to have fun. Deepa was right. Birthday parties didn't come every day!

Speaking of the devil! There she was, smiling at Abhi, leaning into him as his arm rested on her waist. She let him guide her to the table, holding a cocktail in her hand.

'Now that everybody is here, how about we cut the birthday cake?' Abhi suggested. He waved to a guy who soon appeared with a tower-like cake with frosting on the top.

'This is a vodka coffee cake,' Abhi announced. 'Ranvir's favourite.'

Ranvir grinned and blew out the candles.

Cheers went up around the table. The very next instant, the candles magically lit up again and everybody laughed.

'Not fair!' Ranvir groaned at the magic candles.

The gang cheered and whistled as he tried to blow out the candles. Finally, after several tries, he managed to blow them out fully.

Claps followed and everybody sang 'Happy Birthday'. He cut the cake and distributed it. Soon, everyone was digging into the delightful vodka and coffee gooey goodness.

Platters of grilled snacks soon followed—perfectly cooked pieces of chicken, prawn and paneer that had a nice, smoky flavour on the outer coating but were tender to bite into.

After having their fill, everyone wanted to dance. Abhi pulled Deepa towards the makeshift open stage in front of the DJ's booth, which served as the dance floor.

'Come on!' Deepa waved at Ranvir and Simi who were the only two left at the table.

'I'm a terrible dancer,' Simi confessed. There was no point in showing any bravado where none was required. She usually sat out dance parties.

'Then you have company,' Ranvir said, pulling her up to her feet. 'We'll have two terrible dancers stepping on everybody's feet and bumping into everyone.'

Simi let out a gurgle of laughter. Yeah, that sounded like fun.

'Let's show them how we dance!'

She pushed her hair back from her face and held out her hand, following him to the floor. It was not as though she didn't respond to the music. In fact, her feet moved almost instinctively to the beats.

Just to prove to her what he meant, Ranvir purposely bumped into Abhi and Deepa, and the others around them.

'Find your own space, macha!' Abhi teased him.

'Okay, okay!' Ranvir pulled Simi closer, put his warm hand on her back and held her hand. 'This is the way we move,' he said softly in her ears.

They moved to the beats. He laughed it off every time she bumped into him or stepped on his toes.

'You're right! You're a terrible dancer.' He gave her a twirl, making her laugh giddily. 'Hopefully my toes survive the night.'

Simi glanced over his shoulder. Abhi was dancing to the retro Bollywood music, shaking and spinning with wild abandon. Deepa was following his moves.

She was shy to try the same with Ranvir. 'Abhi and Deepa seem to have forgotten their fight,' she whispered in Ranvir's ear.

He gazed at her. 'Lucky for your friend.'

'Lucky for your friend,' she countered with a mock frown. 'I think he'll be the one who tells her he loves her.'

'Uh-huh!' Ranvir shook his head. 'She'll be the first to say she likes him.'

'Want to bet?'

'Yeah, okay bet!'

'You'll lose.'

'We'll see,' Ranvir said, his eyes shining with humour. He swung her backwards before pulling her up towards him in a sweeping motion that made her giddy with delight.

They stayed like that for a few moments, both panting but smiling from ear to ear.

The world around them seemed to have faded. She was no longer paying attention to the music, just him. His fingers slid down her arms and rested below her breastbone, holding her more firmly.

He held her gaze, his glittering eyes so close that she saw nothing but them. As his eyes came to rest on her lips, it felt like something had suddenly changed between them.

She wrapped her arms around his shoulders and clasped her fingers behind his neck, longing to rake her hand through his hair, along his jaw, tracing the sides of his cheeks and his light stubble. She took in his thick eyebrows, the slight crease between them, his straight nose and the slight upward curl of his lips.

He looked so utterly handsome that she couldn't take her eyes off him. There was something so electric about his gaze. She was mesmerized.

He hadn't taken his eyes off her. And then he smiled, the corners of his mouth curling into a deeper grin. Her stomach caved. Why did his smile have to be so perfect?

A shudder coursed through her as he lifted his hand and brought it to her hair, caressing it.

'Some cake,' he said, picking something out of her hair.

Her eyes still lingered on his lips; the full, tempting lips drawing her towards them involuntarily, begging to be kissed.

The music changed.

His eyes flickered. He looked away for a moment before looking back at her. His expression had changed. His face was flushed.

'I have a girlfriend,' he said.

'What?' She was still smiling and looking at his lips.

'I have a girlfriend.'

Her stomach did a flip, and it took her a moment to process what she had just heard.

As he looked into her eyes, her heart thumped wildly as if it was going to burst out of her chest. She took a sudden step back and fumbled. Her ankle twisted and a sharp jolt of pain shot through her leg.

She winced.

He caught her arm. His hand was warm and the smell of his cool lemony cologne drifted to her nose. 'Sit down for a sec,' he said, helping her to the nearest chair.

Her eyes stung with pain the moment her foot touched the ground. But the pain of not being able to meet his eyes was worse. She was annoyed with herself for being so stupid.

'I'll be right back,' he said.

He was gone for a few minutes before he returned with some ice wrapped in a napkin. Settling down next to her, he helped her put her foot over his knee and took off her shoe. One hand wrapped softly around her calf, he placed the ice pack against her sprained ankle.

'Ah!' she hissed.

'How bad is it?'

'I don't know,' she said.

He patted her calf. 'Don't worry. Just stay calm.'

Calm?

Her heart was anything but calm. She'd been thinking about kissing him!

If he hadn't told her about his girlfriend, she might have. Even now, as he held the ice pack against her ankle, she could feel his eyes on her, watching her movements, her expression, but she avoided his gaze, afraid that she might give away her embarrassment.

She looked towards the dance floor to distract herself. The others were too busy dancing to have noticed them. Abhi was cracking Deepa up with his dance moves. The party had helped Deepa's mood lighten up immensely.

The disco lights around the dance floor flashed neon colours on the dancing bodies. Ranvir and Abhi's friends had emptied the four big jugs of beer on their table. The Happy Hour was quite packed by now. It was as if nobody wanted to leave and go home.

'Feeling better?' Ranvir's voice broke into her thoughts.

'A little.' She nodded.

'I should have . . . ' he began, his eyes full of remorse.

Told me that you had a girlfriend?

'We should not have . . . '

Danced?

Gosh! She was so embarrassed, her cheeks felt hot.

'I'm sorry—' he said.

'Me too,' she said, nodding.

'I'd like to start over, Simi.' He offered her his hand. 'Friends?'

She had only two options.

Tell him she was attracted to him and thus they could never be friends.

Or . . .

Pretend she didn't want to kiss him and just be friends.

As she looked into his sharp, glimmering eyes, her heart thundering, the decision was made. 'Friends,' she managed with a smile.

A wave of relief washed over him. 'Good. Let me check with the others and get you home.'

'Yeah.' She nodded. She was right. They were better off as friends.

ELEVEN

As he drove Simi home, the song 'Sooraj Dooba Hai Yaaron' played non-stop in Ranvir's head. He and Simi had danced to it at The Happy Hour.

One minute, Simi and he had been putting a bet on Abhi and Deepa, and the next they had been dancing together, their bodies pressed against each other. Her face was mere inches away from his, her hazel brown eyes shining, her arms wound around his neck; her smile was so dazzling that it was impossible not to stare.

He was spellbound by every subtle feature of her face, the hint of the golden shadow on her eyelids, the deep blush on her cheekbones, her slightly plumper upper lip, the dimple that he wanted to touch.

He felt his heart thumping so hard as if it would jump out of his rib cage.

He touched her hair, and she moved closer. For a moment, he was carried away, forgetting where he was, with whom he was. He saw nothing but her dreamy eyes and the way she was looking at him, and the lips that were a breath away from his.

Then the music changed and he came to his senses.

God knows, he'd been as embarrassed as her about not being in control of himself.

He was happy they'd sorted it out like reasonable and mature adults. He still wanted to be friends with her and not lose her to the insane, spur-of-the-moment feeling— something that had caught him completely off guard.

No damage had been done. They were still friends.

They were safe. All was well.

Simi had said nothing after the incident had been put behind them, except agreeing to being dropped home in his car. He couldn't have left her waiting for a cab or an auto with her injured foot.

Abhi, on the other hand, had hit it off with Deepa. She'd even accepted his offer for a ride home on his bike.

Simi sat silently beside Ranvir, saying nothing. Her intertwined fingers were on her lap. In the dim interior of the car, he could make out the soft lines of her face, her hair draped over one shoulder, her head leaning against the window.

'All okay?' he asked her.

'Yes, thanks for dropping me home.'

'Thanks for coming to the party!'

'I want to know who'll win that bet.' She laughed, the tinkling sound making him feel light and at ease again.

'We'll see!' he said.

The road ahead was clear at this time of the night. He shifted to fourth gear, his hands touching her dupatta that was covering it partially. The car zoomed down the open road.

Just then, Ranvir's phone rang, breaking the silence in the car.

Ranvir answered. 'What's up?'

'Macha! I can't find Deepa's house.'

'What?'

* * *

Instead of going towards Simi's house, they took a detour to Deepa's PG.

'What does Abhi mean they can't find it?' Simi asked, nonplussed.

'Deepa's drunk. Apparently, she is confused and they've landed up in a different building.'

Simi did not know what to do. She'd never been to Deepa's house either. How would they find out where she lived?

It was worse than she'd expected when they arrived, and Ranvir parked his car right next to Abhi's bike. Abhi was waiting by his bike, while Deepa was seated on it, eyes closed, half-leaning against Abhi. He could barely hold her upright.

'I can't drive and search for her place, macha. She's fallen asleep. I can't handle her and the bike together.'

Roused by the commotion around her, Deepa opened her eyes. 'Am I home?'

'Unfortunately, not yet!' Simi said, sighing. 'What's your address?'

She rattled off a building name and street number. Simi dug inside Deepa's bag and found her ID card. The street number on there was different.

The whole street was full of PGs, all indicated by random numbers. It was like a maze, and there were not many people around to ask.

First things first. They settled Deepa in Ranvir's car so that she wouldn't fall over. Then they started asking around for her address.

After several false starts and misses, they finally found her building tucked away in a narrow, poorly-lit lane.

Phew!

'Thank God you came!' Abhi said, after Simi had helped Deepa into her room and tucked her into bed. 'They would never have allowed me inside.'

He was right. The guard at the gate had given them a glaring look and had let only Simi enter the premises. Abhi and Ranvir had to wait outside. Simi heaved a sigh of relief that Deepa was safely home.

Finally, they were ready to head back.

'Thank you,' Abhi said to her and Ranvir. 'I had a lovely night. Thanks again for helping me out.'

Ranvir and Simi exchanged amused glances, neither saying anything about the bet. Instead, they just nodded their heads.

'Sure!' Simi said cheerily. 'We had a great time too!'

Then Abhi rode off on his bike, and Simi got back into Ranvir's car.

It was getting late. She was just about to call home and let her parents know when her phone rang. It was her mother.

Simi picked up the call. 'Hi, Ma!'

'Why are you so late?' her mother asked. 'Did you go shopping with Deepa again?'

'No, Ma. Had to drop Deepa to her house. I'm on my way home now.'

Her mother didn't ask any more questions, and Simi was glad. It would have been tough to make excuses to her mother with Ranvir right next to her.

'Karan had called,' her mother said simply. 'I told him you were out.'

No sooner had Simi hung up the call than her phone rang again. It was Karan.

'Are you still at work?' Karan's voice boomed into her ears.

'Got late at the office.' *At a party.* But she didn't mention that. 'I'm on my way home.'

'Ma said she wanted to talk to you. Have you called her yet?'

Her chest sank with fear at those words. Would his mother propose that they get married without waiting for Karan's promotion? Did she want to speak to her to discuss her bridal attire or choose an appropriate wedding date?

Her breath was stuck in her throat. 'Is it something to do with us?'

He let out a breath, as if he'd been holding it just like her. 'I don't know! But please call her and let me know what she says.'

She promised she would, and he seemed relieved.

He'd transformed ever since the 'proposal.' He was trying to be nice. But was a bit nervous. It gave her a kick to realize he was probably as nervous as she was.

She was used to the version of him who said mean things and didn't share his lollipop. This version was so weird that she still didn't feel like talking to him.

She hung up and found Ranvir smiling.

'I didn't know we were going to be so late. I forgot to call and tell my parents. What's funny?'

'I didn't know you had a boyfriend.'

'What—How did you . . . ? No, I don't have a boyfriend.'

'You were just speaking to him. What's his name?'

Guilt bore into her as he turned to face her. 'Karan. He's . . . I got a marriage proposal from his family. Last week in fact.'

'Oh,' he said shrugging, an unfathomable expression crossing his face.

She felt worse, mortification eating up her insides. 'I should have told you about it back there on the dance floor, but there was nothing to tell.'

He shrugged. 'It's okay that you didn't want to tell me.'

She went on nevertheless. 'I have known him since childhood, but I never thought I was going to marry him.'

'A childhood friend?'

'Karan was not exactly a childhood friend. I never liked him then. We had nothing in common. He was just a pain in the ass. He still is.'

'Why are you marrying a pain in the ass?'

She sensed a teasing tone in Ranvir's voice again. For some reason, her eyes stung. It had been a long day, and she'd been through a lot—from wanting to kiss him to finding out he was unavailable and now having to explain her relationship with Karan. The last thing she wanted was him teasing her about it.

Raising her chin, she turned to look at him. 'Why do you like making fun of me so much?'

He turned to her, looking contrite the moment he saw her troubled expression.

'God Simi! I didn't mean to . . . '

There was a pause and then a long silence as if he didn't know what else to say.

She looked out the window and didn't feel like talking any further.

They finally reached her apartment. He stopped the car and turned to her. 'Simi, I know I really have no business poking my nose in your personal affairs. But I've seen bad marriages in my family. My—' He stopped talking and shook his head.

She wondered what he was about to tell her and why he'd changed his mind. Who in his family had had a bad marriage?

'That door doesn't open from the inside unless you put pressure. It's my dad's old car,' he said with a heavy exhale, getting out of the car and coming around to her side. He opened the door for her and as she stepped out, he said, 'Simi, I'm really sorry! I didn't mean to hurt your feelings.'

She didn't know what to say except she'd been feeling anxious lately. It wasn't his fault her heart was in turmoil.

He let out a long, deep breath and held her gaze. 'I hope you find the right guy.'

I'll never find out if it could have been you.

The thought pulsed through her before she swallowed and looked away.

* * *

Ranvir felt a stab looking at her pained expression.

He knew her ankle still hurt by the way she winced when she moved her foot. It probably started hurting again after she helped Deepa up to her room.

'Let me drop you to your home.'

Simi refused his help. 'No, it's okay. My father would find it very strange if you came to drop me.'

He shook his head. 'I'm just a colleague who's helping you because you're hurt. But if you don't want me to come, I won't.'

Her eyes were dark pools of gratitude and regret. 'I promise it's not because I don't want you to come.'

Don't be silly, he wanted to tell her. Let me help. Stop worrying about what people will think. But he didn't say any of that. 'No problem,' he said instead. 'Will you be able to walk by yourself?'

'Yes,' she said. 'I'll manage. Thanks again.'

He nodded and got back to his car. She walked towards her apartment and slid one last backward glance at him as he turned the car around.

He could still see her in the distance as he started the car. Once he eased on to the road, he switched on the radio for company.

Ironically, at that moment, RJ Shakeel was talking about love and marriage. Ranvir found his thoughts going back to Simi.

I don't have a boyfriend.

First of all, he didn't know how someone as gorgeous as her did not have a boyfriend. And second, why did she have to marry a guy she thought was a pain in the ass?

He'd almost mentioned his sister's marriage, and how he'd been too young then to understand how hurried it was. It had been fixed right after their mother was diagnosed with the illness. He wished his family had not coerced Tina into marriage. He only wished Simi would take his advice and get to know the man she was going to marry.

'Life is a puzzle,' RJ Shakeel went on, his voice drowning out the sound of cars and bikes whizzing past his window.

We love what we can't have and we can't have what we love. We're all unlucky in love sometimes.

He'd heard that quote somewhere.

It felt true but also strange.

He had a girlfriend and yet he didn't even think of Parul on the dance floor. In fact, he didn't remember feeling so happy in so long.

And he didn't know what to make of the feeling at all.

TWELVE

It was only Simi's third day at the co-working space, and already she really liked it.

Though she missed all her colleagues, it was fun to mingle with people from different companies on the floor. Sometimes, the place got so noisy, especially the people who sat across the Murano enclosure, that she had to wear headphones.

At 5 p.m. someone would come around with cookies, and soft music would play in the lounge just outside. On the first day, she'd joined the mill of people gathered in the coffee area, chatting and introducing themselves to each other. The next day, she'd stayed at her desk, tapping her feet to the retro Bollywood beats.

There were meeting rooms with large projectors and pull-down screens. Their usual meeting room was occupied that morning, so they had to go into a smaller one. Champak kept up his irritating questions as usual.

Deepa had a long face throughout the meeting. Her mood seemed downcast again that morning.

Finally, Simi pulled her along for a bathroom break.

'What's the matter with you? You were fine after the party last night.'

It was Pratik. He'd called her and been clear that he loved her. 'I have no idea what to do!' Deepa said, her eyebrows bunched together. 'He told me to give his parents some time. But that's not it, Simi! I'm sure they'll resent me and think of me as the girl who's trying to replace their son's ex-wife. They'll never accept me.'

'Then maybe you need to end this?' Simi asked, trying to help Deepa decide what was best for her.

'The problem is I like Pratik, although I know it won't work out if his parents continue to behave this way. And this morning Abhi sent me a cute message.' Deepa covered her face with her hands and groaned. 'I like Abhi, and I really don't want to hurt him. He was so nice to me, but I don't want to mislead him while I still have feelings for Pratik.'

It made sense, and it was a tough position to be in.

So, for the next two weeks, they decided to stay away from the food court—the only way to avoid running into Abhi—and manage with Simi's lunch dabbas.

Simi was happy to avoid the food court too, because she didn't want to meet Ranvir. She couldn't forget the night they'd danced together.

She needed time to sort out her feelings too.

She'd limped back home that night after Ranvir dropped her at her gate, feeling hollow and even more unsure of her impending marriage.

It had only worsened after her call with Karan's mother, Bhavna, who wanted her and Karan to go shopping for her anniversary party.

'Help Karan pick something up for the party,' Bhavna had said. 'And let him pick something for you. I'd like you both to go shopping together. You both hardly get a chance to meet.'

Simi had rolled her eyes. Karan's taste in clothes was totally opposite hers, like comparing a full suit to a t-shirt and a pair of jeans.

But she'd said yes.

Why are you marrying a pain in the ass?

She never expected Ranvir's words to hit her like they had. She tried to reason out why she was going along with this marriage proposal. Other than the guilt of letting her father down and being worried for his health, she came up empty.

But just thinking about tying the knot with Karan made her heart race so fast that she had to breathe deeply to calm down.

Why was she getting into a marriage she did not want?

And why did Ranvir pop into her head every time she thought about it?

* * *

The Yoga Studio at BizWorks was offering a free week-long trial for their new yoga classes.

Deepa had seen the poster and jumped at the offer, declaring that she needed to get back her peace of mind.

Yoga seemed perfect! So, she'd gone ahead and signed up Simi and herself for the trial.

She was still upset about how things with Pratik stood. They hadn't broken off completely and were still talking to each other, but there wasn't a clear plan on how they could be together.

Simi skipped breakfast to make it on time to the yoga class. The rectangular studio was as large as her living room, and it was full. Colourful mats lay in neat rows on the floor.

Their instructor, Mansi, was a young woman with an enviable figure—long slender legs, flat tummy, and a perfect, toned butt. Not to mention her flawless skin.

'I would be a model if doing yoga every day made me look like that,' Deepa, as awestruck as Simi was, whispered in her ear.

Simi smirked. 'Fat chance that either of us will look like the instructor even in a zillion years!'

Deepa made a face but before she could respond, Mansi asked everyone to close their eyes and begin chanting Om.

The yoga class was calming and relaxing; the deep breathing and full-body stretches were just what Simi needed. Deepa agreed that she was feeling a whole lot better by the end of the class.

They'd just rolled up their mats and set them in a corner when they heard a chirpy 'Hi!' behind them.

Deepa spun around first. 'Oh! Hi!' she said to Abhi. 'I didn't know you were in the class.'

'I came in late,' Abhi said. 'By the way, you look great . . . I mean the yoga pants look great on you.'

Deepa blushed. She'd just bought them yesterday. 'Thank you,' she said.

'Do you have time to catch up before work?' he asked her.

Deepa looked at Simi and back at Abhi and declined. 'I can't,' she said.

'Why not? It's not even 9 yet. They have great dosas at The Dosa Palace. Want to have some? I'm craving a dosa right now.' Abhi grinned and looked at Deepa expectantly. It was obvious that Abhi wanted to speak to Deepa alone, but Deepa continued to dilly-dally.

'I have to get back. You guys carry on,' Simi said, deciding it was best to leave them alone to work it out.

Simi turned around to go to the changing room and ran straight into a rock-solid chest. 'Ooops!' she let out a gasp as strong hands grabbed her shoulders.

Simi looked up in surprise, only to peer straight into Ranvir's eyes. Just the man she didn't want to think about after a relaxing yoga session.

'Hey!' He let go of her shoulders, releasing her. 'You okay?'

'Hey! Yeah!' Simi could feel his heartbeat against her palms on his chest. Withdrawing her hands, and not knowing what to do with them, she tucked a loose strand of hair behind her ear, her heart still thumping. 'I didn't see you. Were you in the class too?'

Ranvir smiled. 'Yeah!'

Her eyes roamed involuntarily over his face, the faint line of sweat over his eyebrows, the upward tilt of his lips. They settled on his eyes and she found herself staring into them.

'Abhi pulled me into it for company,' Ranvir said. 'Good thing he found whom he was looking for. Haven't seen you around much since the party.'

Had she heard him right? Or was she reading too much into such a casual statement? She touched her flaming cheeks, hoping to calm herself down. 'Just a lot of work,' she said. *Besides the fact that I didn't want to see you.*

'Is your ankle better?'

She nodded. 'Yeah, it's fine now.'

She wished she could get the thudding of her heart to stop, but she couldn't while he stood in front of her looking so sexy. It didn't help that he wore a snug grey t-shirt that hugged his biceps and stretched across his broad chest.

She cleared her throat. 'I have to go.' Ignoring the perplexed look on Ranvir's face, she rushed out of the studio back to the safety of her desk.

* * *

A few days later, Simi found Ranvir seated at the same table where she'd seen him on her first day at work, his back to her.

She had to do this. Even if she had stayed away from the food court and tried to keep to her area to avoid running into Ranvir, she still had to return his charger.

And not see him again.

The thought made her throat choke.

Chin up, she made her way towards him, prepared to get it over and done with.

She cleared her throat. 'Hi.'

Ranvir turned around in surprise and smiled. 'Hi!'

Her stomach did a flip-flop. She pulled out his charger from her bag. 'Thanks for this!'

'I've missed this bugger,' he muttered, eyes lighting up.

She felt her cheeks grow warm. 'Thank you for letting me have your charger for so many days.'

'You're welcome.'

'I brought something to say thank you.' Her words came out in a rush of nervousness. She pulled out a tiny packet from her bag and gave it to him. 'You don't have to keep it. It's a crochet butterfly.'

Yeah, it was cheesy thank you. She'd crocheted to calm down her scattered brain and stop thinking about him, and yet made something for him.

He reached inside the packet and pulled out the butterfly.

She'd used soft yarn to give the butterfly delicate, indigo blue, scalloped wings, fuchsia pink circles and maroon antennae with two beads attached to its tips.

He looked at it keenly, touching it, turning it around, admiring it. 'It's so intricate. I've never seen anything like it,' he said. 'Thank you!'

'My grandmother taught me as a young girl.' She knew what he must be thinking now. 'I know!' she said, shaking her head. 'It's such a grandmotherly hobby.'

He gave her an intense look. 'It's beautiful! I love it!' As if that was all that mattered. The fact that it was beautiful and that she'd made it for him.

A soft sense of pride settled in her chest.

'Thank you. Really!' He held her gaze and hesitated for a moment. In fact, he was giving her a weird look.

'What?'

He rubbed his hand over his face and paused as if forming the words in his head. 'Can I ask you for a favour, if you don't mind?'

Did he have something else in mind in return for the charger?

'It's for Abhi actually,' he said, surprising her. It wasn't what she was expecting.

'What about Abhi?'

He sighed. 'He's been wanting to take Deepa out on a date but it's not working out. I don't know why she's avoiding him—'

She'd seen Deepa sulk even more lately. Pratik and Deepa had broken up again, and Deepa was a mess. 'It's because she's still sad about her ex-boyfriend,' she said. It seemed like the best way to explain Deepa's confusion in life at the moment. 'And she isn't sure about Abhi.'

'I guess that's what it is.' He looked crestfallen.

Why was he so upset? She was talking about Abhi, not him.

She eyed him warily as he picked up the conversation and continued, 'Abhi's been losing his mind thinking something is wrong with him. Maybe we could bring them together so they could talk it out?'

'It'll be good for Deepa too. Maybe,' he added cheerfully.

'What do you have in mind?'

'What if all of us pretend to bump into each other?'

What?

His eyes were locked with hers. '5 p.m. Friday. Bring Deepa to the ice-cream stand?'

She was about to say she couldn't meet him but the look in his eyes . . .

'Okay,' she found herself saying.

Running his fingers through his hair, he released a breath of relief. 'Great! He smiled, the corners of his eyes crinkling.

Her heart did a backflip.

As she made her way back to her desk, she wondered if she'd agreed to help Ranvir because of that earnest appeal to help his friend or the earnest desire in her heart to help hers.

Either way, it looked like they were playing matchmakers now.

* * *

Simi and Karan were at a clothing store that sold rich saris, dazzling lehengas and expensive wedding outfits.

Karan's mother had insisted they go shopping together for their outfits to wear to the anniversary party.

While Simi had vehemently declined the idea, her own father had seemed keen to send them shopping together.

'Going shopping with Karan is a terrible idea!' Ayush had teased her but what could be done when Karan's mother and her father seemed hell-bent on it.

Karan held out a lime green flowy outfit to Simi.

'I don't like the colour,' Simi said. 'It's too garish!'

'Let's call my mother. She'll know.'

After that, Simi tried outfit after outfit, and each time she had to video call Bhavna to show her how it looked.

Even though Bhavna wasn't physically present with them, it seemed like she was. What would have taken Simi and her mother an hour turned into a three-hour-long ordeal, which involved trying on multiple clothes and discarding most of them.

They finally came to a consensus about a peach and yellow lehenga and a matching blouse and dupatta.

Then they went over to the men's section and started looking for Karan.

It took forever. It was ridiculous. Karan simply could not make up his mind. His mother and he dithered and argued, and finally picked a suit that seemed to please them both. Simi and he finally headed to the counter to pay.

In front of them were a girl and a guy holding hands, discussing where they would go for their honeymoon.

She pictured Karan and her discussing their honeymoon and felt uneasy.

They weren't formally engaged. But the way their parents were pushing for it, it seemed like a very real possibility. She shuddered and pushed the thought away.

'My mother adores you,' Karan said, his voice breaking into her thoughts.

Bhavna Aunty was okay. Not phenomenally nice but okay.

But Karan's words seemed a little odd in a way she couldn't put a finger on.

'She's found fault with every girl I've met,' he continued. He sounded baffled, to her surprise. Was Bhavna Aunty such a tough mother-in-law to please?

Was that why none of the proposals had worked for him in the past?

She chewed on her lip. This was why it had been so difficult to say no when his father had put forth the proposal. His parents liked her, and her parents liked him.

Had they even considered if Karan and she liked each other? Or had they not asked for his opinion?

'Karan, why do you want to marry me?' The words came out without thinking.

'Uh . . . Um . . . ' he sputtered. 'I guess that's how arranged marriages work,' he said after a pause. He stared at her for a moment, an unreadable expression crossing his face. Then he shifted uncomfortably and looked down at his feet. 'Why do you want to marry me?'

I don't!

'Next!' the clerk called out. It was their turn at the counter.

They moved forward. By the time they were done paying and giving Karan's pants for alteration, the question had been forgotten.

THIRTEEN

Being with his older sister, Tina reminded Ranvir of his mother.

Tina told him about her week as he drove.

He'd picked up some groceries for his father like he did on Saturday afternoons. Then he'd picked Tina from her house and was driving to his father's house.

He enjoyed this ritual and had kept it going since he'd moved out of his home.

Parul would train for her half-marathon over the weekends and Tina's husband, Jas, was always too busy to join them. So, it was usually just the three of them.

It was a ritual he enjoyed and kept up, despite work becoming more hectic at Fintura.

Tina noticed the butterfly hanging from the rear-view mirror. She held it between her fingers, turning it around to inspect it carefully. 'It's so pretty. Where did you get it?'

'A girl at the co-working space gave it to me.'

Her antennae went up immediately. 'A girl at the co-working space, huh? Does she work at Fintura too? And why haven't I heard of her before?'

'It's because I don't talk about work when we meet, Tina!'

'That's right, you don't talk about work! You don't talk about Parul or your personal life. Nothing. You've shut me and Papa out of everything.'

Tina could be melodramatic at times. It was painful when she worked up a rant just like his mother used to.

'Don't treat me like your baby, Tina!'

Tina shrank as though he'd slapped her, and went quiet.

Nobody was allowed to say the word 'baby' in their house since Tina's miscarriages. It had been almost nine years, and she hadn't been able to conceive despite trying every procedure available.

He regretted the words as soon as they were out of his mouth. He hadn't meant to hurt her.

Sighing, he turned to look at Tina.

She was pouting and staring out of the window.

'No, Tina, it's not that I didn't want to tell you,' he said, softening his tone. 'You haven't heard of this girl because I just met her myself! Her name is Simi. She is in the marketing department of Murano, and they also recently relocated to the co-working space.'

She turned to him, interested.

Ranvir remembered how his mother would ask him about every new girl he would meet at school and insist he tell her everything about his friends.

'So tell me about Simi . . . the girl who crocheted a butterfly for you . . . ' Tina said. 'Sounds like someone who's the complete opposite of Parul—'

It seemed like they were back on familiar turf. Tina loved to tease him about Parul—who according to when she'd first met her—was too loud, whether it was her voice or her make-up, too picky about her food, and just not his type.

But over the years, she'd accepted Parul and her ways. Tina's complaint now was that Parul never had time for her or Papa.

'Stop it, Tina! Simi is just a friend.'

Tina waved her hands. 'Well, I'm just saying that Simi seems very sweet.'

Ranvir stifled a chuckle.

Trust Tina to play games with him.

He could sense when Tina tried to throw crumbs so she could rile him about Parul and tease him about somebody else. Except there hadn't been anyone to tease him about in recent years.

Tina was succeeding because Ranvir found himself thinking about Simi again.

Simi.

Sweet, yes. He'd thought so too.

But she was also betrothed and out of bounds.

If he let Tina go on, she'd insist on meeting Simi and deciding for herself what Simi was really like.

Sidestepping her tactic to get him to talk about Simi, he fell back on the usual—dodge and deflect. Besides, he enjoyed teasing Tina. 'Why? Do you plan to learn crochet so you can make something like that for Jas?'

Tina looked horrified. 'Are you joking? Jas would hate something like that.'

Ranvir's shoulders shook with laughter. He was enjoying this conversation so much more now. 'How boring!' he replied.

'Like Parul!' she countered, not one to give up.

Oh! They were out with their bats now! Their back and forth went like ping-pong balls, until they reached their father's house.

'Did you get my favourite ice cream?' Tina asked, finally taking a break from Parul and Jas.

'I only got my flavour.' He grinned when she stared at him. 'What could I do? They were out of butterscotch! And who eats such outdated flavours anyway?'

'Such a cheapo!' she shot back. She tried the door handle, but it wouldn't budge. He needed to get it fixed. 'Now open the door. This car is wonky, just like you!'

He leaned across Tina and jiggled the handle until it finally gave.

She snorted. 'I wonder how Parul even sits with you in this *dabba* car.'

'She doesn't!' He chuckled. It was Parul who'd kicked the door in a fit of rage one day, breaking the handle. He'd meant to get it repaired, but that had never happened. 'If she does, she waits for me to get out and open it for her.'

Tina giggled. 'Serves you right!'

Ranvir parked the car on the street, and they took out the grocery bags from the boot and divided them among themselves. They walked up to the house, still fighting like teenagers.

'This is so heavy,' Tina said, holding on to one of the bigger bags.

Ranvir laughed. 'You should have asked Jas to come to help you. Or at least get you the ice cream you like.'

'Shut up!' Tina said as they reached the door.

Ranvir unlocked the door with a smile. 'You shut up!'

* * *

'Over here!' Lalit shouted from the backyard.

Ranvir deposited the heavy grocery bags in the kitchen. Then picking out the special treat he'd got for his father, he headed to the backyard. Tina joined him.

'Ah! What have you brought today?' Lalit said.

Ranvir handed over the box of Adiyar sweets. The shine in his father's eyes was inestimably satisfying.

Lalit took in the aroma of the sweet box before picking up a piece of paneer jalebi. 'Mmm . . . ' he said, taking a bite. 'This is so delicious.'

'I'd like one too, Papa,' Tina said, grabbing a sweet for herself.

Lalit pointed to the incomplete game of Scrabble laid out in front of him. 'How about a game before dinner?'

'Papa, let's cook and then you can play,' Tina said, pulling him up.

'Why? It is my break day!'

'Then, I'm playing too. Ranvir, can you cook tonight, please? I'm sure Parul cooks at home for you.'

He snorted. Parul would throw a fit if she knew he cooked here. In their early days of living together, Ranvir always insisted on cooking dinner. Cooking was relaxing. It calmed him. But the past few months had been so hectic he hadn't had the time to cook. It gave Parul another reason to resent his job.

'Let's all finish dinner and then play,' Ranvir said.

Tina and Lalit joined to help him. It was fun when they were all together in the kitchen. It reminded Ranvir of the days when he'd come home and find his mother and father in the kitchen; when his father was visiting from Kuwait.

He watched as his father rounded up the vegetables to chop and hummed as he washed the tomatoes in the sink. Ranvir wished his mother was here. And Jas, and Parul. The whole family cooking, laughing, having a good time.

* * *

'Papa, can I ask you something?' Tina said as she served her father some salad. They'd whipped up an appetizing meal—potato subzi and salad made by Tina, dal made by Ranvir, and rotis made by their father.

'Of course!' Lalit said.

'I'd like to start a boutique of my own. My online clients have been asking me to start one.'

Ranvir remembered how his sister would play dress-up for hours in front of the mirror, trying on Ma's saris and lipsticks and carrying her handbags as if she were going to a cocktail party. The spark of excitement in Tina's eyes about clothes was the same then and now. Leave her in a store full of clothes, and she'd get as excited as a child let loose in a toy store.

Lalit glanced up from his plate and peered at her. 'That's nice.'

'Will you lend me some money?' Her voice was shaky.

Lalit paused and put his hands on the table. 'Beta, wouldn't Jas like to do something like that for you?'

Tina focused on the plate in front of her, not meeting his eye. 'I haven't told him yet, Papa.'

Ranvir reached for her hand across the table. 'Is something wrong, Tina?'

She shook her head quickly. 'No, nothing's wrong.'

Ranvir had always suspected that something was wrong between Tina and Jas. It was apparent now by the look on her face.

After only a few years into marriage, Tina had aged considerably. Her hair was thinning. She'd put on weight.

Their mother had been diagnosed right after Tina and Jas had met for the first time. Her marriage had been fixed in a hurry. Sometimes, Ranvir wondered if she'd really wanted to marry Jas. If she was happy with him. Even if something was bothering her, she'd never told them.

Over the years, not being able to conceive had made it worse. She'd stopped looking after herself, exercising, eating right.

The Tina who was staring at the plate in front of her without touching it wasn't the happy, chirpy, bubbly young woman he remembered. She was often withdrawn, testy, anxious, except when she was with him.

'I just want it to be a surprise for him,' Tina said, pushing the food around on her plate.

Ranvir didn't believe her.

* * *

It was the day of the pre-planned ice-cream date for Abhi and Deepa.

After a long round of meetings, Ranvir asked Abhi if he would like to grab a coffee right outside the building at the Nescafe stand. It was already 4.55 p.m. They were supposed to bump into Simi and Deepa at 5 p.m. He hoped Simi still remembered their plan.

'I'm hungry! Let's get some wraps,' Abhi said, pointing to the food court.

'Not today!' Ranvir said, tugging him towards the exit. 'Let's just get coffee.'

'No, macha! I'm really hungry. I barely had any lunch.'

The fool!

Couldn't he just follow Ranvir's lead for once? Ranvir checked his watch.

They had just three minutes left.

If only Abhi knew. But he couldn't help it if Abhi was hungry so he let Abhi lead the way.

A minute later, Abhi changed his mind. 'Never mind! Wraps only remind me of Deepa. I can't even look at a wrap without thinking of her.'

Ranvir fought back a grin. 'Let's just grab coffee outside. Food court will be crowded right now.'

Abhi agreed.

They walked towards the exit which led to the ice-cream stand. He hoped that Simi and Deepa were already there.

'Why are women so complicated?' Abhi whined as he followed Ranvir.

Ranvir chuckled. Since his birthday party, Abhi had talked only about Deepa. Deepa this, Deepa that.

'She was okay until the night of the party,' Abhi had said. 'Next day, she told me her ex wants to get back. Why go back to someone after he's broken up with you?'

Ranvir had listened but didn't know what to say to him, how to console him. He was glad he'd asked Simi for this favour the day she'd come to return the charger.

Someday, he hoped Abhi would thank him for this unexpected rendezvous.

And perhaps, he would win the bet with Simi!

FOURTEEN

Fingers crossed, Simi steered Deepa towards the BizWorks exit with the promise of ice cream to soothe her heartache.

Deepa wasn't up for it, but Simi dragged her along. She hoped Ranvir and Abhi would be there on time. She did not want Deepa to realize they'd planned it.

It was hard to convince Deepa about anything these days. She'd cry at the drop of a hat. Even the lure of tulsi tea didn't stop her from moping over Pratik.

Ranvir was right. This would be good for Deepa too.

As they stepped outside, Simi looked around. There was no sign of Ranvir or Abhi. Had they forgotten?

She tried to kill some time by admiring the sky. It was cloudy again. Perhaps, it would rain.

'What are you looking at?' Deepa said, tugging at Simi's hand.

Relenting, she let Deepa lead her to the ice-cream stand.

'What should I have?' Deepa said with a loud sigh.

'Hey!' A voice behind them made them turn around.

Simi tried to act surprised, but it wasn't easy with Ranvir's 'Hey, we did it!' look, and Abhi's expression of disbelief.

'What are they doing here?' Deepa muttered under her breath.

But not softly enough, because Ranvir said, 'Getting coffee!' as he pointed at the Nescafe stand.

Simi tried hard to hold back her smile.

Abhi gave Deepa a glazed look of sweet reverence. 'Hey!'

'Hey!' Deepa replied and turned to Simi. 'Are we getting ice cream?'

Abhi shook himself out of his stupor. 'Why don't you guys sit? Ranvir and I will get you guys ice cream.'

'How are they here at the exact same time as us?' Deepa hissed at Simi when they were out of earshot. 'I didn't want to run into Abhi again. I feel so guilty when he gives me those moony eyes.'

Simi feigned ignorance. 'Relax! It's just a coincidence.'

Deepa pffted loudly as though she couldn't believe it.

A few minutes later, Ranvir and Abhi were back, holding two cones each.

Ranvir handed one to Simi. 'It's cookies 'n' cream.'

'How did you know it was my favourite?' she said, eyeing the rich chocolate.

'I guessed. Must be destiny!' he said, laughter shining in his eyes.

Despite it being clear that he was joking, Simi choked on her first bite and started coughing.

Ranvir reached over and patter her back. 'Just kidding! It's my second favourite. I ordered two of the same.'

'I love this,' Simi said with a wheeze. 'They were out of coffee burst for you?'

'You remembered!' Ranvir smiled, that smile that made her heart thud.

Next to her, Deepa let out a cry. 'Vanilla? You got me, vanilla?'

'Uh . . . sorry.' Abhi rubbed the back of his neck. 'That's the only good flavour they had.'

'Then how did those two get cookies 'n' cream?'

'I like vanilla and thought you might like it too.' Abhi looked desperately towards Ranvir for help.

'I don't like vanilla!' Deepa said.

Oops!

Ranvir licked his ice cream slowly and shrugged as if telling Abhi he was grown up enough to take care of his own problems.

'Will he exchange it?' Deepa asked.

'Uh . . . I don't know!' Abhi's eyes were filled with panic now.

'Let's go and ask.' Deepa rose from her seat and made her way towards the ice-cream stand, Abhi in tow.

Ranvir started chuckling.

'I'm glad you bought me cookies 'n' cream,' Simi said, eyeing her mouth-watering cone.

'So, you don't like vanilla either.' He gave her a mischievous grin. 'I'm glad I didn't pick that.'

She laughed.

'Come on,' Ranvir said, extending his hand. 'Let's scoot before they get back with their ice creams. I think we've managed at least this one date.'

'Did we have plans for more?' Simi asked, smiling as she let him pull her up.

'Who knows!' Ranvir said playfully. 'It all depends on Deepa.'

They walked away from the ice-cream stand so Deepa and Abhi could be by themselves.

Simi licked her ice cream. 'Mmm . . . ' Ice cream was the best comfort food.

Ranvir slurped a dollop off his cone. 'I love coffee, but my sister has only butterscotch. We eat ice cream every time we go to my father's place.'

'Ayush gets it after dinner every night, and we finish off an entire tub in one go. It's so irresistible!'

'My girlfriend hates it,' he said.

She tried to picture his girlfriend. It seemed difficult to imagine him in love with someone who did not love ice cream.

He sat fidgeting with the collar of his shirt, looking away. Something about his fingers curled around his neckband mesmerized her.

Their dance at The Happy Hour flashed in front of her eyes, and she felt butterflies in her stomach. But then she remembered why she couldn't look at him like that. She dragged her eyes back to his face, to his pinched eyebrows.

'Tell me about your girlfriend,' she said, curiosity finally getting the better of her.

He peered at her. 'What do you want to know?'

Everything! 'How did you meet?'

'We met in college. When college was about to end, she suggested moving in together. It seemed like the best option. We've been living together ever since.'

'A live-in relationship?' This was way more than she'd imagined. 'You're brave!' Simi couldn't imagine living with a guy. She'd never even had a boyfriend!

'No, you're brave for getting married.' It didn't sound bad when he put it like that, with a twinkle in his eyes. 'Trust me, a live-in relationship is far less daring.'

'In what way?'

'It doesn't seem as final as marriage. So, I'm not brave at all! It wouldn't have been possible if my mother had been around, but she'd passed away by then.'

'I'm sorry to hear that.' Simi uncrossed and crossed her feet. 'You're the first person I know who is in a live-in relationship,' she blurted out and immediately regretted it. Why did she say that? Now he'd think she was so crass.

He snorted instead. 'Don't start having any grandiose ideas about it.'

'I've never lived away from my family.' *Forget living with a boyfriend. Forget telling him she'd never had any!*

He chuckled. 'Yeah! I know what you're thinking. Unrestricted parties and a rollicking sex life.'

She blushed at the last bit.

He didn't say anything further, but curious thoughts about his girlfriend churned in her head. Was she pretty? Was she sexy? Did they really have passionate sex?

She crunched into the last of her cone while her thoughts ran wild.

'Tell me about your family,' he said, which seemed like much safer ground.

She told him about Ayush and her parents, and he listened carefully, giving her his full attention, laughing at all of Ayush's antics, the way he was addicted to video games, how he cried about getting a haircut.

Then she told him about Karan and their disastrous shopping 'date'. 'I'm trying to get to know him better.'

She could swear that she saw his smile falter a little.

'I'm glad!' he said.

Maybe she'd imagined it.

'Sir, please, one rose!' A young boy pulled at Ranvir's shirt. He held a bunch of single red roses for sale.

'No,' Simi told the boy. 'We don't want any.'

The boy looked to Ranvir, pleading. 'Sir, please, only one!'

Ranvir paid for the rose and offered it to Simi. 'Come on! Don't be shy!' he teased, back to his old, genial self. 'Here's for pulling off the date!'

Simi couldn't help but blush as she accepted the rose. Awkwardly trying to draw attention away from it, she looked at the ice-cream stand. Deepa and Abhi were nowhere to be seen. Maybe they had managed to pull it off after all.

She couldn't help but think that this—between her and Ranvir—had seemed like a date too.

She stood up. 'I think I better get back.'

His face fell for a split second. 'Going so soon?'

'Work,' she said, although she would have liked to stay a bit longer too. 'Anyway, I hope this was worth it. Thanks for the ice cream and the rose.'

'Thanks for coming!' His mouth tugged upward into an adorable smile.

And her heart kicked up a protest for leaving him and heading back to the office.

* * *

Simi was falling off a cliff, tumbling headlong into a valley. As she hurtled down, big sharp needles of the desert cacti loomed into sharper focus. Above her was the dark sky and the tiny fading faces of her parents, her brother and Ranvir (what was he doing with her family?) who were standing at the edge of the cliff, watching her fall.

'A girl has to adjust,' her mother shouted. 'I'll make sure you get to know him,' her father threatened. 'You must be crazy!' her brother screamed. 'I hope you find a good reason,' Ranvir whispered. But none of them did anything to stop her as she plummeted to the bottom where the thorns awaited her, calling her, promising to poke and draw blood from every pore, every cell of her being.

Simi squeezed her eyes shut and screamed and screamed for help but the valley was soundproof and nothing emerged from her throat.

When she jolted awake from the dream, she was sweating profusely and breathing hard as though she'd been running for her life.

She sat upright in bed for a few minutes. Rubbing her face with her hands, she tried to calm her breathing. It was only a dream, she told herself, still in shock.

When she finally opened her eyes, her gaze fell on the sheet of paper lying next to her pillow—the new crochet pattern her grandmother had sent her, the one she'd printed out before going to bed last night. It was a criss-cross pattern of lines and knots. She focused on them, and slowly, her breathing returned to normal.

She repeated a few lines to calm herself down. All was still well with the world. She was still in her parents' house. She was most certainly not married to Karan. And her grandmother still sent her crochet patterns that made her want to work on them as soon as she was done with breakfast and her morning chores.

She let her eyes wander over the intricate pattern—a beautiful cap with snowflakes. This was why she loved crocheting so much. It gave her something to do with her hands while her brain was in turmoil. Keeping her hands busy relaxed her, sparked her creativity and helped her forget everything around her.

This was just what she needed at the moment.

She put the pattern back on the nightstand, her gaze falling on the rose that Ranvir had bought for her. She'd hid it in her bag when she'd walked in last night and propped it on her nightstand before going to bed.

The ice-cream 'date' flashed through her mind. She pinched her cheeks as if she couldn't believe it.

What if she'd indeed been on a date—her very first? What if the rose had really been for her? What if he'd bought it for *her* and not because he'd had to buy it?

Such foolish thoughts! She couldn't help smiling.

She picked up the rose, still dewy fresh, and brought it to her nose. The aroma was mild and the petals felt soft against her cheek.

She pulled out two sheets of paper from the drawer and placed the rose between them. She then picked up an old book and carefully put the sheets between its pages. She kept the book at the back of her desk, piled a few more books on top of it, and gave herself a pat on the back for the wonderful idea to preserve it.

There! The memories of her only memorable 'date' were in that book, saved for whenever she wanted to look at it and think of it again. Or him.

Then, she went about her morning with a skip in her step.

After breakfast, Simi sat down with her needle and special cotton yarn to work on the crochet pattern. With the pattern paper beside her for reference, she began laying out stitches, feeling lighter and calmer as the neat and tidy pattern formed.

She'd first learnt to crochet when she was eleven, while spending her summer holidays with Ammamma in Coorg. She'd been curious about the needle in Ammamma's hand every year she had visited. It had taken a lot of badgering for Ammamma to teach her the skill.

Ammamma would make her a delicious summer milkshake with berries and bananas. Then they would sit side by side and crochet while the rest of the family bustled about them. Her stitches weren't perfect initially but Ammamma had prodded her on, giving her a beatific smile every time she completed a row and showed it to Ammamma with glee. Slowly, she became better and continued the hobby back at home too, even after the visits to Ammamma's became less frequent over the years.

Ammamma lived alone in a house big enough for twenty people. The help—a husband-wife duo who lived in the outhouse—cooked, cleaned and kept house.

Simi loved her summers with Ammamma. Even now when she picked up the crochet needle, she felt like she had been transported back to Ammamma's house, the porch where they'd sit—Ammamma on her easy chair and Simi on the hammock—the backyard where Ammamma's helper, Mani, would roast groundnuts on an open fire in the evenings, and the large bedroom which she and Ammamma shared because she would be too scared to go back to her own room after listening to Ammamma's ghost stories.

Ammamma didn't have a phone back then.

Now, she had become as technologically advanced as her grandkids. She had WhatsApp and she used email like a pro. She'd formed a large online crochet group and held small crochet meets in her tiny rural town. Ammamma had turned into a crochet star, and her house was full of crocheted things from table runners to wall hangings to sofa covers and throws.

Simi took a break only for lunch and then happily lost track of time until her mother told her to get ready for Bhavna Aunty and Dheeraj Uncle's anniversary.

Simi wore her peach and yellow lehenga, clicked a selfie, and sent it to Ammamma. Within minutes, she got a reply.

My! You look lovely!

Simi smiled as she swirled in front of the mirror. Working on the new snowflake cap had lifted her spirits. Even the fact that she was going to see Karan couldn't dampen her mood today.

FIFTEEN

Karan's sister Kalki greeted them at the door. She welcomed them in with a smile. Her smile brightened when she spotted Ayush. But he just brushed her off with a nonchalant shrug and a dull 'Hi!'.

Bhavna Aunty was dressed in a dazzling cream sari that made even the air around her sparkle. Dheeraj Uncle was wearing a three-piece suit.

The whole house was decorated. Balloons hung from the ceiling with colourful threads, and there was a banner that read 'Happy Thirtieth Anniversary'.

Ayush leaned in to whisper in Simi's ear. 'You've got tough competition to be the most-in-love couple.'

Bhavna noticed Simi and came towards her, beaming, her arms wide open. 'Oh! I'm so happy to see you, my dear!' She engulfed Simi in a breath-crushing hug.

'What about me, Aunty?' Ayush brushed Simi aside and walked towards Bhavna with open arms.

'Of course, beta! Good to see you too!' She swept him in a hug and pulled back to admire him. 'Why do you seem taller every time I see you? I need you to help Kalki. She's been slogging in the kitchen all evening.'

Simi heard an imperceptible groan from Ayush.

Simi was sure if Bhavna had brought Kalki's proposal for Ayush, he would have flat out refused.

She stifled a giggle as a put-out Ayush made his way to the kitchen to help Kalki, although Simi was sure Kalki didn't need it. There were plenty of people milling around to do just that.

Two tray-bearing men walked around the living room with snacks—kebabs and stuffed mushrooms—and offered them to the guests.

Simi was allergic to mushrooms, and the kebabs looked dry and unappetizing.

'Take something, na?' Bhavna said, looking hurt when Simi politely refused the server.

Simi picked up a kebab hesitantly.

'Everything is catered from The Zaika. It's fabulous! Try it!'

Simi bit into it and wondered how she could get rid of it when Bhavna wasn't looking. Just then Dheeraj's voice boomed across the living room.

Bhavna turned around to look in his direction. He was standing on a step stool, holding a champagne flute in his hand and trying to catch everyone's attention. Dheeraj was a boisterous, loud man with a pot belly. Balanced on top of the stool with the glass in one hand and a spoon in the other, he looked comical. Simi hoped Ayush was watching.

Dheeraj wobbled a little. Bhavna let out a shocked, 'Oh my God,' and rushed over to him.

'Ah, there's my darling wife!' Dheeraj exclaimed.

'Get down now!' Bhavna scolded him, but instead he pulled her up to stand beside him.

It was a hilarious sight to watch. Bhavna was struggling to get him back on solid ground.

Finally, he obliged and stepped down. He turned to everyone with a beaming smile. 'Today, on the occasion of our thirtieth anniversary, we're going to dance.'

The crowd whistled.

'I knew the clothes my mother picked would look great on you,' Karan said, coming to stand beside her. He rested his hand on the small of her back.

Simi had not noticed him make his way over.

'I like it too.'

'It looks perfect on you. You would have picked something loose and ill-fitting.'

Annoyed, she pursed her lips. Was he saying her choice was pathetic, but his mother's intervention had saved the day?

The music started. Karan smiled as he held her hand and swayed along. Other people started dancing around them too.

I hope you find the right guy.

She would, if she could stop thinking about the guy who'd said those words!

Why did swaying along with Karan make her think of Ranvir?

Dheeraj and Bhavna were in each other's arms. Bhavna's sari swished as she tapped her feet to the 1980s Bollywood music.

Her own parents were somewhere across the living room, their arms around each other, looking happier than she'd seen them in a long time. They were lost in each other's eyes, smiling at each other, dancing like it was their anniversary.

Simi wondered when she'd be back home. She was bored of pretending that she was enjoying Karan's company and the party.

Finally, the music ended, and dinner was served.

Bhavna managed to get their two families to sit together for dinner. Simi was seated in between Karan and Ayush. The two sets of parents sat opposite each other.

Simi put some rice and gravy on her plate.

From across the table, Kalki directed her question towards Ayush. 'So, what are your plans after engineering?'

'Don't know yet,' Ayush said, relishing the chicken tikka on his plate.

'You mean, you really don't know or are you going to quit engineering as soon as you graduate?' Karan asked teasingly.

Ayush didn't answer immediately and instead called out to the server standing next to their table, 'Can I have some water, please?'

A glass of water was put in front of him.

Ayush took a sip and turned to Karan. 'Bhaiyya, back to your question. You're right!'

Karan forked a piece of chicken tikka and brought it to his mouth. 'Right, as in?'

'I don't know what I'm going to do.' Ayush grinned.

Simi kicked Ayush in the shin to make him shut up, but Ayush kept up the grin, trying to provoke Karan.

Kalki giggled.

As expected, Karan's face turned red. 'I knew I wanted to be a project manager, then VP, then director, and so on.'

Bhavna turned to look at him. 'Oh yes!' She then turned back to the rest of the table, eyes gleaming. 'Karan, tell them!'

Simi's eyes darted to her parents. *Tell them what?*

Karan cleared his throat. 'My boss called me for a special meeting yesterday. My promotion seems to be due any time now.'

Bhavna clapped her hands with delight. 'Isn't that amazing? And, we'll have another party to celebrate his promotion. Right, Karan? Such good news in the family. Are you looking forward to it, Simi?'

When Simi heard the words 'promotion' and 'good news', something happened. Her hands began to shake and accidently struck the glass of water that the server had placed next to her.

It tipped over, soaking Karan's precious suit.

Simi's hands flew to her mouth in horror. She couldn't believe she'd done it again.

Karan whipped up from his seat, shaking with rage. 'Who put this here?' he shouted, snapping his fingers. Two servers rushed to the table.

'Sir, somebody asked for water,' one of them said.

Karan looked like a chimney, smoke billowing from his head and ears.

'Beta! Calm down!' his mother said.

His parents and her parents started making a fuss over him.

Karan turned on Ayush, fuming. 'You asked for that glass of water!'

'I was thirsty!' Ayush said, an innocent look on his face.

It was madness. Simi could not understand why he was raising such a ruckus. It was only water. Karan could just wipe it down or change into something else.

Instead, he started arguing with Ayush and then with Simi, because she tried to defend him.

'Your brother did it on purpose!' Karan glared at Simi when they were leaving.

Nobody else heard but she hated the way he spoke about her brother—as if Ayush had meant for it to happen.

On their way home Ayush doubled over with laughter. 'Did you see Karan's face after his suit got soaked?' They were in the back seat while their parents were in the front— their father was driving and their mother was looking out of the window.

'Stop teasing him so much,' Simi hissed.

She'd said sorry and everything, but Karan had remained angry until his parents had intervened and sent him off to change his suit.

Simi couldn't see why it was such a big deal, but even then, she felt guilty for ruining the mood of the party.

'I don't know what came over me.'

'Chill, Didi! You got nervous, that's all! It's normal. You want to watch *Dear Zindagi* when we get home?' He wiggled his eyebrows, referring to another of his Shahrukh Khan favourites.

'No, I want to get back to my crochet . . . ' Nothing else would get her mind off the sudden and unexpected declaration from Karan.

'Don't worry,' Ayush whispered in her ear so that their parents wouldn't hear. 'Neither will he get that promotion so soon, nor will he marry you!'

She wished she could offer him ghee and sugar for those words to come true.

* * *

Back at work on Monday, as they walked towards the garden café, Deepa gave Simi a blow-by-blow account of the chance ice-cream date with Abhi.

She couldn't stop talking about how they'd gone for a movie afterwards and Abhi had turned to look at her just when the song-and-dance sequence had begun.

'We kissed!' Deepa gushed, then sighed. 'Have you ever kissed and felt like you were hungry for more?'

Simi's cheeks grew warm. The only thing that made her hungry for more was chocolate.

Did a kiss taste like chocolate?

Deepa wanted to meet Abhi for lunch, so they'd all decided to meet at the café since it was a lot quieter than the food court.

The place was bright and airy. Simi's dupatta fluttered in the breeze. The sunlight poured in through the skylight, making pretty patterns on the pastel walls. A lot of the tables were empty.

Simi gasped at the murals—they looked even more gorgeous than the last time she'd seen them.

Deepa and she sat down at a table, and Ranvir and Abhi joined them soon. They ordered burgers and coffee.

Deepa and Abhi had eyes only for each other the whole time, even as Abhi told Ranvir and her that he planned to start yoga thrice a week and make eating ice cream a sort of weekly ritual.

He'd already bribed the ice-cream vendor to stock Deepa's favourite chocolate chip flavour.

'Drinking makes you happy but ice cream is better for the soul,' Abhi quipped, then rolled off shayari about alcohol.

Deepa blushed at Abhi's shayari, finding it very cute and funny.

Simi couldn't help smiling at the two of them.

As soon as lunch was done, Abhi and Deepa excused themselves and headed off down the path that led to the open courtyard beyond the café.

Ranvir crossed his legs and sank deeper into his chair, eyeing them as they left. 'The palms and foliage around the courtyard make it a cosy hangout for lovers,' he said with a laugh. 'They must be going there.'

'How do you know?' Simi teased Ranvir. 'Have you ever checked it out?'

'Haha, would you like to see it?' Ranvir asked, a mischievous grin on his face. 'The benches are well hidden from the main path. They could be kissing as we speak. Perhaps more.'

She blushed at the meaningful look in his eyes. 'Deepa seems so happy.'

'Who would've thought they'd even meet, right?' His smile was contagious.

'Finance meets furniture!' She nodded, making air quotes. 'Such diverse worlds!'

A glint of sunlight made his hair glow. He turned to her. 'Tell me something. Did you always know you wanted to work for a furniture company or was it by chance?'

'Umm . . . Mostly by chance.' She still remembered it like it was yesterday. 'I was travelling in a cab when I saw this ad on a huge roadside billboard. It was for a beautiful diwan bed rolled up high on one side. Very regal!'

He leaned forward, interested, egging her on.

'It reminded me of my grandmother's house, which is filled with antique beds, armoires and dressers passed down from generations. And then I saw that Murano was looking for a marketing executive. I can't explain it, but I felt some sort of connection to the pieces, the colours, the look and feel when I went to the office for an interview. They had a showroom on the ground floor of the building then. It felt like I belonged there somehow. And it helped me come up with exciting campaigns because I understood and believed in the products.'

'Interesting!' he said, raising his eyebrows. He was hanging on to every word, giving her his full attention, like everything she said to him mattered.

'I didn't want to leave my old office when we were getting transferred to BizWorks, because I could visit the showroom on the ground floor whenever I wanted, but it got real stuffy. We couldn't all fit!' She laughed.

'I'm glad,' he said, running his hand through his hair, which distracted her, making her notice his large palm and his long, slender fingers as they moved through his thick dark hair, creating wavy patterns. A lock of hair fell over his forehead just moments after he'd pushed it out of his eyes.

'We wouldn't have met otherwise,' he said, cutting into her thoughts.

If he kept looking at her like this, she would get into serious trouble. Because every time he did, she felt like she was inside a warm cocoon.

Just then, her dupatta flew with a gust of wind and one end landed on his leg. Surprised, she grabbed it and put it back on her shoulder, patting it in place.

'Yeah!' she said, blushing and getting back to the topic of furniture. She could talk about it all day. 'Doing something I love makes me happy. To me, furniture personifies beauty and balance. I can't design furniture, so I chose marketing.'

'It's so nice that you enjoy what you do.'

Something flickered in his eyes just then and warmth crept over her neck.

'Sorry, I've been blabbering.'

'No, no. It's fascinating,' he said, his eyes never leaving hers.

Simi's insides did a skip she'd never felt before.

* * *

Ranvir could bet that very few people chose jobs because they were passionate about something. He'd seen pictures of the furniture in the enclosure where the Murano employees usually sat. The furniture looked so elegant, and he wished he could pick a few pieces for his home. But he knew Parul would gag at the plush, cushiony sofas and carved wooden cupboards. She'd pick steel and sterile over antique and cheerful any day.

'My job doesn't require much creativity, like yours does,' he said, less lightly than he'd intended. 'I can deal with nothing but numbers.'

She leaned forward as if to make a point. 'But your expertise can make your company's results better. Doesn't that make you rather proud?'

He didn't know how she'd picked up on his mood. It did make him proud but it also felt like walking a tightrope. He wished he could change that. 'It used to be balanced. Not any more. I'm swimming so deep in numbers that I can easily miss the shore.'

'If it didn't excite you, you wouldn't work so hard.' Admiration sparked in her eyes.

He did not deserve the praise. He knew there was a price to pay for wanting to make a difference, to satiate one's goals and purpose, and not worry about anything else.

He swallowed, pushing the image of his bank job and Paris vacation away, and forced a smile. 'Life is not only about numbers. The thing you said. So much is about finding beauty and balance where it doesn't exist.'

Their eyes met briefly and in that unfiltered moment, her smile faded. She flushed a little.

'Beauty and balance,' she repeated slowly, pushing a stray lock of hair behind her ear. 'The way it brought Abhi and Deepa together.'

'The way it brought Abhi and Deepa together . . . ' he repeated, feeling at ease. He looked upwards at the glass ceiling of the café, at the leaves peeking through the top, and eased further into his chair, feeling relaxed and happy like he hadn't felt in a long time. 'It's only been one date.'

It had grown quite windy. A few dry leaves brushed his feet.

'But they kissed . . . ' Simi blurted out dreamily, then bit her lips.

He fought back a smile, his gaze sweeping to the dimple that was back on her cheek.

Shaking her head, she cleared her throat. 'Something tells me it's going to work out,' she clarified, her cheeks flushed.

Another big gust of wind swept through the café, and her dupatta blew off her shoulder. This time it landed straight on his face. The next thing he knew, his hair and face and neck were enveloped in its soft, languid caress. It smelled like flowers. He breathed in the intoxicating scent.

Her mouth stretched into an 'O', and she jumped from her chair to retrieve her dupatta. She was thoroughly embarrassed as she stood over him, grinning sheepishly.

He gently held the soft, warm fabric and handed it back to her with a smile.

She blushed, the colour of her cheeks now matching her dupatta, its scent lingering on him long after the afternoon was over.

SIXTEEN

Ranvir hummed 'Aaoge Jab Tum' as he marinated the chicken for the tandoori chicken.

Into a large bowl went the chicken legs, salt, chilli powder, coriander powder and cumin, ginger-garlic paste, and yoghurt. He mixed it all in, rubbing the chicken with his fingers, massaging the flavour into it. Then setting the bowl aside, he started prepping for the onion soup.

Their kitchen in their airy, bright one BHK apartment was tiny with just enough space for one person to move about freely.

Parul stood next to him, cleaning the carrots and cucumbers for the salad.

It was one of those rare days when they were both cooking together. It was a good break from their regular ordering-in.

Cooking made Ranvir happy and calm. Songs played on the Gaana app on his phone. For once, he felt relaxed and at peace.

His phone rang just then, interrupting the music. It was Tina. Setting aside the onions for the soup, he picked up the call.

'Hey! What are you up to?' Tina said chirpily at the other end.

'Making dinner,' he said.

Parul looked up for a moment.

'Tina, Parul says hi, by the way,' he said.

Tina let out a derisive snort. 'Say hi to her too. I just called to thank you for the loan.'

At his father's house last week, he'd promised to transfer her some money for her boutique. 'No need for thank you,' he replied. 'Just wanted to help you get started on your idea!'

She laughed merrily. 'I can't wait! I've already leased a space on Palm Avenue. Keeping my fingers crossed.'

'That's wonderful! Congratulations!'

'Too early for congratulations yet,' Tina said, her voice taking on a grave tone.

'Everything will be fine, Tina!'

'I'm hoping to be able to return your principal with interest soon.'

'Don't worry about it right now. It's too early to think of all that. Call if you need anything else.'

Tina sent him air-kisses as usual and disconnected.

The music on Gaana came back on.

'Baawra Mann . . .'

Parul's hand hovered over the chopping board. 'Thank you for what?'

'It was Tina,' he said. 'She wants to start her own boutique. Papa and I lent her some money.'

Parul's eyebrows bunched together. 'Was Jas not able to lend her the money?'

'She has problems asking him. You know how things are between them.'

Parul doubled down on her chopping. 'I don't see why we have to sacrifice our happiness just because she has issues with Jas.'

'What are you talking about?'

'What about Paris? You were saving to go! Now you have another excuse not to go because you've given your savings away.'

Ranvir shook his head. 'I can't go this year because I can't take time off. And I'll start saving again.'

'Oh!' she said, her eyes narrowed. 'I didn't know you'd already counted this year out.'

He let out a sigh of resignation. He knew they'd been thinking about the Paris trip for some time. But he thought he'd made it clear that they would have to postpone it.

She looked at him sadly, her eyelids hooded with exhaustion. Gone was the happiness that had bound them together five years ago, even if it was to make Zubin burn with jealousy. She seemed to be too tired to even try to put on an act now, especially since there was no one watching.

Had she given up on him? Had they even loved each other, or had it all been a game of convenience, played to hoodwink her friends, his friends, and especially her ex-boyfriend, Zubin?

'Look, let's not ruin our evening.' He put his hands on her shoulders. 'Come on, we haven't cooked a meal together in a long time.'

She shrugged his hands off and stared back at him, her eyes brimming with angry tears. 'I know our life is not important to you, Ranvir. That's why you left a cushy job to take up something that has'—She shook her head as though she couldn't believe it—'that has such an airy-fairy launch date, brings in not half of what you used to make, and now you've given away what you saved for us. For *us*.'

'Parul, come on! She's my sister. I'll save up again. Paris is not going anywhere, right?' he pleaded. 'You know how hard it is for me to go on a vacation with this launch.'

'What launch? Huh? A launch that can take from six months to a year? How long am I supposed to wait?'

'You've got to trust me on this. We will get a break soon.'

She was in his face the next moment, waving her hands, the steel of the knife dangerously close.

'Put the knife away!' he ordered.

But she ignored him. 'I'm tired of waiting! It's always you or your family. I wish I didn't have to deal with any of this.'

He tried to hold her hand, trying to stop her from waving the knife around, but she was unstoppable.

'You know why I stopped going to visit your dad and sister?' she went on.

He wished she didn't twist everything and spoil this beautiful evening with an ugly fight. 'Calm down, Parul!'

'No! I will not calm down. Because I hate that I have to—' She jerked her hand away from his grip. 'Let go!'

The next moment, the knife whipped across him.

He heard the rip of his shirt and felt an excruciating pain in his abdomen as Parul staggered backwards.

It took him a second to realize what had happened. She stopped shouting. Fear flashed through her eyes as she looked down the front of his shirt.

'Oh God!' she said, the knife falling from her hand and clattering to the floor. 'Your shirt!'

He looked down at his shirt. It was soaked in blood. He pressed a hand over his abdomen to stop the bleeding and the pain that was searing through his muscles.

'I've . . . I've cut you.' She trembled. 'I've cut you!'

It was as though everything was happening at once. She was screaming at the top of her lungs. His vision blurred.

In a last-ditch attempt to stop her screaming, he clenched his teeth and shook her.

'Let's get to the hospital. Now, Parul!'

She nodded, horrified.

He picked up his phone, switched off the song and rushed to the door.

* * *

A week later, Ranvir and Abhi were seated at the food court. Ranvir had got back to work after the stitches on his abdomen had mostly healed.

He'd told Abhi it was a small kitchen accident, and Abhi had left it at that.

'It feels like I wasn't alive until I met her,' Abhi told Ranvir, talking about his new love life, as he chomped on his favourite wrap. 'I'm so glad we bumped into each other while getting ice cream. We haven't stopped talking and texting since then.'

Deepa and Simi joined them soon after.

'What happened to you?' Deepa shouted across the table as soon as she saw Ranvir.

'Nothing much!' Ranvir shrugged, trying not to look at the love birds with a twinge of envy. 'Just a minor kitchen accident.'

'His girlfriend and he had a knife fight,' Abhi joked.

Simi took a seat beside Ranvir, eyeing him with concern. 'Are you okay?'

He did not want sympathy from his friends. 'Haha, of course we didn't have a knife fight,' he said, trying to make light of the situation. 'Abhi is just jealous because nobody's ever this concerned about him.'

Abhi made a face at him and took another big bite of his wrap.

'I wanted to eat at my desk and finish some work but the temptation of the wrap that Abhi said he'd save for me pulled me here instead.' Deepa grinned smugly, putting her hand on Abhi's arm.

'Awww!' Abhi said.

Ranvir couldn't help feeling envious. 'Come on, guys! Save it for when you're alone.'

'Jealous?' Deepa joked, giving him a wink for good measure.

'Who wouldn't be? I can't take it any more. Maybe I should find a different table.'

Deepa tapped his hand across the table. 'Simi could give you company.'

Ranvir bit into his large sandwich. It was a struggle to finish. He didn't know why he always ordered Subway sandwiches. Maybe because they were just simpler and faster to order.

Simi had ordered appam and stew. Her food smelled delicious.

'Where's my wrap?' Deepa asked, eyeing Abhi's plate. 'Did you call me here for nothing?'

Abhi pushed his wrap towards Deepa. 'That's your half.'

'What? You didn't save a whole wrap for me?'

'They were out of wraps by the time we came. Come on, babe!'

'You come on!' she complained. 'I came to eat the wrap and you didn't save one for me.'

Abhi gave her a hurtful glance. 'You came for the wrap, not for me?'

Their argument went on back and forth.

It was like a switch had been turned on. One moment they were sweet lovers, the next, they were fighting over something trivial.

Ranvir just didn't get it.

Simi looked at him as though she wanted to ask him something, but the argument at the table kept them from getting in a word to each other.

* * *

Simi sighed as Abhi and Deepa squabbled over the wrap as if it was the last one on the planet.

It had been just two months at BizWorks, and she'd already missed Ranvir all week. She so badly wanted to ask him what had happened. But she didn't have his number, and there was no way to find out.

It was so unfair!

And now, she couldn't even get in a word with Ranvir alone with the two lovebirds dragging their argument.

Ranvir turned to her. 'Have a paper and pen?'

She looked at him curiously.

'Any paper will do.'

She searched inside her cramped bag, and finally dug out a piece of paper and pen. She handed them over to him.

She wondered what he was up to. She could make out he was drawing something. In a few minutes, he was done. He turned the paper around to show her. They were cartoon stick figures showing Abhi and Deepa arguing, with little speech bubbles over their heads.

Give me the wrap, one of them said. *Catch me if you can*, said another. There were more speech bubbles with Abhi and Deepa striking funny poses. *I have been kidnapped. I'm chilli chicken.* And so on.

Simi looked up from the paper. 'That's them!'

'Yup!' He waved the paper in front of them until they stopped scowling at each and looked at it.

'That's us?' They read the lines out loud and slowly broke into grins, defusing the fight.

Abhi turned to Deepa apologetically. 'I'll save a full wrap next time. I promise.'

Deepa squeezed his arm in return. 'Have I told you that I love you even if you don't?'

Ranvir turned to Simi, looking relieved. His lips spread into an adoring smile that managed to completely disarm her, and make her realize that it was the first time all week that she'd smiled.

SEVENTEEN

It was Saturday, and Simi's father had invited Karan over. He wanted him to be a part of the barbecue dinner they did as a family every few weeks. Although Simi didn't want to meet Karan, she had agreed to inviting him. Perhaps, her father was right. They needed to include him in more family activities so she'd get a chance to know him better.

Ayush, in turn, had invited one of his college friends.

'Can't you wear something else?' her mother asked, noticing that Simi was still in the t-shirt and pants she wore at home.

Simi refused to change. 'He's getting to see the real me. It's just a casual party, Ma.'

When the doorbell rang, Gauri plumped up the cushions once more, ran a quick hand over her head to tidy her hair, and patted her sari. Venkat took his position on the couch, pretending to read the newspaper.

Simi and Ayush smiled at the unnecessary show.

It was only Karan!

Karan stood at the door holding a bouquet of six impeccable white lilies bundled together with a yellow ribbon. He offered them to Simi.

'So sweet of you to bring flowers,' Gauri gushed. 'Come in. Sit down.'

Venkat rose from the couch to welcome him.

Ayush whispered to Simi, 'Isn't he a tad too dressed up?'

Karan was wearing a dressy copper-coloured long silk kurta over cream pants, looking like he'd come to a festive bash instead of a casual barbecue dinner.

To give him credit, Karan always showed up looking a bit flashy, while Simi's family never dressed up for anything.

'Sh . . . ' Simi whispered back to Ayush, hoping Karan hadn't heard.

But she agreed with her brother. Karan had definitely overdone it.

Ayush's friend, Jamwal, rang the bell soon after. Ayush never invited friends home, so it was a pleasant surprise.

Venkat shook the young lad's hand and asked him to feel at home. Jamwal seemed like a nice, quiet guy. He said hello to everyone around the room, thanked them all for inviting him and then left with Ayush to check out his room.

Venkat had set up the barbecue grill in a corner of the balcony. Simi and her mother had spent last evening chopping the vegetables and marinating the meat and fish. The cauliflower florets, corn cobs, potatoes and paneer were all chopped and placed in large bowls, ready to go on the grill.

Venkat lit the charcoal and headed to the kitchen to help gather all the food.

Simi took Karan to the balcony where her father had put chairs for everyone to sit, away from the grill—a black, shiny bowl on three legs.

'This thing must be fun,' Karan said, as light smoke filled their balcony.

Simi smiled, thinking of the mouth-watering food. 'It's yummy! Worth the time and effort.'

Venkat came back, holding large trays and bowls of the marinated vegetables and set them up on a small table next to the grill.

Gauri brought out tall glasses of juice and some beer bottles.

Ayush and Jamwal came out too. Jamwal asked her father questions about the grill and offered to help.

Venkat seemed to like Ayush's new friend. He went to great lengths to explain how the grill worked, how it was better to keep the hot coals on one side, so that the nicely browned vegetables could be moved over to the cool side so they wouldn't burn and overcook.

He took pride in telling Karan and Jamwal that once they tried his hot dogs, they would never eat them elsewhere.

After some chitchat, Ayush and Jamwal went back to Ayush's room with their mocktails, to play on his PS4. Simi offered to bring the food to their room when it was ready.

Gauri, Venkat and Karan chatted a bit while waiting for the charcoal to heat up.

Karan caught Simi alone for a few minutes when her parents were in the kitchen. 'Your brother is funny. Did you see how he was showing off his friend?'

Surprised at the sudden comment, Simi didn't know what to say. Jamwal was only being sweet and sociable. Ayush was not showing him off. Why pick on Ayush? What had he done to irk Karan?

'I think they're good friends. Ayush wasn't showing off. He was being nice,' she said when she couldn't take it any more.

'He's not always nice to everyone,' Karan smirked.

'What do you mean? What has he done to you?'

Just then Venkat walked back in with some oil to brush the vegetables and meat, and Karan dropped the subject.

'You having a good time, Karan?' Venkat asked jovially.

'The best so far! Can't wait to try some grilled potatoes.' Her father smiled.

When the coal was ready, Venkat started setting the vegetables neatly on the grate.

Slowly the heady aroma of charcoal and the grilling vegetables infused the air around them.

Venkat was delighted when Karan tried to turn over the paneer slices with a tong. One of the pieces broke and slipped through the grate into the smoking coal but Venkat laughed and spurred him on.

After many attempts he finally managed to flip one, and whooped. 'I'm good at this!'

Simi sipped on her cocktail and ignored Karan. She didn't get how he made such little effort to be nice to her but tried so hard to suck up to her father.

After the vegetables were finally ready, her father put the meat on the grill. The aromas were delightful.

Simi bit into the wonderfully browned and succulent vegetables on her plate, relishing every bite. As did the others. Venkat had decided to keep the hot dogs for last.

After the meat was cooked, Venkat placed the sausages on the grill and toasted up the buns.

Simi topped each hot dog with ketchup, mustard, onions and cheese. She set up a plate each for Ayush and Jamwal and started towards Ayush's room.

'I'd like to use the bathroom,' Karan said, catching up with her.

'After tasting this food, I want to buy a grill for our house,' Karan said amiably. 'Your father is a terrific cook. But don't expect the same from me,' he quickly added with a smile. 'I've never stepped into the kitchen.'

Simi imagined Bhavna Aunty serving him all his meals and picking up the plates when he was done.

'Don't expect me to bring your food to you,' she retorted.

'Like you're doing for your brother?'

Her mouth twisted. 'I don't do this every day.'

Karan gave a non-believing shrug and went to the bathroom.

Simi turned towards Ayush's room, a little miffed at Karan. They had invited him so that they could interact with each other, but the more she talked to him, the more irritated she became.

She walked to Ayush's room, still thinking about Karan and his obnoxious comments. One hand balanced the plate which was heaped with hot dogs, grilled meat and vegetables, and with the other she pushed open the door.

And froze . . .

Ayush and Jamwal were sitting on Ayush's bed, their arms around each other, kissing. They broke apart just as Simi entered.

It was Ayush who jumped and stood up first, Jamwal recovered next, staring at the floor, his face stricken. It took her a few shocked moments to process what she had seen.

Ayush's eyes darted around the room awkwardly, finally settling on her, a gamut of emotions on his face. Shock. Fear?

Simi didn't know where to look. She was as shocked as him.

'Don't you knock?' he asked, his stinging voice startling her out of her stupor.

Her face flamed with embarrassment. Setting the plate on the nearest desk, she bolted out of the room.

She should have done something. She should have said something. But it was all in hindsight. The sight had caught her completely off-guard.

She ran straight into Karan who'd just emerged from the bathroom.

He gave her a curious look. 'What happened? You look like you've seen a ghost.'

Simi closed her eyes and took a moment to compose herself. When she opened them and looked at Karan, she was afraid that he would still see that something was amiss.

She needed to sit or lie down. Her legs felt wobbly.

'It looks like something you saw in Ayush's room,' Karan said perceptively. 'Were the boys watching porn?' He paused and grinned. 'Or were they making out?'

'Stop it!' she hissed.

* * *

Things were terrible the next morning too. To Simi, it felt like waking up in a world in which her brother and she had stopped talking to each other. Ayush avoided her at breakfast and went off to a friend's house to study. She hardly saw him all weekend.

She knocked on his door on Sunday night, determined to talk. They had to stop behaving like strangers.

He didn't answer.

'Hey!' she said, opening the door and peeking inside.

He was bent over some sheets of paper. A textbook lay open in front of him on the table. He continued to ignore her.

She went over and stood by his desk, letting her fingers linger over his table lamp. She had helped him make it with an empty wine bottle for a school project.

The light from the lamp went out. Maybe she had accidentally pulled the plug.

'Will you stop touching that?' he said, pushing her hand away and thrusting the plug back into the socket. The lamp came on again.

'Ayush, I didn't mean to—'

'Please!' he said, holding up his palm. 'Can we not talk about it . . .'

His words hit her hard. She tried to swallow a lump in her throat as tears stung her eyes. 'Why didn't you tell me?'

He lowered his head between his hands, shutting his ears. 'I didn't want to tell anybody, all right? Not even you!' His tone was brusque, laced with anger and hurt. 'You should have knocked. I didn't ask you to come then. I didn't ask you to come now. Just leave me alone!'

'I'd never do anything to hurt you,' she whispered, tears blurring her vision and threatening to spill.

His face remained lowered. 'Please just go!' The words held a tone of finality and seemed to plunge into her heart like a knife.

Tears coursed down her cheeks. But there was nothing she could do to make him talk to her.

She turned around and rushed out of his room, not wanting to cry in front of him, but unable to prevent herself from turning into a weeping mess before she got back to her room.

EIGHTEEN

Monday morning rolled in, all gloomy and overcast, just like Simi's situation. The suffocating thought of Ayush not speaking to her ate up her insides.

She woke up to see that Ayush had already left for college. She left for BizWorks as usual and immersed herself in work all morning. At lunch time, she dragged herself to the food court with Deepa.

Ranvir and Abhi had already started eating by the time Deepa and she put down their trays on the table.

The usual chitchat went around the table. Ranvir was having his usual Subway sandwich and coffee.

Abhi serenaded Deepa with one of his favourite Rumi shayaris.

Deepa clapped her hands when Abhi finished with a sweeping bow.

Simi had ordered a plain dosa, but it seemed like a chore to finish it. She wasn't hungry. The sambar was too bland, and the dosa, which was usually her favourite, was all soggy.

Ranvir nudged her arm. 'What happened?'

Simi shrugged as if she didn't know what he was talking about.

'You're not eating?'

'It's not as good as it usually is,' she said simply.

Deepa and Abhi were busy among themselves across the table.

When she couldn't eat any more, Simi pushed the plate away and wiped her hands.

Ranvir finished his sandwich and gulped down the last of his coffee. 'Want to go for a drive?'

'Now?'

'Yeah! I have to pick something up.'

A drive sounded like a good idea. Leaving Abhi and Deepa to themselves, she and Ranvir returned their food trays and went to the basement where Ranvir's car was parked.

It was a relief to get out of the office, where it had felt stuffy all day. Outside, the sky was overcast, and the weather was quite pleasant for late February.

Ranvir lowered the windows, switched on the radio and they were off. A soft breeze hit her face. It calmed her. It had rained before lunch and the cool air smelt of wet earth.

After a few minutes, they turned into a narrow street. 'Let's get some sugarcane juice,' Ranvir said, parking next to a juice shop and holding up two fingers at the boy standing in front. In no time, the boy brought out two tall glasses of juice.

Ranvir offered one to Simi. 'This is my favourite.'

She took a sip and felt the cold, sweet, sugary liquid ease down her throat. 'It's good.'

Her gaze fell on the butterfly hanging from the rear-view mirror. 'You hung that.' She'd been so lost in thought that she hadn't noticed it till now.

He finished his juice in one go and turned to her, a white foam covering his upper lip. 'It would have been rude of me to accept a gift and put it somewhere I'd never see it again. It just hangs here so perfectly, as if it was made for this spot.'

A smile played on her lips. 'I'm honoured.' She pointed to his lip. 'The juice gave you a moustache.'

The corners of his eyes crinkled. He wiped his mouth. 'Gone?'

She nodded and returned her glass. 'I liked it.'

'The moustache?'

She couldn't help a smile. 'The juice.'

His lips curled upwards as his eyes swept over her face. 'My pleasure. It's the best! Nothing quite like it anywhere else.'

'What did you want to pick up?' she asked, remembering the reason they'd come.

He peered at her for half a beat and said, 'Your mood!'

Suddenly, her throat closed up, her cheeks burned and her eyes stung.

It was the way he had said it.

Like he cared. As though he could read her moods, and knew exactly what she needed.

Her eyes were welling up fast.

He'd done so much to make her feel better already, and yet she was about to cry. Like, bawl her heart out and never stop. Wish the weekend away.

He tucked a finger under her chin and turned her face towards him. 'Is it that boyfriend of yours?'

She couldn't breathe. Before she knew it, the tears rolled down, wetting her cheeks.

He leaned over, patting her head like she was a baby. 'Now, now,' he said, his voice a soothing rumble. 'Tell me what happened.'

That was all she needed.

Like a fountain, it gushed out of her, the words pouring out in jerks and jolts, bits and pieces. By the time she finished telling him that she had walked in on Ayush and Jamwal, and about Karan's remarks about her brother, her face was buried in his shoulder, her tears streaming down uncontrollably.

Cupping the back of her head, he tilted her face so he could look at her, his eyes deep pools of loving kindness. 'Why are you crying?' He wiped her tears with the pad of his thumb. 'Your brother has just made a choice!'

'But he won't talk to me,' she said between sobs.

His lips lightly skimmed her forehead. 'It's okay . . . It's okay. Give him some time.' He patted her head as she pressed her face against his chest.

'This is a difficult time for your brother. He probably just wants someone to hear him out and help him understand it all. That's where you come in, as someone he's really close to. But you have to be patient, understanding and supportive.'

She took in his words like a sponge absorbing water.

'If you give him time to come out on his own, he will. And you'll be happy you gave him the space and love he needed until he was ready.'

It was all so much to take in, and yet his words resonated deeply, filling her chest with the wisdom and truth of it all. She needed this talk. She needed to hear that her brother was not shutting her out, he was perhaps just as shocked and confused as she was.

She could feel Ranvir's heartbeat against her cheek. There was something so calm and soothing about his voice. She could stay like this forever, pressed against him, hearing his heartbeat like she could her own. After what seemed like forever, she sat up, leaving a big wet patch on his shoulder.

He smiled, that crinkly smile of his that she loved. 'Are you feeling okay?'

She nodded, grateful for the talk.

They'd just started back for the office, when a gigantic rainbow arched across the horizon, a soft radiant burst of colours brightening the bluish-white sky,

'A rainbow!' he shouted. He reached over and held her hand, squeezing it with delight.

'It's beautiful!' she said, excited at something so rare in the middle of the day.

'My mother used to love rainbows,' he said. 'Seeing one always reminds me of her.'

She squeezed his hand back. It felt good to hold his hand.

'My mother used to say—only two things are important. We all need each other. And we need someone to love us unconditionally.'

Her heart clenched when she detected a crack in his voice. She swallowed as she noticed his moist eyes.

She was still lost in thought when they reached back. He stopped the car and switched off the engine.

'Let me get your door,' he said. 'It's jammed.'

He leaned towards her all of a sudden. Their cheeks brushed, sending a shiver down her spine. He was so close, she could smell his clean, soapy scent.

'Thanks for coming on the drive,' he said, his voice low and deep.

'Thank you for taking me,' she said, keeping her eyes on his jaw, which was only inches from hers.

They remained like that for a long moment. Simi said nothing, her fists opening and closing in her lap of their own accord. She felt her heartbeat slow down. Her eyes were still on his face, taking in his features—his long, sharp nose, his full lips.

I have to pick something up.

What?

Your mood.

He had made her feel a thousand times better already. A rush of emotions swept through her and the next thing she knew, she had wound her arms around him and buried her face in the hollow of his neck.

What am I to do with this beating heart that seems to have a heart of its own? It won't listen. I can't force it or fight it. It won't obey. It won't back down.

In that moment it felt as if she never wanted to let him go.

* * *

Ranvir let her hold him. It felt so good to be held, to be heard, to be understood. It had been so long since he'd spoken about his mother, and it had made him feel so much better, probably even more than his talk had helped her.

Her hold was soft and warm and felt as vulnerable as his. He inhaled the flowery fragrance of her hair and buried his face in her thick, luscious waves. There was so much more he wanted to tell her about his mother.

For the first time in a long time, he felt like he'd made a true friend. Someone he felt totally comfortable talking to. Someone who wouldn't judge him, mock him, or ridicule him for the silly things he loved, like coffee, rainbows, cartoon stick figures, and, at this moment, an impulsive hug.

He couldn't tell how long they stayed locked in each other's arms.

Then she slowly pulled apart. Her eyes were misty, and her cheeks were flushed. Her lips trembled softly.

They kissed. Something tells me it's going to work. He remembered how she'd blushed at those words.

In that moment, he wanted to kiss her too and tell her that everything was going to work out.

Instead, he leaned over and twisted the door handle open for her.

Something pulled in his abdomen then. He winced as sudden pain shot through his stitches.

Worry exploded in her eyes. 'What happened?'

He pressed a hand to his abdomen until the pain eased.

'Does it still hurt?'

'A little,' he admitted. 'Sometimes.'

'I'm so sorry about the accident.'

'I probably deserved it!' He chuckled as he told her how the knife accident had really happened; it seemed a lot easier to talk about it now than it had been before.

'You can't be serious!' she said. 'You fought over Paris?'

He laughed, then pressed his hurting abdomen. 'Unfortunately, I'm not so good at making someone happy.'

She smiled, a slow, languid stretch of her lips, and shook her head. 'That's not true! You make me happy . . . '

NINETEEN

Parul refused to talk to Ranvir after the knife incident. Every evening, when he got home, she'd lock herself in the bedroom and pretend to sleep, leaving him the couch. She spent the weekends away at her parents', and Ranvir wondered how they would find their way back to each other.

It was obvious she did not want to broach the subject of Paris, but why was she avoiding him?

Meanwhile, Fintura's board of directors had decided to launch the app in two months, and Ranvir had become busier than usual.

Tina had already starting planning for her boutique. She had everything in place to open it in a few months. Their fights over ice cream continued at his father's place.

With Parul not around on weekends any more, Ranvir started spending more time with his father, getting his plumbing fixed, the broken tile on his roof replaced, and doing all the odd jobs around the house that he'd not tackled for ages.

His father and he cooked elaborate lunches on Sundays, for which Tina usually turned up too. But mostly, Ranvir just pottered around his childhood home, rummaging in the old shelves until he found his old books, art sketchbooks and things he'd long forgotten.

His mother had preserved his old sketchbooks over the years, books that had his pencil sketches, and the smaller notepads he'd used for doodling.

He started sketching again in the evenings, while his father played Scrabble against himself.

It was a relief to see that he still loved doing what he used to. His father was quite surprised to see his renewed interest in sketching too.

One day, Ranvir packed up his sketchbooks and took them home.

He started sketching during lunch at the office sometimes, when he wasn't busy working. He made funny figures that resembled Abhi and Deepa. But mostly he drew Simi—Simi eating dosa or noodles, Simi groaning at the two fighting at the table. Her loopy earrings featured in his sketches often, and she loved it when he tore out the page and let her keep it.

Sometimes, late at night, he would just pick up the sketchbook and draw something. He would get so lost in it that time would just fly by.

* * *

The Holi bash at BizWorks on Friday was nothing like Ranvir had imagined. It was being held two days before the actual holiday. Abhi and Deepa had coaxed him to join the party.

Holi parties were happening events in Bangalore though he hadn't attended any before this.

The central courtyard was teeming with colourful bodies dancing to the beats of the dhol and blasting Bollywood Holi songs. Pots of colours and flowers sat in several corners. Abhi and Deepa had got passes for the four of them. It promised to be a fun-filled evening.

Food counters with thandai, chaat, gujiyas and samosas were set up in one corner.

Ranvir stood at the entrance, looking around in confusion, totally unprepared for the loud music, the swaying bodies and the unrecognizable colourful faces. Now that he was here, he didn't know what to do. Moreover, he couldn't recognize anyone he knew.

A moment later, someone came up to him, waving her arms enthusiastically. It was Deepa, whom he recognised by her voice and silver nose ring. She held his hand and dragged him in.

A hand came out of nowhere and patted his face. A cloud of yellow powder wafted in front of him. He grabbed the mischief-maker's hand and turned around, only to look straight at Simi, whose face was streaked with purple and yellow. Her hair was tied up in a ponytail and she was wearing a colour-streaked t-shirt that he guessed might have previously been white.

'Happy Holi!' she screamed, smearing the colour on his face with both her hands. Ranvir just stood there gaping while she dipped her hand into a nearby pot and smeared more colour on his shirt, lightly running her hands along his chest and back.

He smiled at the official initiation into the party. Now, he was sure he looked like everyone else.

A balloon hit his head, taking him completely by surprise. He turned around to see Abhi aiming another one at him. Deepa was armed with a *pichkari* and she had a go at him too.

'Come on, join the party! Don't just stand there!' Simi yelled, laughing and offering him a pichkari too. He took her lead and went after Abhi first, spraying water at him until he was crouching in surrender.

The crowd became hysterical as 'Teri akhiyon ka vaar' blasted from the speakers, swaying and bopping to the beats.

There was nothing graceful about this kind of dancing, but it was exciting and pure fun. It brought Simi and Ranvir closer until they were bumping into each other and laughing.

Simi screamed with delight when a spurt of water hit the back of her head. She hugged Ranvir in her excitement. He pulled her into him and turned around, protecting her from the next barrage of balloons.

'So sorry!' she smiled mischievously, one eyebrow green and the other pink.

They stared at each other for a few moments before another balloon hit, landing with a loud plop on his back this time. They escaped before they were hit again, and made straight for the food counter. His stomach was growling already.

Her colourful wet t-shirt was sticking to her like second skin, showing off her curves. He tried to look away but failed. She shivered as she reached for a thandai and downed it, followed by a gujiyas which she crunched slowly. 'This is good!'

He turned his gaze back to her face, guilt flashing through him when he realized that despite her colourful and drenched appearance, she was still sexy as hell. 'Yeah! It's good,' he said, even though he hadn't even tasted the gujiya yet.

The corners of her mouth curled into a deeper grin. 'The colours look good on you,' she said in a teasing tone.

He ran a hand through his hair and looked at her sheepishly. 'I've never played Holi before.'

'Oh! I'm glad I got to show you how it's done,' she said, taking another bite of the gujiya. 'Aren't you hungry?'

He was ravenous. He picked up a gujiya and bit into its crunchy, flaky crust. The filling inside was utterly moist and delicious, melting in his mouth.

She smiled as she saw him savour it. 'The thandai is good too!'

He drank a whole glass of the thandai spiked with alcohol and wiped his lips with one finger. 'Yeah, this is good.'

They had a couple more glasses as they watched everyone enjoying themselves. He felt tipsy and happy as the alcohol kicked in. They tapped their feet to the songs, waving their hands and shaking their bodies to the music. Simi smiled and waved at Abhi and Deepa, who seemed to be joined at the hip.

Ranvir felt something in his hair and ran his hand through it. Suddenly some colour flew out of his hair and into his eye, making it burn. 'I think I got some colour in my eye,' his hissed, rubbing it.

'Let me look,' Simi said, pulling his head down so she could peer into his eye. She blew into it a few times but it was of no use.

His eyes continued to burn. 'Water!' he croaked, his eye stinging now.

She tugged at his hand. 'Come.'

'Where are we going?'

'To get washed up.'

She led him to the ladies' bathroom.

'Here?'

'Everyone's busy with the party. The place is empty.' She pulled him inside and shut the door.

Then bending him over the sink, she washed his face and eyes. 'Hold on,' she said, getting some soap from the dispenser. 'Let me wash your hair too.'

He stood bent over the sink while she lathered his hair with soap and massaged his scalp.

They then dried his hair with paper towels.

'Better?' She smiled at him.

'Yes.'

Suddenly, she laughed and splashed some water on his face.

He turned to her in surprise. 'What?'

'Who says Holi is over?' She splashed some more.

Naughty!

Well, if it wasn't over for her then it wasn't over for him either.

Dodging the water attack, he made for the next sink, filled his palm with water and splashed it on her. She tried to grab his hand to stop him. They tussled, each trying to stop the other.

He grabbed her waist, his chest pressing against her back, and lifted her off the ground, pulling her away from the sink. She laughed and yelled, wriggling in his arms.

Kicking her legs in the air, she laughingly instructed him to put her down.

He was having a blast. He wasn't going to let her go so easily—the night was still young, and she so mischievous.

He held on tight, every bit of him wanting payback.

* * *

Simi had never felt so hot and cold at the same time. Every part of her tingled under his touch, goosebumps prickling her skin. His arms were around her waist as he lifted her. She was out of breath and turned on.

Her cheeks grew hot as she tried to prise his arms loose, but her struggle pressed her further against him until she could feel every hard muscle in his body. There was not much to separate their bodies, their wet t-shirts doing nothing to alleviate her embarrassment at his proximity. Every part of her felt alive and naked, as if it was his bare skin touching hers. His breath was warm against her neck, and his throaty laughter rang in her ears.

Her stomach flipped as his lips grazed her ears. 'Tell me when Holi is over.' His voice was a sexy whisper turning her insides into mush.

She couldn't take it any longer. Cheeks flaming, she squeezed her eyes shut. 'It's over. I promise,' she begged. 'Put me down.'

He finally put her down and turned her around to face him, keeping himself between her and the sink, guarding himself against sudden water attacks.

He bent down then, his hands on her shoulders, looking straight into her eyes with an intense, scorching gaze that made her insides go into a tizzy.

She laughed and shook her head to dislodge the indecent thoughts circling her brain. 'I think we have had too much thandai.'

'Yeah, we have!'

That killer smile again! She could die just watching him!

Gazing into his shining eyes, she blurted out, 'I like you . . .'

He wound his arms around her, pulling her into his chest, his gaze dipping to her mouth.

She came up on her toes just as his face moved closer to hers.

Everything around her blurred, the room, their surroundings. There was only him and her.

She didn't even know what she was doing.

She moved towards him involuntarily.

One moment, his dark intense eyes were piercing into hers and the next, all she could see were his lips—the chocolate she had longed to taste. The oxygen she needed at that moment.

She brought her lips to his, hesitating at first, then kissed him softly, gently.

He closed his eyes, a sound of pleasure emanating from the back of his throat.

If kisses were like chocolate, kissing him tasted sweet and spicy, the sweetness of thandai mixed with his spearmint breath.

Her heart melted into a puddle.

She felt brave, daring.

Fumbling at first, she took her time to savour his lips, one by one. A groan escaped him as she nipped his bottom lip lightly. He responded to her, his lips opening up to let her in, allowing her to explore unhurriedly as she figured out her rhythm.

It felt like a slow dance—pleasurable, sensuous, setting every cell in her being on fire. As his lips caressed hers, her heart knocked about in her chest, her breasts tingling.

She lifted her arms, her hands moving of their own accord, one diving deep into his hair, feeling its silkiness, the other caressing his chest, where she could feel the thumping of his heart, just like hers.

Did he want her as much as she wanted him?

Nothing made sense except the sigh that escaped his mouth, giving her immense pleasure to know that he was enjoying what she was doing.

His hand reached up to touch the soft spot beneath her ear. A shudder coursed through her as his fingers stroked her neck, her arm, the heat of his palm searing her everywhere he touched. She moaned, letting herself melt into him, feeling like she was floating on clouds.

His heart thudded against her chest, his heartbeat matching hers, like both their hearts had gone crazy.

She'd never forget this kiss. Her very first.

Delightfully better than she'd imagined.

As he kissed her back, as every breath of his mingled with her own, nothing else mattered. All she knew was that she wanted more.

'Simi!' They heard someone calling out before the bathroom door swung open and Deepa barged in just as they broke apart hurriedly.

Deepa paused when she saw Ranvir standing a few inches away from Simi, staring at the floor. 'What's he doing here?'

Ranvir's hand flew to his eye. 'Ah!'

'Some . . . Something got into his eye,' Simi stuttered. 'I was helping him.'

Deepa came closer and peered into his eyes. 'Is it better now?'

With a quick 'I'm fine' Ranvir left the bathroom, and Simi buried her head in her hands with a silent groan.

'What?' Deepa asked.

'Nothing.' *Thank God Deepa hadn't seen them kissing.*

TWENTY

The aroma of chicken biryani wafted up Simi's nose as she let herself into her home after the Holi party.

Gauri was humming in the kitchen. She peeked inside to see her mother preparing raita.

'Hi, Ma!'

Gauri turned around, took one look at her wet clothes and coloured face and gasped. 'What is this?'

Simi giggled.

'Change immediately or you'll catch a cold.'

Simi gave her mother a hug from behind instead.

'Silly girl! Now you're getting the colour on me too.' Gauri pinched Simi's cheeks playfully. 'Hungry?'

Hungry for more . . .

Her mind was still on the sensuous kiss with Ranvir, which had tied her up in knots and left her feeling weirdly hollow. What had she done!

She squeezed her eyes, shutting out the images of the evening.

Thankfully, Deepa had been pretty cool about seeing Ranvir and her in the bathroom together. Not much later, the party had ended and they'd all exchanged goodbyes in the courtyard. Her heart had pounded the whole time as Ranvir and she had stolen awkward glances at each other around the others.

'Are you not hungry?' Gauri interrupted her thoughts, her hands on her hips. 'Did you eat a lot at the party?'

Simi shook her head. 'No, Ma! I am hungry. What's special with the biryani today?'

'Ayush's exam results are out. He got a distinction. But he's been cooped up in his room, so I thought I'd make something special.'

Simi felt a rush of happiness. She wanted to run into his room to congratulate him but decided against it. Ayush's mood had improved since the night of the barbecue party, but he was still quiet and withdrawn. Even leaving him alone had not quite worked.

If you give him time to come out on his own, he will.

She remembered Ranvir's words and sighed. She'd give Ayush all the time he needed. If only he'd let her in and talk to her.

At the dinner table, her father couldn't contain his excitement over Ayush's marks. He only had one more semester to go until graduation.

'This year is turning out to be great!' her father remarked. 'First, Simi gets a proposal, then you get a distinction. By next year, Simi will be married, and you'll have a job.'

'Oh, Papa!' Simi whined. 'Can we not make everything about my marriage?'

Venkat rubbed his hands. 'Karan loved the barbecue dinner. I think we should do something else. How about all of us go on a trip to Coorg and visit my mother? She would want to meet him too.'

Simi groaned. From the corner of her eye, she saw Ayush bend down. His head disappeared under the table. Just as he came up again, she caught the telltale signs of laughter on his face.

Was he laughing at her?

Well, if her plight made her brother laugh, so be it.

Simi whined some more and received more advice from her father, who was never known to back down from parental gyan. And every time she felt worse, she could see Ayush's face lighten up.

All for a good cause, it seemed.

After dinner, her mother put the brownie batter in the oven and plopped down in front of the TV to watch her favourite show on Travel Network. Beautiful scenes of Paris played on the screen. The Eiffel Tower and the Seine River.

Simi remembered Ranvir's Paris trip as she settled down and put her head on her mother's lap.

'A honeymoon to Paris would be so lovely. Simi, why don't you bring it up with Karan.'

Simi turned to stare at her mother.

'What? Not now!' her mother clarified. 'Maybe when the marriage talks happen.'

Simi sighed as she watched the show.

'What is it?' her mother asked, stroking Simi's hair as she oohed at the Grand Palais.

'I don't like Karan.'

'What do you not like?'

'Everything . . . I don't know. I don't like him.'

'Simi, what's wrong with you? What are you blabbering about?'

Her mind strayed back to the moment in the bathroom. Ranvir and her. The way she'd felt in his embrace, the longing she'd seen in his eyes, the pure bliss she had experienced while kissing him. She didn't have any of those feelings for Karan.

'I want to marry a man I like.'

Gauri stopped stroking Simi's head. 'Do you like someone else?'

Yes, I like Ranvir . . .

The words were on the tip of her tongue. She wished she could tell her mother she liked Ranvir. But what would she say?

Yeah, Ma! I like this guy, but he has a girlfriend. I've never felt this way for anyone else. Today, we got carried away and kissed . . .

Have you lost your mind? her mother would say.

She had lost her mind, indeed!

She turned around in her mother's lap and sighed, dreaming about a life that seemed impossible—a life with someone she loved and who loved her back.

The oven pinged, signalling that the brownies were done, just as the front door opened and Ayush walked in with something in his hand.

'Ooh, ice cream!' her mother whooped, nudging Simi aside and rising from the couch. 'Perfect with brownies.'

Simi caught Ayush's eyes, and they exchanged a happy smile.

Simi's heart did a tiny leap of joy.

The smile was a sign! A sign that her brother might talk to her again.

Suddenly, she was happy. All seemed well with the world. At least, her little world.

Beaming, she brought out the bowls and helped her mother serve the delicious ice cream with brownies.

The three of them sat on the couch and dug into the cold ice cream melting into the warm brownies.

Heaven!

* * *

After the Holi party, Ranvir walked into his house to the aroma of pizza. He'd expected Parul to be in her room already but going by the noises coming from the kitchen, she seemed to be in there.

'Hey!' she said, when she saw him peeking into the kitchen. She was propped up on a bar stool. A box of pizza and a beer bottle sat in front of her. An empty bottle was kept beside it.

She shot him an unexpected smile, which took him by surprise. She looked happy.

She patted the bar stool next to her. 'Come, let's eat. You're early today! And you look . . . Well, colourful! Except your face . . . '

The image of Simi washing his hair and face flashed through his mind. *And that kiss!*

He ran a hand through his damp hair. 'Yeah, there was a Holi party in office.'

She looked a bit surprised. 'I've never seen you play Holi before . . . That's a new you!'

He gave a self-deprecating laugh.

She finished her beer and asked, 'You hungry?'

'I ate something at the party.'

'Oh!' She pouted. 'I ordered a large.'

'I'll have it tomorrow.'

She got off the bar stool and walked to the refrigerator. She pulled out two bottles of beer, handed one to him, and settled back on the stool. 'Sit down.' She patted the empty stool next to her again.

He sat down and took a sip. The cool liquid refreshed his parched throat. He put down the bottle and looked squarely at Parul. 'We have to talk.'

'Me first, actually!' she said mid-bite.

She finished swallowing the pizza and sipped some more beer before turning to him. 'What do you think of Turkey?' She began ticking points off on her fingers. 'It's a short trip. It's cheap. And my company has a special deal to Turkey this month.' She did a little dance with her hands. 'I can't believe it!'

'Turkey?' He frowned. 'Didn't you want to go to *Paris*?'

She made a pouty face. 'I did! But then this deal came along, and it just looked so much better that I've changed my mind.' She touched his cheek and ran a finger along his jaw. 'Just think about it, jaan! I know you had to help Tina and all. But just imagine, we can still go and celebrate our anniversary next month!'

He caught her hand as it made its way down his neck and fisted his shirt. 'Parul, no!'

'What, no?'

'Our company just made an announcement a week ago. We're launching in two months. I can't go! This is an important—'

She scoffed. 'This has to be a joke. I thought you were never going to launch. And now that I've made new plans, you're launching?' She started laughing hysterically.

Ranvir took in a deep breath. This was not going to be easy. 'This is not the time to joke, Parul.'

'I'm not joking!' she yelled.

He tried to remain calm. 'I told you I can't go'

She got off the bar stool, her eyes fiery. 'You can't go or you don't want to go? How selfish of you, Ranvir! I supported your job change even when it ruined our life and now you expect me to not ask for anything from you?'

'Parul, what's gotten into you?'

Her eyes welled up. 'You know what? I've had it! I don't care. We're doing this. Tell your boss you need this. You've been working like a dog for almost a year. I know you need this. *We need this*, Ranvir!' She wiped her eyes and blew out a sharp breath to compose herself. 'I've already booked our tickets and stay. Tell your boss you're going . . .'

He shook his head in despair.

In two strides, she was next to him, reaching up to cup his face with her hands and pressing her lips to his. 'Jaan, please!' she whispered. 'Say yes if you love me?'

Nothing he said was making her see sense. It felt like they'd reached a point where they wanted different things in life. He got that she wanted to feel loved, something that had been missing from their lives lately, but if only she understood that he also needed patience and understanding. Although he knew it was too much to ask of her.

'Life will get better. Please, Parul! Please try to understand. I've worked so hard to prove myself. I can't throw it away. If you want it so much, why don't you go by yourself?'

'You can't do this to me,' she yelled. 'Who goes on a holiday to celebrate their anniversary by themselves, huh?'

He was too tired to fight her.

Suddenly, she gave up, sagging against him, limp and spent.

'We'll talk later,' he said, taking her to the bedroom. He helped her get into bed.

'Stay with me,' she said, grabbing his hand.

He prised his hand out of her grasp. 'Get some sleep, Parul.'

She closed her eyes and in minutes, was snoring softly. He left the room, closing the door behind him.

Back in the kitchen, he regarded the mess.

A long night lay ahead of him. He had to make up for all the time he had lost because of the Holi bash. Letting out a huge sigh, he put away the extra pizza in the refrigerator, threw away the box and wiped down the kitchen counter.

When he was done, he lay on the couch, every bit of him drained and exhausted. He'd come in, wanting to talk to Parul about what he'd been feeling lately. About where their relationship was heading.

It was hard to process what had been going on with him over the last few weeks. So much had changed. Something had shifted inside him.

He'd been fighting his attraction for Simi. Until today, when he had kissed her in a moment of weakness.

He pressed his head between his hands and sighed.

TWENTY-ONE

On Monday, Simi and Deepa walked into the food court to find a pasta brand conducting a promotional contest.

A few tables had been set up in a corner and people were being invited to participate.

Curious, Deepa dragged Simi over to check it out.

'What's Bella Notte?' Deepa asked, reading the card displayed on one of the tables with a covered plate of spaghetti.

The lady at the table smiled. 'We have organized a game based on the "Lady and the Tramp" song, ma'am. Two people have to eat from the same plate of spaghetti without using their hands. The team that finishes in sixty seconds wins.'

Everyone around looked interested but no one came forward to participate.

'This looks like fun,' Deepa said, squeezing Simi's hand. 'Let's see if Abhi and Ranvir want to play too!'

The two had not come for lunch yet. But a few seconds later, Simi spotted Ranvir, followed by Abhi, heading their way.

Simi stared at those broad shoulders and that chest that had felt incredibly solid when they'd been pressed together in the bathroom. She tried to avoid Ranvir's eyes as he approached them.

Deepa made a beeline for Abhi, pointing to the game. 'Shall we play?'

'Really?' Abhi looked amused. 'Do we want to waste lunch hour?'

Deepa pouted, and a few moments later, he caved in.

Simi and Ranvir watched them head towards the counter. Abhi had just settled down at a table when Deepa came back. 'You should play too!' she said to them.

'Nah!' Simi and Ranvir said together.

'One more team is required,' the game host called. 'Does anyone else want to join?'

'Come on,' Deepa said, tugging at Simi's hand. 'Be a sport!'

Simi glanced at Ranvir.

Ranvir shrugged and nodded.

They went along and took their seats. Five teams were playing. A plate heaped with spaghetti was placed in front of each team.

'All set? Get ready . . . Set . . . ' the game host said, holding a whistle to her mouth, ready to start the timer. 'Go!'

Ranvir turned to Simi right at that moment. 'About the Holi party . . . I'm sorry. It was—'

'Yes, I know,' Simi blurted out, realizing that she was holding on to her breath from the moment he started. She'd been trying to sort this talk out in her head all weekend, and thinking the moment she saw him that she didn't know how they were going to deal with this—this elephant in the room. She was so stupid for kissing him. For being swept away.

'I shouldn't have . . . '

Right! She swallowed nervously, fidgeting with her fingers. 'Me too. I'm so sorry! It was the thandai.'

An awkward pause. 'I mean, you have Karan.'

Yes, she had Karan. And, he obviously had Parul. Both of which were painfully true.

She nodded emphatically, blinking as her heart pinched with guilt and shame. 'Yeah! That day was . . . a mistake.'

He was suddenly tongue-tied.

'Fifty-eight. Fifty-nine . . . Sixty! Times up!'

They looked down at their plate at the same time. They hadn't touched the spaghetti.

'Looks like we lost!' Ranvir said to Simi as the game host walked around to each table.

Her lips wobbled. 'We're awful.'

He searched her eyes as they rose from their seats. 'We're okay, right?'

'Yes . . . ' she said, a tad overlightly.

He seemed relieved. 'Shall we get some lunch?'

Unable to think clearly, Simi decided to just get what Ranvir was getting, and they both got sandwiches.

'Ayush and I are talking again,' Simi said as they walked back to their table.

'Really?' He looked truly happy for her. 'That's great news!'

She hoped she and Ranvir were really going to be okay too.

Deepa and Abhi caught up with them just as they sat down.

Deepa eyed them as she neared their table. 'How can you still be hungry?'

Abhi clutched his stomach. 'I'm feeling so full, I think I'm going to burst.' He groaned.

Deepa explained how they'd dug their faces into the plate and tried to gobble as much spaghetti as they could. 'We had to literally swallow it and half of it got stuck in our noses. What about you guys? Did you finish?'

Simi quickly changed the subject.

As they were exiting the food court after lunch, Deepa pointed to a corner. 'Look! A photo booth! Let's take pictures.'

Abhi and Ranvir went to check out the new installation. It seemed like another gimmick.

Deepa sidled up to Simi as soon as the guys were out of earshot and whispered, 'Wish it was a dark, closed booth like they show in the movies. Abhi and I would have enjoyed some private cosy time in there.'

'It's open for that very reason, so couples like you don't hijack it,' Simi shot back, giving her a knowing smile. 'Looks like you two haven't been able to keep your hands off each other!'

Deepa leaned in. 'That's why we're moving in together.'

Simi's eyes popped. 'What? When?'

'We couldn't wait!' Deepa said.

'Really?'

'Next month.'

'Congratulations!' Simi said, overjoyed for her friend.

Deepa blushed. 'Let's get our photos before there's a long queue.'

They moved ahead to the photo booth. When it was their turn, they decided on a group photo first. Simi had Deepa on one side and Ranvir on the other.

The four of them smiled into the camera just as it clicked.

'You guys should take a photo too,' Abhi suggested.

Ranvir and she stood side by side then, holding on to the props. Simi wore fake glasses and Ranvir wore a hat.

Despite the pain she was hiding, she would always remember being pressed against Ranvir's side, the warmth of his hand on her shoulder, her hand tugging at his waist.

* * *

'What?'

Deepa gave Simi a peculiar look as they walked back to the office together after parting ways with Ranvir and Abhi.

'What's that look in your eyes when you're with Ranvir? Since the Holi party you guys are behaving so weirdly.'

Simi stopped walking and turned to Deepa. 'There's something I have to tell you.'

'What?'

'Ranvir and I kissed that day in the bathroom.'

'What!'

'Yeah . . . I got carried away.'

'Sweetie, he has a girlfriend,' Deepa warned softly.

Simi pressed a hand to her heart. 'I know. It just happened. For the first time, I could imagine myself with a guy like him if it weren't for his girlfriend. But it won't happen again.'

She knew Parul was Ranvir's reality. She was only a friend.

* * *

March flew by pretty quickly.

Ranvir was increasingly busy, and had skipped lunch the last couple of weeks. Even when he did show up, he didn't stay too long.

Abhi and Deepa moved in together by the end of the month, and invited Ranvir and Simi over for a housewarming dinner.

They were all supposed to go together after work on Tuesday evening.

Simi and Deepa were waiting for Ranvir and Abhi to join them in the lobby but only Abhi showed up, telling them that Ranvir had received an unexpected phone call and would join them later.

Abhi and Deepa's home wasn't flashy but comfortable. A jumble of colourful cushions adorned the angled two-seater sofa in one nook, pink candles stood on a small table between them, thick curtains hung over the windows for privacy, and love songs played on Abhi's phone. The ambience had a heavy romantic vibe to it.

Deepa had set up their small dining table with paper cups and plates. Finger food and bottles of beer had been ordered. It promised to be a fun evening.

'We couldn't wait to move in together,' Abhi said.

'It felt like we were playing hooky from office every afternoon. And on weekends we had to request our roommates to give us some privacy. It was getting too much,' Deepa added.

Simi was happy for her friend. It seemed what Ranvir and she had bet on had really come a long way. She couldn't wait for Ranvir to come and settle on who had won the bet. She was sure Abhi had confessed his love to Deepa first.

But she knew that Ranvir would challenge that just because it would be something fun to do. Ranvir, however, had still not come.

Four hours later, Ranvir had still not showed up. They'd finished the beer and dinner, but there was no sign of him. Not even a call to let them know his plans.

Abhi tried his phone. It rang, but Ranvir didn't pick up.

Simi wondered what had happened to him. It was so unlike him to not show up at all.

TWENTY-TWO

Ranvir rubbed his eyes at the scene in front of him.

When Parul called him at work and told him his father and sister were at home, he didn't believe it.

And yet, here they were. This was the first time they'd ever come to the house he shared with Parul.

Tina rose and came to him as soon as he stepped in. 'Where have you been? We've been here since ages!'

'Hi, son!' His father beamed.

It was all so strange that it took Ranvir a while to absorb it. The house looked different too—less stark and bare, more homely, perhaps.

Parul had arranged big white lilies in a vase he'd never seen before. On the table, there were large steel bowls of chole, pulao, salad, roti, the sort of spread he'd have expected his mother to come up with.

'What's going on?' he asked, confused.

'I'm so glad you're home early!' Parul said, coming over and kissing him on his cheek. She looped her arm around his and led him inside. 'Why don't you get changed and come for dinner? We've been starving. Right, Papa?'

Papa?

Since when had she started calling his father 'Papa'? In fact, he did not remember her calling him anything, except Uncle that one time they'd met.

They sat down to dinner . . .

His father admired everything around him. His sister was all praises for the food, which Parul had obviously taken a lot of time to decide on and order. Ranvir remained silent as his father and sister went on and on about how they'd always admired Parul for her poise and style, according to his sister, and her simplicity, according to his dad.

Parul glowed at all the compliments and basked in their open adulation. After dinner, she pulled out the gifts she'd bought for them—an elegant watch with a leather strap for his father and an expensive scarf for Tina.

A scarf? Tina never wore anything but her traditional churidar-kurta. When would she wear a scarf?

But Tina was all smiles. She asked for Parul's opinion on how to wear it. She wrapped it around her neck and preened. They settled back on the couch. His dad was offered another drink, and Ranvir wondered if it was perhaps too much already.

Parul spoke non-stop about her office and work. She'd been promoted recently—something he didn't recall her telling him.

'Congratulations!' Lalit beamed, giving her a wide smile he reserved only for a few occasions.

Ranvir got up to go to the kitchen, and Tina quietly followed him while Parul and Lalit continued to chat.

'What's going on?' Ranvir asked her. 'You guys seem to be under Parul's spell.'

She pinched his arm, making him squeak with pain.

'She's trying to be nice. We're tired of waiting for you, Ranvir.'

'Waiting for what?'

She laughed. 'To get married, of course.'

He coughed. 'Married?'

'She was talking about you guys going to Turkey.'

'That's not to celebrate anything . . . '

'Then?'

He pulled her ponytail loose like he used to do when they were kids.

'Ah! What was that for?'

'To mind your own business.'

She laughed mischievously. 'Why do you think she invited Papa also?'

He winced, itching to throw a spatula at her head. 'Tina,' he said instead. 'What are you going to do with that scarf?'

'Wear it, of course!' she said smugly.

'On your bag?'

She playfully tapped him on the shoulder with a ladle.

'There you are!' his father said, when they walked back to the living room. 'Come, one last drink before I go home. A toast to the Turkey trip!' his father said, rising from the couch. 'Parul told me she will manage a good deal for me too. I think it's wonderful that she cares for you and wants you to take a break.'

Ranvir couldn't believe Parul had roped his father and sister into this. He fumed while Parul quickly filled four shot glasses.

'Yes, Papa. I've told him so many times.' Parul stuck the glasses in each of their hands, and then raised hers. 'To the Turkey trip and many more family gatherings like this.'

'Many more!' his father cheered, downing his glass.

* * *

Ranvir shut the door and turned to Parul. 'That was a cheap stunt!'

His father and sister had finally left. They had tried to convince him, and at one point even pleaded with him to go to Turkey. His father had laughingly threatened him that he wouldn't be allowed to come home if he didn't go for the trip.

By the end of it, he'd had enough.

Parul merely smiled. 'What did you expect me to do? Our relationship is five years old. Do I have no say in this? What have I done wrong?'

'You didn't have to get them involved in this.'

Her eyes were wide open, staring at him as if she did not understand what he was talking about. 'I did what I thought was best.'

'You don't even care for my father or my sister. All you care about is yourself. You've never even met them more than a few times in all these years.'

She cocked her head. 'Maybe I decided it was time I changed things around.'

'Maybe you should have stuck with Zubin.' He didn't know where that had come from.

She froze for a moment and clenched her fingers. 'Maybe I should have. Maybe I shouldn't have wasted my time on you.'

'Maybe that's right!'

'Ugh!' she screamed, and, in a mad rage, rushed across the room to grab a cushion. She ripped it open and white stuffing flew out.

'Stop it!' Ranvir yelled.

'No, I've had enough! You stop it!'

He strode towards her and grabbed her hand. 'Are you out of your mind?'

She tried to get out of his hold. 'Let me go! I just want to go!'

'Go then.' He let go of her. 'Nobody's stopping you from going. You're free to go wherever you want, do whatever you please.'

'Are you breaking up with me?' Shock flared in her eyes for a moment and then settled into a mad gleam. 'No, no, no. *I'm* breaking up with *you*,' she yelled. 'I've tolerated you for so long. You good-for-nothing, son-of-a—' Eyes tearing up, she glared at him.

He met her defiant stare, calm enough to say what he should have said a long time ago. 'I think we should break up, Parul. You don't deserve me.'

'You bet I don't deserve you!' she spat. 'You're a terrible boyfriend!'

He couldn't deny that, but he still wished she was just saying that to spite him.

She scoffed. 'I hate you! I can't believe I stayed with you all these years!'

It took all these years, but realization finally hit him like bricks crashing on his head. How long had it been since they'd wordlessly moved apart? How long since she felt that way about him? How long since they had stopped loving or even liking each other?

This whole living together had been a mere transaction. A veil. A charade. A cheap shot at convenience.

For what?

She didn't care. They had gone without talking to each other for days, without so much as bothering about each other. They'd been living like two strangers. They didn't love each other. Maybe they never had. All this had been a mistake.

He'd lived in it with his eyes closed, as if in a dream. A bad dream. Reality looked so different.

Parul dragged her hands across her face and gave him one last scathing look, fire still burning in her eyes. 'I will move out by the weekend. I hope you're happy!'

With that, she turned around and strode off to her room. The next moment the door banged shut and the whole house fell silent.

TWENTY-THREE

On Wednesday morning, Ranvir was sitting at a sleek grey table in one of the conference rooms at Fintura. There were two pairs of eyes, belonging to the two founding partners, staring back at him.

He'd done his research. He'd considered the financial implications of the market, weighed the pros and cons, and had come armed with data and reports that suggested that the new app had some serious cause for concern.

The market research had indicated bad news. He had to warn the founders of the impact of the economic downturn, because he believed it would be vital to the success of the launch.

If the founders went for his plan, they could, no doubt, avoid the financial risks. But not approving the plan, on the other hand, would mean they could potentially face losses. He trusted his instincts and was expecting a charged discussion.

'So, you're telling us we shouldn't launch now,' said Kuldeep, one of the founding partners. He gestured to the report Ranvir had prepared, which sat on the table in front of him.

Ranvir cleared his throat and went over the figures in the report. 'It shows that the market is unstable, and banks will not be willing to lend money to consumers in a few months when things get worse, because they won't be confident of their capability to pay back.'

They looked on gravely as he concluded his findings.

'If we postpone the launch, we'll be in a much better position to deal with the market conditions.'

'That's a risk we'll have to take,' Kuldeep said, tapping his pen on the desk and exchanging a look with his partner.

'It's a big risk,' Ranvir stressed. 'And I propose that we wait until the credit sentiment picks up.'

Nayan, the other partner, was about to say something when Kuldeep intervened. 'What time frame are we looking at?'

Ranvir met their curious gazes. 'Six months.'

'Delay for six months?' Nayan exclaimed.

Frowning, Kuldeep crossed his arms on the table. 'That's not possible. The investors are already on our backs.'

'We've already delayed it too long!' Nayan said. 'And the competition may take up our space if we don't push it out fast enough.'

'The launch has to go on as per schedule,' Kuldeep said with finality. 'So, whether it requires building bank confidence or promoting consumer opportunities, this has to get done. We'll discuss this at our next investor meeting, but right now, I don't think we can make any changes to the launch date.'

The meeting continued for another thirty minutes as they went back and forth on the issue and worked out what could limit the risks until the market bounced back.

At the end of the meeting, Kuldeep and Nayan seemed okay with some options Ranvir put forth.

'Good luck!' Kuldeep clapped Ranvir on the back, pleased with the talk. 'I'm confident you'll take care of it!'

Ranvir wasn't as confident that he would find a workaround with barely three and a half weeks left to go, but he could try his best to make it work. It just meant that these few weeks would get even crazier!

* * *

Ranvir was at his cubicle, plugging into his spreadsheet, a cup of espresso cooling at arm's length. It was almost lunch time, and his stomach was growling, but he'd decided to take a break only when he was done putting this together.

A knock made him look up. It was Abhi.

'Hi! Coming for lunch?'

Ranvir pinched his eyebrows with his fingers. 'No! I'm going to eat at my desk. Lot of work.'

'Come on, macha!' Abhi grabbed the seat across his table. 'You are too busy these days. Deepa has brought some home magazine. You can help us decide which bed to buy.'

'No, bro! I can't. Not today. Please.'

'You didn't even come to our party,' Abhi complained. 'Deepa was really upset. We were waiting for you.'

'Sorry,' Ranvir said, truly meaning it. 'I got delayed with that phone call and then I had to go home.'

'Go home?'

'Yeah, Parul invited my father and sister, and I didn't know what was going on when she called me.'

Abhi scowled. 'At least you could have picked up my call. We tried you so many times!'

'Sorry. Things were just a bit tense. And I got really busy afterwards!'

Abhi's face fell. 'That's all you have to say?'

Ranvir knew that moving in together meant a lot to both of them, and he'd really wanted to be there to be a part of their celebration, but he had been so swamped with work lately. Plus, he was still coming to terms with his break-up with Parul.

He shrugged, his eyes going back to the spreadsheet on the screen. He had calls lined up back-to-back and a report to finish by evening.

When he looked up again, Abhi had left.

Ranvir let out a sigh and got back to work, with every intention of making it up to his friends as soon as he had some free time.

TWENTY-FOUR

Simi always looked forward to coming into work, treating lunch hour as a happy time when she spent time with Ranvir, discussing mundane things and laughing at his silly jokes.

It was truly absurd how she felt this way every day.

A part of her knew how close they were getting. A part of her brain kept warning her that he had a girlfriend, and she, for all practical purposes, was engaged and shouldn't cross a line. But the fact was that meeting and talking to him gave her so much joy that she couldn't even think of stopping.

She appreciated the fact that he was a wonderful listener. He remembered everything she told him, encouraged her to talk about her family and dreams. She had never had this before, someone to whom her ideas and thoughts mattered, someone who was truly interested in what she had to say. Each time they finished lunch and went back to their offices, she felt a sinking despair as though it was the last time she was experiencing this kind of joy. Even the thought of not seeing him the next day brought her sheer misery.

She fretted when he was too busy to come for lunch or go out for sugarcane juice. She was hurt that he didn't show up at Deepa and Abhi's home, and envious of Parul, a person she had never met, for being the reason that he didn't make it.

She grudged Parul for being the only person who was with him all the time; for not having to depend on his coming to work to see him or talk to him. Though he hardly spoke about Parul, she knew the relationship mattered to him, and she couldn't prevent the pain it caused her.

Or that she couldn't get away from marrying Karan.

As the days progressed, it became increasingly evident that it was a marriage of convenience. She and Karan barely called each other or exchanged messages, and the only time they met was when their families asked them to arrange something. Karan seemed willing to marry her, but only to fulfil his parents' wish.

It seemed she was marrying him for the very same reasons.

* * *

At lunch, Simi watched Abhi and Deepa across the table and felt a fresh surge of longing for the good old times. She hadn't seen Ranvir in almost a week.

Her heart skipped a beat when she heard his voice right beside her.

'I hope I'm not too late.' Ranvir was carrying a plate of donuts for everyone. He set the plate down on the table and smiled. 'Sorry about the party.'

Both Abhi and Deepa ignored his peace offering.

Deepa pushed the plate towards Simi. 'I don't like donuts.'

Abhi sniffed at the plate. 'Me too.'

Ranvir looked crushed. 'I'm sorry I couldn't come, guys. I've been so busy, I haven't had time to breathe.'

Abhi rose from the table, pursing his lips. 'Actually, we're busy too.' He gestured to Deepa. 'We have to go and look for new curtains. We shouldn't waste our time.'

Deepa winked at Simi as she rose too. 'Maybe we'll end up buying some Murano furniture for our home.'

Simi smiled and wished them luck. It was surprising that they had completely disregarded Ranvir, who looked disappointed.

'Come on, I said sorry? Couldn't they forgive me?' he asked.

'They're your friends, Ranvir. We missed you at the party. You didn't even tell us you weren't coming.'

Ranvir ran a hand through his hair. 'Parul invited my father and sister, and I had to go home.'

She paused. She didn't know his father and sister had also been there. 'A phone call would have helped.'

'I couldn't, okay? Besides, it was just a casual party.'

'Yeah, but we waited for you all evening.'

'Oh! So now you want to lecture me too about how busy I am and have no time for anything?'

'Who said anything about lecturing you?' She rose. 'You know what? I'm sure you have work to get back to.'

She barrelled out of the food court and had barely made it to the exit when he came up running behind her and grabbed her arm. 'Hey! Hold up for a sec.'

She stopped and turned around.

'Can we go to their place this weekend?' he said, peering into her eyes.

'I can't,' she said. 'It's Karan's birthday.'

'You mean the boyfriend you don't even like!' Ranvir snapped. 'You'll go to his birthday party over your best friend's house?'

She couldn't understand what had come over him all of a sudden. 'First of all, I already went to their house. It was you who didn't turn up. And second, you're squeezing my arm.'

People were stopping to stare at them having a heated conversation in the middle of the exit passage. He let go but politely asked her to accompany him to the exit near the staircase, where it was a bit quieter.

It was empty. He closed the door behind him and sat down on one of the steps, gesturing to the space next to him.

She sat down beside him.

'I'm sorry! I didn't mean to yell at you. I don't know what's wrong with me,' he said, burying his head in his hands.

They remained silent for a few moments before she cleared her throat. 'So what happened at home that day?'

'I don't want to talk about it.

'Why not?'

'Why are you marrying Karan, Simi?'

She crossed her arms across her chest. 'How does it matter to you?'

He tipped a finger under her chin, raising her face until she was looking into his eyes. 'Do you love him?'

She held his gaze defiantly. 'Not everyone gets to be with the person they love.'

'I hope they do . . .' he whispered.

In a blink, he swept down, pulled her towards him and kissed her, so deeply that tears sprang from her eyes.

She wanted to push him away. Instead, she found herself wrapping her arms around his neck and kissing him back.

God, she wanted him so badly!

That kiss tipped her over the edge. It solidified her feelings for him. There was no going back now. She couldn't keep denying to the world that she wanted to be with him and only him, especially not while she was unofficially engaged to someone else. It wasn't fair to Karan at all.

She moaned when he nipped her lip softly. 'Ranvir . . .' she whispered as his hands roamed her back, sank into her hair, and pulled her to his chest.

When they pulled apart to catch their breaths, she caught his gaze, her cheeks wet.

'God, Simi!' He groaned. 'Why is it that we want the things we can't have and can't have the things we want?'

She wiped her tears. 'I—'

'Parul wanted this trip so much that she called my father and sister home to back her up.' The words tumbled out of his mouth. 'They want me to do what she wants . . .'

The mention of Parul felt like a red-hot iron searing right through her heart, scorching her dreams, stabbing her hopes.

She should have known better. Deepa had warned her too.

But she loved Ranvir so much that it was unbearable. She'd tried to stop her feelings for him. God, she'd tried so hard!

Yet, he was all she kept coming back to.

But it looked like he would always belong to Parul. Her heartache turned into bitterness.

She couldn't help herself. 'Then go, if that's what you want,' she said, choking on her words. 'She is your girlfriend. She's part of your life.'

'What are you saying, Simi?'

She shook her head. 'Do you love her? If you loved her, you'd have the courage to tell her what you wanted!'

His eyes flashed with resentment. 'You're marrying Karan. Do you love him?' He tipped her chin up so she'd meet his eyes. 'And yet, you haven't done anything about him!'

She flinched at the acidity in his voice. What did 'you haven't done anything about him' mean? Did he want her to be the reason for his break-up? Or him to be the reason for hers?

'What should I have done about him?' she asked him. 'What are you trying to tell me?'

For once, he had nothing to say.

Finally, she rose, the silence too much to bear, her heart bursting with feelings she could not express.

There were so many things she wanted to say to him.

I love you, she wanted to scream at the top of her lungs, but what was the point of a declaration that was already a dead cause.

One chance! That's all she'd ever wished for.

But fate had never intended him for her.

She pulled herself up from the steps, her chest heaving with pain, her eyes stinging with tears. She yanked open the door and left without a word.

TWENTY-FIVE

The taste of her salty tears still lingered on Ranvir's lips. The feel of her forehead joined to his, her warm breath on his face as he pressed his lips to hers.

Every bit of that angry kiss was still fresh in his memory, blood rushing to his veins, his heart thumping wildly.

A part of him had resisted her but the heat in her eyes and her trembling lips had been his undoing.

She'd kissed him back, clinging to his shirt. A tiny spark of joy had coursed through him. No matter how much he had tried to stop himself, it had been impossible. He couldn't remember ever feeling so starved.

Her hands had gone around him, and she'd put her fingers into his hair. He had groaned and pressed her body against his, opening her mouth to his, deepening the kiss, stealing as much closeness as he could.

It didn't seem enough for either of them.

Not everyone gets to be with the person they love.

Her words had touched him. He wanted her to have everything, the love and hope she deserved, if he could give them to her.

Instead of acknowledging how much she meant to him, he'd been gripped by guilt when they'd pulled apart.

He'd ruined their friendship by saying hurtful things, and kissed her even though she was engaged to someone else.

What should I have done about him? What are you trying to tell me?

He didn't have words. And even if he had said that he was falling for her, would it have changed anything? Because she'd still not changed her mind about Karan.

And then she was gone.

He remained on the empty staircase, unaware of how long he sat there, feeling hopeless and empty.

He didn't deserve her.

* * *

It was late evening, and Ranvir was still in the office when his phone rang. He took a look at the name on the screen and picked up immediately.

'Tina?' It was very unlike her to call him at work. 'What's wrong?'

'I can't go to meet Papa today.' Her voice sounded shaky and her nose seemed blocked.

'Are you okay?' Just last week he'd told her he wouldn't be able to meet Papa for the next two weeks at least. It had made him feel less guilty when she'd agreed to go alone. 'You know I can't make it.'

'Yes, I know!' she blurted out. 'But I can't either.'

'Why? What happened?'

The phone went dead.

Tina had hung up without explaining. That was so unlike her. She had never missed a meeting with their father.

He knew something was wrong.

Shutting his laptop, he picked up his bag and headed towards the car.

* * *

The door to Tina's home swung open, and Ranvir stood face to face with his brother-in-law. 'Jas?'

'Surprised to see me?'

'Yes . . . I mean, no. Where's Tina?' He walked in and peered inside the living room, but she wasn't there.

He walked towards the bedroom just as Tina came out of the bathroom. Ranvir was horrified to see her. 'What happened to you?'

A purplish black bruise covered her eye.

'What are you doing here?' she said, as shocked to see him as he was to see her.

Jas strode towards them, pointing his finger at her. 'So you called your brother over?'

'I didn't call him.'

'Then why is he here?'

Tina turned to Ranvir. 'Ranvir, it's not what you think. I hit my eye against the door. It was an accident,' she pleaded. 'Can you please leave?'

'Leave?' He couldn't believe her.

Jas shoved him, sending him teetering towards the wall. 'Didn't you hear what she said? Just get out!' His voice boomed.

Ranvir blocked further attack with his arm and refused to move. 'Not until I know why Tina has a black eye and couldn't make it to Papa's.'

Tina started to cry. 'Ranvir, please go.'

Despite trying to contain his rage, Ranvir found his temper rising. 'What did you do to her?'

'I did nothing. Ask her if you don't believe me.'

'This can't be nothing! Tina, pack some clothes,' Ranvir said. 'Come with me!'

'Really?' Jas laughed. 'And where are you taking her?'

Ranvir glared at him. 'Home.'

Tina looked on, fear flashing in her eyes.

In an unexpected move, Jas grabbed Tina's arm, and pushed her towards Ranvir. 'Sure, take her with you but she's not coming back until she gives up that stupid boutique idea of hers.'

'I'm never giving it up,' Tina said in a shaky voice.

'Don't I make enough for you? Why do you need to open a store and serve customers?'

'We already talked about it. I want to pursue my passion.'

He scoffed. 'Passion! Bullshit! It's all a charade. You want to disrespect my family. You don't care about anyone but yourself.' He wagged his finger at her. 'Let me warn you, it won't work. Not with me!'

Tina turned around and headed to the bedroom. In a few minutes, she came out with a small suitcase and a handbag. 'Let's go,' she said to Ranvir.

Jas fumed. In a sudden flash of anger, he strode towards Tina, arm raised, but Ranvir's quick reflexes stopped him from hitting her.

'Don't you dare!' Ranvir glowered at Jas. 'You think opening a store is being disrespectful to your family? Hitting the woman of the family is even more disrespectful. Hit her and you disrespect your entire family.'

Jas lowered his hand and just glared as Tina rolled her suitcase out of the door. They left the house, leaving Jas with venom spewing from his eyes.

Once in the elevator, Ranvir said, 'What a maniac! Was he always like this?'

She still looked pretty shaken up. 'You have no idea!'

'Why didn't you tell Papa or me? Why did you suffer this silently?'

'I thought doing something of my own would give me freedom and peace. I didn't know my decision would irk him so much. Thanks for coming for me. I don't know what I would have done without you.'

He pulled at her ponytail lovingly and then hugged her. 'You're safe now! Don't worry.'

She wrapped her arms around him and hugged him back.

For now, all that mattered was that Tina was leaving with him. He was glad he'd decided to come and check on her. What if he'd done nothing after her call? What if he'd let her stay with this monster? He shivered at the thought.

As they reached the ground floor, Tina's phone pinged. It was a message from Jas.

THINK TWICE BEFORE LYING TO ME, BITCH!

Tina sobbed all the way home and wouldn't say a word.

Ranvir let her be, angry with himself for not being able to help her earlier.

Everything around him seemed to be blowing up in his face.

How had he become so busy that he had neglected the very people he loved? His eyes strayed to the butterfly swinging below the rear-view mirror, and his thoughts flew to the other person he'd fought with earlier today.

He parked by the street, and they walked to the door, Tina holding her dupatta partially over the side of her face to cover her black eye. He felt sick as he walked beside her.

His father was stunned and speechless when he saw Tina. 'What's with her—' His hand flew to his mouth. 'How did this happen?'

Ranvir didn't answer the question. 'Tina is going to stay with you from now on, Papa.'

'Why? Where's Jas?'

'He's the asshole that did that to her.'

'Jas did that to you?'

Tina nodded.

The words poured out of Tina. They'd been having an argument about the boutique, and he had pushed her against the door.

'We should talk to him,' Lalit raged. 'How could he—'

'There's no use, Papa,' Tina said. 'He doesn't want me to start the boutique.'

Lalit shook his head. 'What rubbish! Why can't you start your boutique?'

'I think she should stay here until we can sort this out,' Ranvir cut in.

'Stay here?'

'Until we sort things out,' he made it clear.

'Sort this out, how? Jas and she should sort it out. How can we interfere?'

Ranvir shook his head, burning with rage as he remembered how Jas had raised his hand at his sister. 'If we'd interfered earlier, Papa, this wouldn't have happened.'

His father's eyes welled up. 'I wish your mother were here. She'd know what to do.'

Ranvir wished his mother were here too.

'I know what she'd do,' Tina said. 'She'd tell me to do what my heart told me to do.'

Lalit groaned. 'But it's not that easy, beta! You can't stay here forever. You must return to Jas. We have to sort it out before it turns ugly.' He made his way over to the telephone. 'Let me call Jas and talk.'

Ranvir held his hand and stopped him. 'No, Papa. How can you send her back to that—' He held back the expletives.

It wasn't going to be easy, but he could not throw his sister back to that monster after what he'd done. If his father couldn't take care of her, he would.

His father looked troubled but finally nodded. 'Yes, let her stay until we sort it out.'

TWENTY-SIX

Simi had almost forgotten that Karan's birthday was coming up until her mother asked her what she wanted to gift him.

A week before his birthday, Karan's parents had invited them to their house. Of course, she couldn't say no, despite not wanting to go to their house at all.

Kalki greeted them at the door. For once, she looked excited to see Simi more than Ayush, hugging her as soon as she entered.

Kalki's braces were gone, and her hair was longer than when Simi had last seen her.

'Hi, beta! Where's everybody?' Gauri asked Kalki.

'We were waiting for you, Aunty!' Kalki said, leading the way into their plush living room.

The balloons and streamers from Bhavna and Dheeraj's anniversary party came back to mind. The room looked a lot less flashy today.

Bhavna was speaking to someone on the phone, and Dheeraj was seated on the couch, having a cup of tea.

'Right on time,' Bhavna said, disconnecting the call immediately and waving to Simi's parents to take a seat. Then she gave Simi a once-over, a twinge of disapproval clouding her eyes, which she swiftly brushed under a wide smile. 'Beta, this colour doesn't flatter you,' she said about the lavender pink churidar set that Simi was wearing.

Simi's mother had said something along the same lines, that the colour made her face look pale and washed out. But she'd paid her no heed. She didn't want to put any effort into her appearance for Karan's birthday.

If he liked her the way she was, good. If not, it wasn't her problem.

Dheeraj waved Venkat into the seat next to him, while Bhavna poured him and Gauri two cups of tea. The men sipped their tea and got into a conversation instantly while the women huddled together and whispered among themselves.

Ayush had wandered off into the balcony for some fresh air.

Simi leaned towards Kalki. 'Where's Karan?'

'He's gone to office to get his charger,' she said.

The mention of the charger unexpectedly brought on a sudden rush of memories.

You're marrying Karan. Do you love him?

She shook her head and swallowed as Ranvir's words came back to her.

Kalki waved her hand in front of Simi's face. 'What happened? Are you okay?'

She nodded, feeling herself sway a little. 'Yes, just a little frazzled because of work.'

'Bhaiyya will take care of everything,' she said with a knowing smile that sent Simi's brain into a tizzy.

What did Kalki mean? What was Karan going to take care of?

Not giving her any more time to ponder, Kalki pulled her by her arm. 'Come, let's go to my room.'

A shocking bright pink wall stared right at Simi as soon as she entered Kalki's room.

The rest of the walls were mossy green. Simi disliked both colours.

'My room was refurbished recently,' Kalki said, showing off the colour-coordinated wardrobes, the lights, lamps and even the bedspread. Everything in her room was a shade or two lighter than the same pink or green.

A massive board had several of her childhood pictures and a few recent ones.

'Sit down,' Kalki said, patting the bed.

Simi sank into the soft bed and smiled at Kalki. 'Nice.'

'What colour would you like for your bedroom?'

This conversation was all too strange. Kalki had never spoken so much, neither asked her so many questions.

'I like light shades.'

Kalki giggled. 'Then you'll be shocked to see Bhaiyya's room.'

That made Simi curious again. If this was Kalki's room, she wondered what Karan's looked like.

'I'll take you to Bhaiyya's room,' she said, knowingly. 'But first, let me show you this.'

She went to her wardrobe and pulled out a velvet case.

She sat down on the bed beside Simi, settled the case between them, and opened it.

There was a shimmering necklace inside; so dazzling that Simi's eyes grew wide. 'Are these . . . ?' *Diamonds . . . ?* She swallowed the rest of her words.

'Do you like it?'

Even before Simi could respond, Kalki pulled out the necklace from the case and held it up in her hands. 'Turn around.'

The next thing she knew, Kalki was placing the necklace around Simi's neck and clasping it at the back. Simi shivered as the cold metal touched her skin.

'There!' Kalki said, leading her to the mirror. 'Look! You look like a princess.' She leaned towards her conspiratorially then. 'Bhaiyya likes—'

Someone cleared their throat. She stopped mid-sentence and both of them turned towards the door. Karan stood there, leaning against the door jamb, his hands folded across his chest, smiling. 'I see you two are busy.'

Kalki laughed. 'I was just showing off my new necklace.'

Karan came closer, held Simi's shoulders and turned her around. 'Of course, it looks beautiful. Would you like something like this for our wedding?'

Simi blinked. 'What?'

'Let me check if Ma needs anything. I'll be right back,' Kalki made an excuse to leave Karan and her alone.

Just then Bhavna called out Karan's name.

'Be here. I'll be right back,' Karan said, disappearing to the living room.

'Show me Karan's room,' Simi said to Kalki, unable to curb her curiosity.

Kalki happily led the way to another bedroom down the corridor. Simi stood at the threshold to Karan's bedroom, her mouth agape. It was awash with navy blue and gold accents. Every surface—the walls, wardrobe knobs, light trimmings, curtain rod brackets—had these colours. The heavy brocade curtains were drawn completely to block out sunlight.

The dark space suddenly made her feel claustrophobic. 'He likes his room dark and cold,' Kalki explained.

Simi imagined herself waking up in this room every morning and shivered at the very thought. It brought goosebumps on her skin. She rubbed her arms vigorously.

'Let's go back to the living room,' she heard herself say to Kalki. 'Our parents must be looking for us.'

'Ah! There you are!' Gauri said, when Kalki and she got back to the living room. 'I was just about to call you. You look tired, my dear,' she said, rising from the couch.

She brushed her mother's hand aside. 'It's nothing, Ma.'

'Well, then let's have dinner,' she said. There was a consensus in the room as everyone rose from the couch and headed to the dining room.

Simi was thankful for her mother's guiding hand as she led her to the table. 'What's wrong?' her mother whispered when they were out of earshot. 'Is everything okay?'

'Yes, Ma. I'm fine.'

Karan took his place next to Simi and made a show of removing the glass of water kept next to her plate. Ayush sat on her other side. The parents made themselves comfortable around the table. Simi seemed to have lost her appetite. The food had been ordered from a nearby restaurant. The gravies looked too thick and the subzis seemed too oily. She managed to eat the rotis, soaking them into as little gravy as possible.

Bhavna had never cooked in her life, she claimed now to the group at the table. 'My mother never cooked, and my sisters don't cook. Actually, none of the girls in my family cook.'

Gauri looked aghast.

Dheeraj complimented his wife on her other skills; the word 'other' emphasized with a wink.

Bhavna giggled like a schoolgirl and swatted his arm playfully. 'You're such a naughty man . . . Not everybody is used to your sense of humour. Don't scandalize everyone.'

Dheeraj grinned.

Simi did an inward eye roll. Beside her, she could hear Ayush's imperceptible grunt.

Venkat smiled awkwardly. 'I think we all know how playful Dheeraj was even during service. He was called the—' He stopped with an awkward pause.

Dheeraj peered at him. 'And you know what they used to call Venkat at the bank?'

Bhavna looked at everyone around the table and raised her hands to the sky. 'You've never told us, Dheeraj!' she said with a mock pout. 'Come on, we have to know.'

'Our new boss mistook him for the chaiwallah. *Ek chai lana* . . . And then he was known as the chaiwallah.' Dheeraj's belly laugh caused an awkward hush at the table.

Only Bhavna smiled indulgently at her tactless husband.

Simi noticed her parents' faces fall. They looked at each other and back at everyone, trying to hide their discomfort.

'It's time to cut the cake,' Karan announced, finally breaking the mortifying silence.

Kalki escaped to the kitchen to bring the cake.

Simi excused herself to go to the kitchen to help her.

When Simi returned to the table it seemed like the situation had defused.

Venkat's face looked even. Gauri was calm but there was a fake smile on her lips. Bhavna and Dheeraj were in good spirits, oblivious to the blundering table conversation. The storm had passed.

Everyone sang happy birthday, and Karan blew out the two- and eight-shaped candles on the gigantic red velvet cake.

He cut a slice, brought it to Simi's mouth, and announced, 'Today is not only my birthday, I also got my promotion!'

Simi's eyes flew open.

Just as she bit into the piece of cake, Bhavna jumped up from her chair. 'How would you like to be my daughter-in-law, Simi?'

Simi took in a deep, shocked breath. The cake got lodged in her throat. She choked and coughed until she was out of breath. 'Water . . . ' She could barely form the words.

The rest was a blur.

Karan thumped on her back. Kalki ran to get water. Suddenly there was chaos all around.

And then that queasy feeling returned. Her stomach churned. A loud rumbling made itself known in her belly.

The next moment she heaved and rushed to the bathroom while everybody watched in shock.

'What happened?' she heard her mother scream.

But she was already in the toilet, throwing up her dinner.

She was so exhausted when she came out that she collapsed on the couch, feeling drained.

'What happened?' Bhavna asked.

'I hope there weren't mushrooms in any of the dishes,' she heard her mother say out loud.

Her mother had created the perfect excuse. As the others gathered around to analyse and rip apart the menu, Simi closed her eyes and tuned out.

When she woke up, she was being helped to the car.

On their way home, her father only spoke about the wedding proposal. Swept along by the image of a wedding at last, her mother gushed at her father's euphoria.

In the midst of all the incoherent babble, Ayush turned to her in the back seat, and whispered, 'Didi, are you okay?'

'Not okay,' she heard herself whisper back, unable to recognize her strange hoarse voice. 'Far from okay . . . '

He threaded his fingers through hers and held her hand all the way home.

TWENTY-SEVEN

Parul had packed and sent most of her stuff to her parents' place a couple of days after their fight. She had moved out the night of the argument.

She'd shut Ranvir out of her life, leaving him out in the cold.

If she hadn't broken up with him, he would have done it. After all, they'd been living a dream that was empty and hollow.

She was in her bedroom, packing the rest of her things.

The refrigerator was empty. Empty takeout boxes lay in the waste bin. He cleaned up the kitchen and settled down on the couch, waiting for her.

A few hours later, she emerged, rolling her suitcases out.

'I'm not coming back,' she said, her eyes full of hate.

A part of him knew he deserved it.

He was tired, overworked and hopelessly in love, but not with Parul. He'd been negligent and had cheated on her. He was a terrible boyfriend. He deserved that she wanted nothing to do with him.

Parul stared at him, her lips set. She wanted out.

He wanted it too. He was in love with Simi. He finally had the guts to admit it, if only to himself. He'd shut down his feelings far too long.

He looked at Parul and limply nodded.

Parul walked out and closed the door behind her. The door clicked shut and just like that she was gone. Just the way she had come into his life.

For a moment, he was sad, thinking of everything they had been through together, wishing he could have changed to make himself more worthy of her. But it felt like making excuses for his happiness, for the kind of freedom and peace he hadn't felt in a long time.

He allowed the peace to flow through him.

And, being alone again, he picked up his sketchbook, turned to a new blank page, and started sketching.

* * *

That weekend had left Simi anxious and sad. Her father had already started talking about the wedding arrangements, and calling card printers and wedding halls.

Simi couldn't believe Karan had got an unexpectedly early promotion.

How would you like to be my daughter-in-law, Simi?

The words played in her head on endless loop, making her queasy. Even something like crochet, which would always calm her down, was not helping at all.

The wedding was in two months. *Two months!*

The very thought of that made her rush to the bathroom again. She vomited into the toilet bowl, tears streaming down her cheeks, but she came up empty. She felt sick to the stomach but there was nothing left in her system because for the last two days she'd hardly eaten.

On Monday morning, Simi took a cab to her old office in Koramangala instead of going to BizWorks.

'Hi, Simi! Great to see you,' the receptionist greeted her.

Simi smiled at her. 'Hi Jessie! Is Vandana in?'

'I think she's in a meeting. I'll tell her you're here.'

Simi wandered around the showroom. She had left just six months ago, yet the sight of the three hundred or so sq. ft room filled with furniture, the smell of leather, the feel of the grainy wood, made her nostalgic.

Alongside their signature home furniture was the new collection of office furniture. Her boss, Vandana, had once asked her to be its marketer. She wondered if the opening was still available.

'Hey, Simi! What are you doing here?' Vandana stood behind her, beaming.

Simi started out hesitantly, then decided to come straight to the point. 'Vandana, you wanted me for the new office division. Do you still need someone for the position?'

'You're interested!' Her eyes shone for a moment before they narrowed. 'Come to my office.' Once they had sat down, she said 'Look, Simi, I won't lead you on. It's nothing like the home division. The products are still new, very slow pick up, and we're not doing too well yet. On the other hand, we do need more capable hands. And yes, the spot's still open.'

Simi couldn't believe her ears. 'You mean I can join?'

'I can put in a word with Nandan. I'm sure we can work it out. We'd love to have you back here.'

Simi knew she'd love that. She'd been thinking about this all night. Leaving BizWorks would mean not meeting Deepa every day and working in a cool office space. But it would also mean not running into Ranvir. After Karan's proposal, it made sense to not see Ranvir any more.

Plus, here she'd have more creative freedom. Working with Champak had always dampened her creativity and choices. Working on a new project would mean truly testing her skills and a chance to prove herself. Besides, this office still felt like home.

'Still miss this place?' Vandana raised an eyebrow.

'As a matter of fact, I do.' Simi smiled back.

'I knew it! Come along!' Her boss led her to the first floor to show her a tiny, empty desk. It was in a cramped corner at the end of a narrow corridor, nothing like the beautiful large spaces she'd grown used to at BizWorks.

But it still made her feel like she was back home!

* * *

'What do you mean you're going to be working out of the main office?' Deepa's voice blasted through the phone. 'Why?'

All the words came pouring out of her. She told Deepa she was getting married, and she'd decided to not see Ranvir again.

'You can't be serious!' Deepa yelled back. 'What happened?'

All weekend, Simi had been numb and in denial about Karan's proposal, but nothing could change the fact that in two months she would be married to him. She had fought her emotions all weekend and asked herself if that was what she wanted.

Every inch of her had protested, begged to find a way out. But there had been none.

Her marriage to Karan was inevitable. She knew it wasn't for love, but her family was very happy with the match.

She knew what love truly felt like because she'd felt it with Ranvir, and she'd seen it in Deepa and Abhi's relationship.

She'd fallen in love with Ranvir. But she'd said yes to Karan.

She had to stop seeing Ranvir, and there was only one way to end this longing for the man she loved but could not have.

'I can't meet Ranvir and pretend I'm fine . . . I won't be able to. I can't think of another way,' Simi told Deepa.

She'd woken up that morning and realized she wanted to move out of BizWorks. That was the only way to stop herself from going into a downward spiral of guilt, hurt and regret.

That's why she had asked for the transfer.

'I hope you understand,' she told Deepa. 'The only way to forget this ever happened is if I don't see him ever again.'

Deepa made a disapproving sound. 'You don't have to go away. You'll forget him, you'll see.'

'I won't forget him,' she said sadly. 'That's why I want to stay as far away from him as possible.'

'Oh, you silly girl,' Deepa said with a long sigh, finally giving up. 'You did so much for Abhi and me, and I'm so sorry I can't do anything for you. If there's anything—'

'No, it's not your fault,' Simi said. 'I'm the one who messed up.'

TWENTY-EIGHT

A few days before the Fintura app launch, Ranvir ran into Abhi and Deepa at the food court. It had been almost two weeks since they'd had lunch together.

He'd missed their lunches—the hour when they forgot work for a bit and laughed at silly things like Abhi's shayari or Deepa's musings on 'perfect boyfriend material'. Simi and he loved to settle the fights between the two, which happened often. And when Abhi and Deepa slipped away to be alone, he and Simi would talk about just anything under the sun.

He'd missed Simi the most.

Deepa looked surprised to see him as he made his way to their table with his Subway sandwich and coffee.

'You finally found time for us,' Abhi said, frowning, as he unwrapped his sandwich.

'Where's Simi?' Ranvir asked.

'You're such a workaholic, macha! Forget about us. You don't even know Simi left, do you?' Abhi said.

His mouth fell open. He didn't even have an inkling. He'd been so busy that he hadn't been able to take even a lunch break.

'What do you mean she left?'

'She doesn't work here any more.'

What? But why? The news shook him.

'She never said she was leaving!' He'd missed her terribly since their argument on the stairs. He meant to apologize when he met her, but he hadn't expected not to see her again.

Abhi nodded empathetically. 'She asked about you at her farewell.'

She had a farewell? 'Why didn't you call me?'

'I did call you, macha! You cut my call.'

Ranvir ran his fingers through his hair in disbelief. 'So, she's gone? Where?'

'She got a transfer to the office closer to her house.' Sighing, Deepa reached for the glass of water next to her.

It brought back an old memory of Simi when Ranvir had first met her at this very food court.

And subsequent times, the way she blushed at the drop of a hat and blurted out the first thing that came to her head. Even more so lately, he'd missed their conversations, the things that always brought a smile to her face. And his.

He felt at ease with her, the way she spoke out her thoughts and her expressions that told him exactly what was on her mind. She didn't judge him, laugh at him or scoff at his love for his work, like Parul did. He didn't have to pretend in front of her.

He remembered the time he'd told her he hated making plans for weekends. Or the future. She'd laughed and told him she'd never given a thought to the future either.

And now, she was gone forever?

He couldn't believe that she wasn't coming back.

Nothing would be the same without her!

'Can I have her number?' Ranvir asked Deepa, wondering why he'd never asked Simi himself.

'Sure.' She gave him Simi's number, adding very subtly, 'She's getting married in a few weeks.'

God! That felt like a stab in his chest.

The conversation at their table dragged on listlessly, and as the lunch time wore on, it felt horrible without her.

As he lay in his bed that night, Ranvir pulled out the phone to call Simi, his fingers itching to hit the call button.

What would he tell her?

He was such a terrible friend who hadn't even made time for her. He was so consumed with work that it had taken him weeks to know she'd left.

Ultimately, better sense had prevailed. It was best if he didn't call her.

He didn't want to impinge on her new life.

If she wanted to, she could have got his number and called him too, but she hadn't. It meant she wanted things the way they were.

Understandable.

They had spent some wonderful times together, and he didn't want to ruin it by calling her. He had no right to disturb her peace and happiness just because he was finally free.

He'd hold on to her memories; their friendship would remain in his heart.

* * *

The marketing role for the new office furniture at Murano gave Simi a lot of satisfaction. Her small team had created a social media content plan and strategy, and Vandana had given the go-ahead to try out even the whackiest ideas.

She often missed the BizWorks office, especially at lunch time, now that she'd gone back to eating home-cooked meals at the smaller cafeteria with her team members.

One day, she walked in and noticed a tall guy with his back to her at the reception. Her heart almost skipped a beat, thinking it was Ranvir.

She stood rooted to the spot for a whole minute, exhaling only after he turned around and she was sure it was someone else.

She still remembered the day she'd met Vandana and gone back to BizWorks to tell her team that she was moving back. It was all very impromptu. Deepa and the rest of the team had cut a small send-off cake right at her desk. Then, at lunch, she'd hoped to meet Ranvir and tell him too, but he hadn't picked up Abhi's call.

Apparently, Ranvir had taken her number from Deepa, but Simi still hadn't heard from him.

Maybe he felt it was best to stay away from each other, like she did.

I think so too, she said to the preserved papery rose tucked inside her book, which she opened every night, just because . . .

It felt like a reminder of happier times that would never return.

The wedding plans were in full swing. Thankfully, being busy at work helped. Simi used office work as an excuse when she didn't want to discuss the wedding. She went home late every day, had dinner and went to sleep. Even as she lay in bed, waiting for sleep to come, she wished she'd wake up and realize this was all a dream.

The only silver lining was that Ayush and she were talking a lot again. They watched movies like before. He teased her too, like always. They watched *DDLJ* again, right after all of the Internet celebrated the movie's twenty-fifth release anniversary.

Ayush walked into her room one day and saw the photo she'd kept. It was from the photo booth. She'd propped it up behind her crochet needles and thread.

'What's this?' he asked, picking up the photo from her desk.

She snatched it back from him. 'Friends at work.'

'Then why is it hidden here?' He wiggled his eyebrows at her. 'Someone special in there?'

She laughed at his silliness although he'd hit the nail.

She missed Ranvir. Soon, she'd miss her parents and Ayush too.

She'd remember Ayush's teasing, and his habit of buying ice cream for all of them every night. Most of all, she'd miss his laughter and the way he settled between her mother and her on the couch, his head on his mother's lap and his legs on hers, while her mother watched her favourite travel channel, Simi did her crochet, and he played games on his phone. What a sight they made!

Why was it that a girl had to leave everything behind, she wondered, shivering just thinking about the ghastly blue room in Karan's house. Why should she be the one to leave her cream walls, her mother's brownies after dinner and the movies with Ayush? Why should she be the one to have her whole life turned upside down?

TWENTY-NINE

At home, Simi was chilling on the couch in ratty pyjamas that had seen better days, with her latest crochet earrings pattern from her grandmother. It was after dinner.

Gauri was peacefully settled in front of the travel channel again, and Venkat was in the kitchen, getting a glass of water when the doorbell rang.

They weren't expecting anyone at this hour.

Venkat opened the door and gave out a shout. 'Hello, Karan! Gauri, look who's here!'

Simi turned her head towards the door and made a hurried attempt to cover her hideous pyjamas with a cushion, but despite her best efforts, Karan's eyes fell on her clothes and widened in shock.

Shit! There was also a hole in the armpit area! She'd forgotten about that. She kept her arms lowered determinedly and flashed him a smile.

Karan gave her a half-nod in return, his mouth just about stretched in a smile. 'Hello, Uncle and Aunty. Hello, Simi.' He strode in purposefully and settled on the couch.

Simi wondered what this unexpected visit was about.

Gauri rose from the couch. 'Will you have dinner if you haven't eaten, beta?'

'No, thanks, Aunty! I have something important to tell you all.'

Venkat and Gauri exchanged curious glances. Simi too straightened in her seat. Karan's gaze slid to her before he turned his full attention to her parents.

'This is difficult for me to say . . . ' he began. 'But I think it's in our best interest if I bring this up now.' He cleared his throat. 'Actually, it's better if I show you.'

'Sure, beta,' Venkat said.

He pulled out his phone and opened something up. Then he gave the phone to Venkat.

'It's a video—' Venkat paused mid-sentence, his eyes growing wide. He looked shocked, then angry. 'What is this?'

Simi just looked from Karan to her father, getting worried.

Gauri took the phone from Venkat's hand. 'Let me see.' She instantly clapped a hand over her mouth. 'How—'

Simi rose from the couch and took the phone from her mother.

It was a short clip. She hit play.

On the screen, Ayush was kissing Jamwal.

Simi gasped. This looked like one of Kalki's Instagram stories. How did Karan get hold of this?

Her head was reeling. 'How did you find this?'

Karan stared at her.

'Ayush!' Venkat called out.

'I think these things bring a bad reputation to families,' Karan said smugly while Venkat paced the floor, waiting for Ayush. 'Children post nonsense on Instagram thinking no one in their families will find out. But what do you know!'

'How did you get on Kalki's Instagram?' Simi asked numbly. 'Whose—'

Venkat turned to her, waving a hand. 'Simi, stop asking foolish questions. Call Ayush.'

Simi could not get her legs to move.

Ayush walked into the living room then, oblivious to the cause of the commotion.

Gauri unexpectedly began to cry.

'What is this?' Venkat stormed towards Ayush and thrust the phone in his hand. 'Isn't this the boy who came home for the barbecue?'

Ayush's gaze slid to Simi before he pressed play. All the colour drained from his face as he watched the video.

'What is this about?' Venkat repeated. 'Is he . . . are you . . . ?'

'I just thought I should let you know,' Karan went on, while father and son stared at each other. 'I should be going now.'

After Karan left, Venkat yelled at Ayush, and Gauri cried. Ayush just stood there and took it all, not saying a word. Simi's words were stuck in her throat too.

Her heart went out to him.

After his father had run out of steam, Ayush looked at him and said, 'I love him.'

Simi felt proud of her little brother for having the guts to tell their parents.

Venkat imploded. 'Shame on you for such actions! And do you know who found this? Karan! The boy who is going to marry your sister. Now, they know about it too. They'll laugh behind my back. Perhaps even cancel the wedding. You'll ruin your sister's life! If this happens, I will break your legs. You will never step out of this house again. I will not have this kind of nonsense in my house . . . '

The barrage of harsh words continued but Ayush said nothing.

Simi felt scared when he didn't react at all. She wondered what was going on in his mind.

She wanted to stop her father, but didn't dare to.

Finally, Ayush quietly went back to his room. Venkat slumped on the couch next to Gauri.

Simi returned to her room too, and the whole house fell silent.

* * *

At 7 a.m., Gauri barged into Simi's room. 'Ayush is not in his room!'

Gauri knew that Ayush had left the house in the wee hours, since both Venkat and she had been up till midnight.

The bigger question was: Where was he? Where had he gone?

Sitting by the edge of Simi's bed, Gauri wiped her eyes and whispered tearfully, 'I hope he's okay.'

Simi scooted across the bed to hug her. Though she was comforting her mother, she was terrified of where Ayush might be or what he might have done.

THIRTY

Simi rushed out of the bathroom as her phone rang, hoping it was Ayush.

But it was her grandmother. She swiped to connect the video call.

Ammamma's calm and smiling face appeared on the screen. She was wearing a big red bindi, her silvery white hair was tied up in a bun, and a pair of gold earrings glittered on her earlobes. She peered at Simi through round gold-rimmed glasses. 'How are you, beta?'

Simi felt tears sting her eyes, wishing she could tell her grandmother about Ayush's disappearance, but she bit back her words. There was no point in worrying Ammamma as well.

'Where's everyone? It seems so quiet out there!' Ammamma asked.

'All are busy as usual,' Simi said, hoping Ammamma wouldn't ask to speak to Ayush like she sometimes did. She didn't want to lie to her grandmother.

'Guess what I'm making today?' Ammamma said.

'What?'

'I'm making Ayush's favourite achar. Kaccha mangoes are in season, no?'

'They're my favourite too, Ammamma.'

Ammamma smiled, the corners of her wise eyes crinkling, the creases etching long and deep patterns across the sides of her face. 'Don't worry! I'll send some achar for you too.'

After a few minutes, Simi hung up, heaving a sigh of relief that her grandmother had not asked about Ayush.

Though, it wouldn't be too long before they'd have to tell her.

Simi felt queasy thinking about Ammamma's reaction.

A little while later, Karan arrived. Venkat had called him over to help out.

Karan walked in purposefully and tried to act as if he had the situation under control. 'I always felt there was something odd about him, Uncle,' he said tactlessly.

Gauri swallowed her tears. 'Don't say that, beta!'

Venkat's bloodshot eyes revealed how little sleep he'd got last night. 'Where do you suggest we look for him first?'

Simi had never seen her father look so helpless. He stared earnestly at Karan, hoping for a magic solution to the problem.

'Let's go to the police, Uncle!'

'No, no, let's look ourselves before we go to the police,' Venkat said.

'Simi and I can take my car and scout the neighbourhood,' Karan suggested.

Venkat nodded. 'Meanwhile, Gauri and I will contact all his friends and see if they have any idea where he might be.'

* * *

Simi felt stuffy in Karan's car.

Before they set off, he pulled out a cigarette and lit it. 'Hope you don't mind,' he asked customarily before lighting it, without waiting for her reply.

There was a Clint Eastwood-style squint in his eyes and a deep frown on his forehead as he drove around the area without any luck.

'I didn't want to say this to your parents but this search of the neighbourhood won't work. We should go to the police.'

That's what she didn't get about him. He acted cordial and agreeable in front of her parents when he clearly didn't want to.

'How did you find that video?'

'I know Kalki's Instagram password,' he snapped. 'Why does that matter?'

'Were you spying on Kalki?'

'Must you ask so many questions, Simi?' His smile was devilish. 'I was just casually looking through her Instagram, and I happened to see it. They seem to have common friends.' He shrugged. 'Anyway, long story! I recognized Ayush, and I had to warn your parents.'

'You could have told me, Karan! You didn't have to go to my parents.'

'Told you?' Karan scoffed. 'It's alarming how lightly you are taking this, Simi.'

'It isn't that alarmingly serious, Karan!'

Karan gave her a weird look. 'There was a gay guy in our college. At least he was the one we all knew about. Believe me, I had that expression of disbelief the first time I heard about him.' He smirked. 'The other boys, not so much. They shut him up in the bathroom until he was crying like a baby. They—'

Bile rose up her throat. 'Stop!' she said, feeling so sick she was sure she'd throw up.

'Do you know what would happen if my parents came to know?'

Simi couldn't stop herself. 'What would happen?'

'They'd . . . They'd . . . There would be no wedding!'

'Why do you want to marry me, Karan?'

'Stop asking silly questions, Simi. Why does anyone marry? To settle down. To please their parents, to have children. Isn't that why you're getting married too?'

'I'm not sure any more.'

'My parents won't be sure any more either. I mean think of the shame he's brought on all of us.'

'Shame? He's my brother. He's run away and all you can think of is the shame? He has nothing to be ashamed about.'

'There is no escape from the shame he's brought upon us.' He ran a hand over his face and let out a gusty breath. 'Whether he's dead or alive!'

Horrified, Simi turned to him. 'What did you say?'

He ignored her and peered at the road.

She raised her voice. 'I asked, what did you say?'

'Oh come on, Simi,' he said. 'Calm down! There's no need to get so emotional! A good beating will set him right.' He snickered. 'Serves him right. Anyway, all this drama is too much. I'm going straight to the police station. We'll tell your father after we've filed a complaint. It's a good thing you're with me.'

'Stop the car!' she yelled.

'For what? We're not there yet.'

'I said, STOP THE CAR!'

The car came to a screeching halt. 'What's wrong with you?'

She opened the door and got out. 'Go home, Karan. We don't need you to take care of this for us.'

He looked like she'd slapped him on the face. 'You're crazy!' he yelled, his eyes simmering with rage. 'You both are crazy! In fact, you and your brother deserve each other!'

'Go to hell!' Simi mumbled as he drove off. She was so mad, she wished she'd punched him.

She didn't care if Karan's family did not approve of Ayush, or if she wasn't going to marry him.

Ayush meant the world to her, and she would find him on her own if she had to. If only she knew where to look.

Where could Ayush be? Where in the world would he think of being right now?

A cab came to a stop right next to Simi and a gentleman stepped out.

The cabbie peered at her. 'Taxi, ma'am?'

'No.' Simi shook her head. As she watched the cab leave, it struck her.

Of course!
That's where he'd gone.

* * *

It took about seven hours.

Simi felt calm as she stepped out of the cab right in front of an old single-storey bungalow with a patch of garden in the front and a picket fence.

She paid the driver and rushed towards the house.

The old armchair on the porch was still rocking. Someone had been sitting there right before she'd shown up. Curious, she knocked on the main door.

In a few minutes, Ammamma was at the door, an apron tied around her waist, a gravy-laden ladle in her hand. Her eyes popped. 'Oh my dear Lord! What are you doing here, Simi?'

Simi hugged her. 'Came to see you, Ammamma.'

'Came to see me? Alone?'

'Yes. May I come in?'

Ammamma stuttered and let Simi in.

Simi looked around the living room. As soon as she'd got out of Karan's car, she'd called her parents and told them she was going to Ammamma's.

She wasn't wrong. His shoes lay in a corner. An Agatha Christie book lay on the table next to the couch.

Simi turned to Ammamma. 'He's here, isn't he?'

Ammamma feigned ignorance. 'Who are you talking about, dear?' But soon gave up when she saw Simi's expression. 'He came in the morning. He wouldn't tell me anything. Just showed up and went to his room. Woke up, had breakfast . . . ' She sighed. 'Come, let's go to the kitchen, and you can tell me what's going on.'

Simi followed her grandmother into the kitchen where a pot of chicken gravy was simmering on the stove. A plate of kneaded flour sat by the corner. Ammamma had been busy, cooking dumplings.

'Shall I put on some tea?'

Simi took off her shoes, wiggled her toes, and rubbed the crick in her neck from the long drive. 'Yes, please.'

'How did you know he was here?' said Ammamma with a twinkle in her eyes.

'You hinted at it.'

'Me?' Ammamma looked surprised. 'When did I say anything?'

'This morning, when you called me, you said, I'll send some achar for you. Not, I'll send some achar for you and Ayush. Besides, the fact that you were making achar was a giveaway in itself.'

Ammamma lips curled upwards. 'You're a smart girl!'

Ammamma got busy shaping the rest of the dumplings while the tea brewed. She placed them in a steamer and set it on the stove. They then went back to the living room with their tea.

Simi settled on the couch and took a sip of her favourite tea, a special brew she got only when she visited Ammamma. She felt all the tiredness in her bones melt away.

'Now tell me everything from the start,' Ammamma said.

Simi began telling her, all about when she'd first found out about Ayush's boyfriend, until yesterday when Karan had shown her parents the video. Somewhere in the middle, the mention of Ranvir popped up, and she told Ammamma how Ranvir had first helped her come to terms with it, and also supported Ayush.

Ammamma listened with utmost attention, nodding her head and encouraging Simi to go on. Finally, when Simi finished talking, Ammamma rose from the couch and said, 'That's all? This is what Venkat got all hassled about?'

Simi stared in disbelief as Ammamma plodded back to the kitchen solemnly.

Really? That was all Ammamma had to say?

She followed Ammamma into the kitchen. 'What do you mean, that's all? We were . . . We were worried, anxious . . .'

Ammamma lifted the lid of the steamer and poked a dumpling with a toothpick to check if it was ready. 'All done. Let's eat?'

Simi was amazed and impressed that Ammamma had remained so calm. 'Call Ayush, so we can have lunch,' she simply said.

* * *

Simi went to Ayush's room, the one he always slept in when he visited Ammamma.

She knocked on his door, waited for a few minutes, before peeking inside.

A large window right across his room faced a thick grove of trees. The curtains fluttered in the breeze, which made the room cool and airy. Ayush lay on the bed, with an arm over his face.

'Sleeping?' she asked as she stepped in to take a closer look.

He removed his arm and sighed. 'How did you find me?'

Just seeing and hearing him again was such a relief. She couldn't help but smile. 'Long story. Come, first let's eat. I'm starving!'

He got out of bed with a groan and followed her.

'Here is the sleepy head! Sit down,' Ammamma said, gesturing to the wonderful spread on the table.

They had barely sat down when somebody knocked on the door.

Ayush was about to get up and rush back inside, but Ammamma grabbed his arm and stopped him.

Simi went to open the door, and her mouth fell open when she saw her parents.

'You're here!' Venkat shouted, glaring at Ayush. 'Do you have any idea how much worry you put us through?'

'Venkat, sit down and have lunch with us,' Ammamma commanded.

Venkat turned down the offer. 'I did not come here to eat.'

'I insist! In fact, let's all sit down and have a good meal before we start shooting each other down. At least with our stomachs full, we'll have a better chance of surviving that.'

'Stop joking, Ma!' Venkat said, scowling, but sat down nevertheless to a plate of steaming hot dumplings and chicken curry.

Gauri took a seat right next to him too.

'Now, we'll eat first before any discussion,' Ammamma said. 'I will not have anyone arguing and fighting while eating the food I cooked.'

Venkat shut up and focused on his plate. In fact, everyone focused on the food, heads bent.

Ammamma cleared her throat. 'I want to tell you all a beautiful story while we're eating. But I insist on no interruptions. You enjoy the food while I talk.'

Everyone at the table exchanged knowing glances. Ammamma always meant what she said and despite being the soft and lovely sort, she held a lot of respect in the family. All her children and grandchildren loved her but were also slightly afraid of her.

'You remember my cousin, Jeet?' she began. 'He was my father's older sister's son. We were very close. Jeet loved men too, and of course, because I was his favourite cousin, he told me first. I laughed at him, the silly girl I was. Jeet stopped talking to me after that. We grew distant, and for several years, we never spoke until I met him again. By then, he was married with two kids. We reconnected, and I asked him what had happened. He said he'd been miserable for many years until he told his wife the truth. They finally made peace with it after all these years.'

Venkat lifted his hand to say something but Ammamma stopped him. 'I want Ayush to be happy, that's all. Do you not want that?'

Venkat stared at the plate in front of him. 'But Ma, what about the people?'

'Who are these people who are more important to you than your own son? What would you rather have—people who don't have anything to do with you, or your son, who just wants you to accept him for who he is?'

Gauri's glance darted from Venkat to her mother-in-law. Nobody said anything.

When lunch was done, and everyone had washed up and gathered in the living room, Gauri came up to Ammamma. 'This has been a shock for us, Ma, but Venkat—'

'I've kept the cab waiting, Ma,' Venkat said, interrupting her. 'I'm glad we found Ayush. We should be leaving now.'

'Papa, can I stay with Ammamma for a few days?' That was the first time Ayush had spoken since Venkat's arrival.

'No.' Venkat glared at Ayush but Ammamma's stare beat him down.

'Let him stay if he wants to,' Ammamma insisted.

Venkat looked at his mother, his eyes turning moist. Finally, he sighed. 'As you wish.'

'Me too, Papa,' Simi said. 'I want to stay back too.'

After Venkat and Gauri left, Ayush sagged on the couch and broke into sobs. Simi gathered him into her arms and shushed him softly. 'Hey!'

'I'm sorry for running away,' he said, in between hiccups.

She smoothed his hair and hugged him tighter. 'That won't change the fact that you're my brother. I love you no matter what. I mean it.'

Ayush hugged her back and together they rocked in silence in each other's embrace.

Ammamma smiled at the easy love between her grandchildren and trundled back to the kitchen.

THIRTY-ONE

Ranvir threw the gym bag on the seat next to him and got behind the wheel of his car.

He felt so much more clear-headed after the gruelling HIIT workout. It had been almost a month since he'd started going to the gym five days a week after office and signed up for yoga thrice a week in the morning. A lot of things had changed since Parul left him.

The new Fintura app had launched. Even with teething problems, they had managed to tide through the bad times. While his analysis had been correct, the trust they'd managed to gather with some of the partner banks had paid off.

They'd connected thousands of banks and customers. Operations were running smoothly.

Ranvir started his car and opened the window to let in some air.

The butterfly on his mirror swayed with the slight breeze.

'What else do you make?' he had asked Simi, when he had stopped by the side of the road one day for sugarcane juice.

She'd raised an eyebrow at his question. 'You mean, what other grandmotherly hobbies do I have?'

He would have stared at her if she hadn't been looking straight at him. Perhaps watched that dimple imprinted on her cheek for longer as it played hide and seek with her bashful smile.

Her hair had fluttered in the light breeze, and she had pushed the errant strands off her face. 'I make a lot of things with crochet. Decorative things that have no purpose except to remind me that I still enjoy the things I enjoyed when I was younger.'

'You're very good at it.'

'It feels like travelling back in time to my teens, making fun patterns with Ammamma. It seems like I haven't grown since then.'

He chuckled. She was so unassuming, making fun of herself like it was the most natural thing to do.

He sighed at the memory, bringing his hand up to touch the butterfly, longing to feel the hands that had touched it before him. There was a man selling roses on the sidewalk. He wanted to buy one for Simi again like the day when they'd gone out for ice cream.

Parul had balked at the single rose he'd given her for their first Valentine's Day. It seemed like eons ago. She had compared it to the large bouquet of roses her ex-boyfriend Zubin had given her the year before.

Ranvir pulled on to the road. He was going to his father's place to spend the entire weekend with him and Tina as he did on Fridays after work and gym. They would play Scrabble, cook and watch a movie.

They even ate ice cream after dinner, and he remembered Simi every time he did. He wondered what she was doing now. Was she married already? He shook his head to get rid of the memories.

He tried hard to not think about her and spent more time sketching and drawing, making sure he wasn't fixated on work like before. Simi was right. He needed to sort out his life. He needed to make time for friends and family, and his hobbies.

'Will you help me shop for furniture?' he had asked Tina one day, a few weeks after Parul had left.

Tina had been delighted to accompany him to a store where he had picked a few things he loved—a comfy floor cushion for the living room, a small table and two chairs, and some pots of green to add some colour to his home. Parul had arranged for movers to pick up her leather couch and other furniture, and the rest he'd given away. He felt more at peace at home now than he'd felt in a long time.

'What are you drawing?' Tina had asked him one night at his father's house as they'd settled down after dinner.

Lalit was in the backyard, playing Scrabble on his iPad. Tina pulled out her notebook to work on her latest dress design. They were enjoying ice cream as they did every single night that Ranvir stayed over.

'Just doodling.'

Tina licked her spoon of butterscotch. 'This is so yummy.' She never tired of it even after all these years.

He couldn't help remembering Simi as he scooped another dollop of cookies 'n' cream—Simi's favourite flavour, now his.

Ayush and I finish off an entire tub in one go. It's so good!

He smiled to himself remembering the twinkle in Simi's eyes as she had admitted to eating ice cream every night with her brother, just like he enjoyed it with Tina. Simi was right. It was really good, which was why it was a temptation he gave into on weekends.

He hadn't been able to stop thinking about her when he'd visited Abhi and Deepa's new home. They'd avoided any conversation about Simi but that didn't stop him from wondering where she'd sat the day she'd visited, and what she'd thought of their home.

Now, he'd never know.

* * *

Everyone had gathered for the opening of Tina's boutique. Lalit and Ranvir flanked her as she cut the red ribbon. The guests clapped and entered the newly refurbished 400 sq. ft area decorated with soft lighting and racks filled with beautiful new outfits that Tina had designed just for the opening day.

They'd invited a few neighbours and a few of Tina's online customers. But of course, Jas had not shown up.

Lalit was so concerned about Tina's marriage that he'd pulled Ranvir aside a few days after she came home. 'Do you think she's going to end up like my friend Parag's daughter?'

Ranvir laughed. 'The one with no sex in their marriage?'

'Yes, the one who's divorced!'

That had seemed like a long time ago. Tina had cut off all contact with Jas and refused to listen to his demands to give up her passion, and had filed for divorce.

Lalit had tried to reason with her but she'd made up her mind.

Here she was, dressed in a beautiful peacock blue evening gown, her hair styled into a French bun. She smiled at her guests and fielded questions about Jas with such ease that Ranvir found it rather amusing.

When somebody asked her why Jas hadn't come, she simply said, 'We have different dreams for our lives. And no, he couldn't make it to mine.'

Ranvir smiled as he heard her say that for the third time. It was as if Jas was never in her life.

Lalit was taking care of the cocktails, serving them to the guests, and pouring himself generous drinks too.

After everybody had left, Ranvir and Tina sent Lalit home, and set down to clean up before calling it a day.

'So pretty!' Ranvir said, eyeing the gowns on display, and the small jewellery collection Tina had set up to complement her outfits. She had sold some of the pieces and booked most of them.

She gazed at him lovingly. 'I haven't had a lovelier day!'

'Wish Ma were here,' they both said in unison.

'She'd have been so proud of you, Tina,' Ranvir said. 'I'm sorry Jas never supported you.'

Tina looked up from one of the boxes she was packing up. 'Life is always as it is meant to be, and it teaches you something even if it doesn't feel like it in the moment.'

Ranvir squeezed her hand softly. 'I agree.'

'I'd never have been able to start this if it hadn't been for those fights with Jas,' she said. 'So, this turned out to be for the best!'

She was so different now from the Tina with the black eye—more confident, poised and sure of herself.

'What about you?' she asked Ranvir. 'Is Parul coming back?'

Life is always as it is meant to be. 'Our relationship had been dying much before Parul wanted to go on the trip. She wasn't happy. Neither was I.'

'Sorry to hear that,' she said like she truly meant it. 'Though Ma would be happy to see the new you—successful, handsome and . . . single,' she concluded with a laugh.

'I would do anything just to have another moment with Ma,' Ranvir said, sighing. As that truth left his mouth, another truth crystallized inside him.

He'd thought about Simi a lot in the recent past. Yet, he hadn't tried hard enough for another chance with her.

THIRTY-TWO

Abhi patted Ranvir's back as he joined his table for lunch.

'What's that big grin for?' Ranvir said. 'Did you just get a promotion?'

'Better than that. I got a status promotion. I'm not single any more, macha! I'm getting engaged.'

The sandwich sputtered out of Ranvir's mouth. 'Engaged! Wow!'

'Yeah!'

Deepa joined the table. 'What's wow?'

'Heard you guys are getting engaged.'

'Yes,' Deepa said, her eyes shining but she made a face at Abhi. 'He couldn't even wait for me to get here so both of us could break the news to you.'

Abhi tsk-tsked. 'You're here now, na?'

Ranvir chuckled. 'Guys, stop arguing. It's fantastic news!'

'You should come with your girlfriend,' Deepa said.

Ranvir ran his fingers through his hair. 'That's complicated.'

'Why?'

'Because I don't have a girlfriend. Parul and I are not together any more.'

Abhi looked like he'd been hit by a bat. 'What?' He stared at Ranvir. 'When did this happen? Why didn't you tell me?'

'Or us?' Deepa jumped in.

'It was all during the launch, so I didn't get a chance. Besides you two were never free.' All of that was partly true; the main reason was that he didn't want to talk about it. Nobody except his father and Tina knew that Parul had left. He wanted to be left alone and didn't want to explain what had happened.

Abhi crossed his arms over his chest. 'That's not fair, macha! You and Simi knew everything that was going on with us. Not fair!'

Deepa curled a stray strand of hair between her fingers. 'Speaking of Simi . . . ' she added slowly. 'I wish she were still here.'

Ranvir wished the same.

'The Murano office at Koramangala is stuffy as hell,' Deepa went on. 'I don't know what she likes about it so much.'

Ranvir wished Simi had never left.

She should have been here to hear this news. After all, it was him and Simi who had brought Abhi and Deepa together.

If only . . .

* * *

Murano's small marketing team had gathered in a room for its afternoon meeting with steaming cups of coffee.

Starting with the current campaign investments and results, they moved on to the video demo that Simi had suggested for their new range of ergonomic office chairs.

Simi was excited to discuss the new campaign she'd been working on for the past few weeks.

After her presentation, the small team of three pitched in with suggestions and more ideas.

After they were done with the meeting, Vandana looked pleased and gazed around the room appreciatively. 'I think we're good to start the new video campaign next week. Good work, everyone!'

As they dispersed towards their respective cubicles, Vandana called Simi aside. 'Good work, especially you, Simi! We've done really well with the new office range in the last few weeks. Today's idea was brilliant!'

'Thank you, Vandana!'

There was a skip in Simi's step that morning. The video campaign looked really good, and everyone thought it was a great new way to talk about ergonomic chairs. The idea had struck at her grandmother's place when she saw her working on her crochet with a wooden tray propped on her armchair.

It had given Simi an idea for their own range of ergonomic chairs, and she'd discussed it with Vandana immediately upon returning to work. The team had been excited to work on it.

Simi's fingers were crossed. All that the campaign needed now was a great start.

Although different from working with the home furniture range at BizWorks, she felt happy and more valued in a smaller team here.

Since she joined, the team had created several new campaigns and optimized the earlier ones. They'd even begun looking at influencer programmes. Things were moving along well.

When she got back to her desk after the meeting, her phone rang. It was a call from the reception.

'Someone is here to meet you, Simi.'

'Coming down in a minute,' she said.

The familiar figure at the reception made her stop her in her tracks.

It couldn't be . . . him!

There was a moment, a lurch in her stomach, a fizz of anticipation, when they looked at each other nervously, not knowing what to do.

He slowly walked towards her while she stood there gasping for breath. He reached her, looked at her for a moment and then slowly put his arms around her. She let herself be drawn to him as he pulled her closer and held her, as if to say he'd missed her.

She'd missed him too.

'Ranvir! What are you doing here?' She pulled apart, flustered, not knowing what to make of this.

Her heart thumped as her gaze skimmed over him. He was wearing a navy blue shirt and jeans, looking tall and lean, his arms and chest looking more chiselled.

His eyes crinkled. 'How have you been?'

Suddenly she was conscious of her plain attire, a maroon kurta and cream dupatta that she'd carelessly thrown on that morning, her hair loosely tied in a bun, her dry lips that could have done with a dab of lipstick after lunch.

'I'm fine.'

'I came looking for a couch.'

'Oh!'

'And I wanted to see you.'

'Oh!' *Was there no other word she could use?*

'Can we sit someplace quiet?'

'Sure.' She led him to the cafeteria, aware of him at her heels, aware of all the eyes that turned to them as they picked a table.

'Deepa is right. This place is stuffy!'

He was amusing. It came back in a flash how much she enjoyed his company. How easily he made her laugh.

She fidgeted with her dupatta nervously. 'Coffee?'

* * *

He'd held his breath as she'd walked towards him, coming down sooner than he'd expected. Seeing her again after so long had felt like *déjà* vu.

Wisps of silky bangs framed her oval face, and the rest was tied up with a band that he wished he could pull apart so he could remember the way her hair bounced in waves over her shoulders.

She wore no make-up, and yet her clear, sparkling eyes lit up her face, making it radiant. She wore a simple maroon kurta and a cream dupatta that trailed the floor behind her. It made him want to lift the dupatta off the floor and adjust it on her shoulders, but he kept his hands firmly by his side, not taking his gaze off her.

Her eyes searched his face as she came closer. 'Ranvir?' she said, sounding like she couldn't believe he was here. 'What are you doing here?'

He'd told himself he needed a couch when he'd driven all the way from Whitefield to Koramangala on a whim. When all he'd really wanted was just to see her. Especially when Deepa had inadvertently told him where she was. Or perhaps, she'd wanted him to know.

He swallowed, happy he'd decided to take a chance. Happy to see her. 'How have you been?'

'I'm fine.' She licked her lips self-consciously.

'I came looking for a couch.' *Not entirely true.*

'Oh!'

'And I wanted to see you.' *That was really the only reason.*

'Oh!' She seemed nervous to see him.

'Can we sit someplace quiet?' He hoped she'd say yes. He hoped she could stay longer.

'Sure.'

It felt like *déjà* vu again, walking to a cafeteria with her, except this one was small. The tables were cramped, the seats were tiny.

'Deepa is right. This place is stuffy!'

Her laughter lightened his chest. He felt infinitely better just because of the dimple that appeared on her cheek.

They sat down, their knees almost touching. The edge of her dupatta fluttered under the table, grazing his hand.

It felt so good to see her, sitting so close that he could smell the perfume she was wearing.

He caught hold of her soft dupatta under the table and rolled it between his fingers, holding it for a moment before letting it go, and nodded when she asked him if he wanted coffee.

Yes, please! Anything to sit right next to her and talk to her again like the old times. He wanted to know everything that had transpired since she'd left BizWorks.

She told him about her family, that her brother and parents were fine. Nothing more. But what about her wedding?

The question hovered over his lips, unasked.

'You came alone?' she said, as he still mulled over it.

Huh?

'I mean . . . to look for a couch? Did Parul not want to see it too?'

'I came alone,' he said, then paused. 'Parul and I broke up.'

Her jaw fell open. 'I'm sorry!'

'Don't be . . . '

He caught himself staring at her furrowed eyebrows, wanting to smoothen them with his fingers, wanting to glide his hand along her cheek and hold her hand across the table.

She continued to look at him dolefully.

He swallowed. 'What about you?'

It was his fault that he'd told Abhi he did not want to hear about her or what was going on in her life. And so, Deepa and Abhi had not discussed Simi when they met.

But now he was dying to know. He wanted to know if he was too late.

THIRTY-THREE

To Simi, it felt like yesterday that Ayush had gone missing, and she and Karan had argued in the car.

But after a pleasant week at Ammamma's, she'd been happier than she'd been in a long time.

When she arrived home, she was shocked to see Karan and his parents sitting in the living room talking to her parents.

She froze at the door. Ayush stopped right next to her.

Venkat beckoned her inside. 'Come in, beta. We have a few things to discuss.'

Before anyone could say anything, Babita jumped at the opportunity to go first, 'First, we have to discuss Ayush. Karan told us what happened. If he were my son, I would have—'

'But he's not your son,' Simi cut her off. 'He's my brother, and we don't have to discuss his personal life.'

'Look at how she's talking,' Babita muttered to her husband. 'What sort of daughter-in-law speaks like this?'

Gauri immediately got on the defensive. 'Please don't be upset, Babita. She's tired. They've had a long drive. We'll talk to Ayush and sort it out.'

'I'm not tired,' Simi said.

Dheeraj turned to Venkat. 'This is not our office I know, but I have a certain standard to maintain. Unless you can assure me there won't be any more problems, I'm sorry we'll have to reconsider the wedding.'

'Reconsider?' Simi snapped.

Ayush held her hand to stop her from charging at Karan's parents. 'Don't worry on my account,' Ayush said to Karan's parents and his. 'There won't be any more problems.'

Simi shook off his hand and faced Karan's family. 'I'm sorry but no assurances can be given. We're talking about real life. This is not a bargain deal. If you can't take my family as we are, then we don't want this wedding.'

'Simi!' Venkat fumed. 'Go to your room.'

Simi put her hands on her hips. 'I'm not going anywhere.'

Babita rose from her seat. 'Chalo, ji! I don't think we should waste our time here. I told you from the beginning we should have considered somebody else—' She swallowed the rest of her words. 'You were the one who told me it was a good match.'

Dheeraj glared at her. 'It was because your son wanted to marry a Muslim girl. Why else would I be in such a hurry?'

Karan blanched and turned to his father. 'So, you knew about Zara? That's why you wanted me to marry Simi?'

His mother shot him a guilty look.

'What?' Simi exploded.

Venkat looked upset. 'Dheeraj, what does this mean? Did Karan not want to marry Simi?'

'So what happened to your girlfriend? Did you ditch her?' Simi snarled at Karan.

'This isn't about me!' Karan snapped. 'It's about your brother.'

Simi crossed her arms across her chest. 'If it's about my brother then it's also about you. And I think you're a coward for not marrying the girl you love.'

Karan barged towards Simi.

Ayush grabbed Karan's hand as Simi ducked. 'Stay away from my sister. If you touch her, I'll kill you.'

Karan backed off.

Ayush glared at him. 'I may not fit into your norms, but at least I admitted that I loved someone.'

Venkat was shocked. 'Ayush!' he yelled.

Ayush stood silently next to Simi, refusing to meet Venkat's eyes.

He might have relented, but Simi wasn't done. She'd tolerated enough. Even her brother had been bold enough to admit his love. She'd accused Karan of being a coward, but wasn't she guilty too for not speaking up for herself?

'I don't like you, Karan,' she spat. 'I don't want to marry you. Whether you approve of my brother or not, I DO NOT approve of you.'

Babita's jaw fell open. 'I've never seen a girl from a respectable family speak this way!'

Dheeraj rose too and turned to Simi's father. 'Venkat, is this how your children show respect to us? I didn't expect this from your family.'

'Respect you? Marriage is a two-way street. Your son never wanted to marry my daughter. It was just a transaction to please you. I'm sorry, we don't want such boys in our family,' Venkat shot back.

Dheeraj shook with anger. 'Venkat, don't forget our friendship. Don't let our kids destroy the relationship we share.'

'Or what will you do?' Venkat laughed bitterly. 'You have nothing on me, Dheeraj. I trusted you. If you were really my friend, you would have told me the truth. My daughter's happiness is everything to me, just like your son's is to you.' He joined his palms together. 'So, please leave!'

Dheeraj stared at him, open-mouthed.

'Chalo, ji!' Babita tugged at her husband's sleeve.

Karan's family left in a huff. It was only after they were out the door that Venkat collapsed on the couch.

Gauri fetched water for him. He drank it and looked at his children teary-eyed. 'I messed up.'

Gauri sat down beside him and rubbed his arm. 'Nothing terrible has happened. Our daughter is fine.'

Venkat hugged her and wept. 'I was blind. My mother was right. Who are these people who are more important than our children? If all this hadn't happened, we would have never known what a big mistake we were about to make.'

'Better late than never, Papa,' Simi said, sitting near his feet and hugging him. 'At least now I don't have to pretend I like Karan.'

'Me either.' Ayush smiled, taking his place next to Venkat's feet. There was a long pause before he turned to Ayush, his eyes moist, and patted his shoulder lovingly.

A month later, Simi saw a photo on Kalki's Instagram of Karan with a woman. The caption read #BackTogether. He, like her, had decided not to listen to his parents.

* * *

Simi smiled at Ranvir, who was sitting next to her in the cafeteria, looking deeply into her eyes, intently listening to every word, their hands on the table, their fingers touching.

'So, the marriage was called off. We all just went back to our normal lives, as if that day never happened. Ayush is about to finish his graduation, and Papa and Ma have left his life decisions to him. They don't want him to suffocate, like Ammamma's cousin, Jeet, in a relationship that's not meant for him.'

Ranvir reached for her hand across the table. 'I wish I could say I'm sorry to hear that you didn't get married, but I'm not! I didn't want you to marry Karan.'

She laughed. 'I did what you told me to do. I did what made me happy.'

Ranvir held her hand in his, pausing for a moment. 'Did leaving BizWorks and *me* make you happy too?'

'Ranvir, I—'

'Why did you leave?' he asked softly.

She remained silent for a beat as he gazed into her eyes, looking at her with so much longing it broke her heart. 'I thought it was the best thing for both of us,' she said finally.

'You were wrong.' His voice was a whisper.

His phone rang and he shook his head. 'I have to get back to the office.'

She rose along with him, her hand still in his.

'Simi,' he said, giving her palm a light squeeze. 'Can I call you sometime?'

She looked up into his eyes and what she saw there made her heart skip a beat. 'Yes.'

He had barely left her office when her phone pinged with a message.

Can I take you out to a movie tomorrow? We have a lot to catch up on.

But what about office? she typed back.

Let's play hooky:)

She couldn't believe it! Ranvir playing hooky from work? It was a first!

THIRTY-FOUR

Ranvir stuffed a piece of toast and omelette into his mouth. He was already late.

'What's the hurry,' Tina asked him, serving him another slice of toast and omelette.

'I have to go,' he said. He'd stopped staying over at his father's place on weekends for the last few weeks.

'Where are you going again?' his father asked, looking up from his newspaper.

'Need to get the car door repaired, and I have a few errands to run.'

His father rolled his eyes and hid his face behind the newspaper.

Ranvir finished his breakfast and took his plate to the kitchen.

Tina barged into the kitchen just as he was finishing washing his plate. 'So, who is she?' Her hands were on her hips.

'Who?'

She squinted at him. 'The one you're running away to on weekends.'

Simi's hazel brown eyes flashed in front of him and her words when they had met last weekend, 'When can I see you again?'

Her office was now too far away to see her at lunch. They'd met up over the last few weekends for lunch and a movie. She'd messaged him early that morning with a sexy click of herself in her PJs, holding a cup of tea in her hand. He wished he could have met her for breakfast.

Tina clicked her fingers in front of his face, snapping him out of his reverie.

Ranvir smiled sheepishly. There was no point hiding from his sister, who could read him like a book. In fact, she'd been on his case ever since he'd started disappearing on weekends over one pretext or another. Either the plumbing in his house needed fixing, or his car needed servicing.

'I will bring her to meet you,' Ranvir said. In fact, he couldn't wait to introduce her to his father and sister. Whenever she was ready. For now, they just wanted to hang out without any real pressure to meet the families.

He headed out of the kitchen before Tina could harangue him for more details.

'At least tell me her name,' Tina called out.

'Simi!' he shouted back.

* * *

Simi never thought she'd ever think so much about what to wear, but this time, it was different.

Ranvir was coming to take her to Abhi and Deepa's engagement party, but she still hadn't selected her outfit.

She finally settled for a red and gold silk churidar kurta with a beautiful crepe dupatta. She twirled in front of the mirror for the fiftieth time.

They were going as a couple, and they hadn't told their secret to even Abhi and Deepa.

Simi had invited Ranvir home so she could introduce him to her parents. Her father had been nervous ever since she'd told him about Ranvir, but they all wanted to meet him. She could hardly wait for him to meet her family too.

She looked flushed, like a rosy-cheeked teenager going on a big date. Her hair had grown past her waist. She gathered it and brushed it until it shone. She lined her eyes with kohl, put on some eyeshadow, and dabbed her lips with gloss. She checked her watch. It was almost time. He should be here now. She was ready but nervous.

The doorbell rang, and she was the first to get it.

The sight of Ranvir took her breath away.

He was wearing a black shirt with a few buttons open at the neck. His hair was neatly combed. When he smiled at her, he looked so devastatingly handsome that her heart wouldn't stop pounding.

How did she get so lucky?

Ranvir's eyes travelled slowly from her face to her toes and back up again, looking at her as if he was seeing her for the first time.

'Ranvir?' Ayush came up from behind her. 'You're here.'

Ranvir held out his hand to Ayush.

'Simi's been talking about you all day,' Ayush said, shaking his hand. 'She made me clean up my room, dust the house and stock up on ice cream.'

Simi pinched Ayush's arm. 'And I told you not to talk too much . . . '

'Ah!' Ayush twisted in pain. 'Let go.'

* * *

Ranvir stared at her, words escaping him. She looked breathtakingly beautiful.

She smiled at him with that dazzling smile of hers that lit up her entire being. She was wearing a red and gold kurta, her eyes were lined lightly with kohl and her eyelids were dusted with a shimmer of gold.

He couldn't believe they'd made it this far. They'd been going out for a month now and every time he saw her, he couldn't help think how lucky he was. Finally, when she'd asked him to come pick her up for Deepa and Abhi's engagement, he knew she meant she wanted him to meet her parents. His hands were clammy as she took them in hers.

'Are you going to stop staring and come in?' she said.

Ayush snorted. 'I did not know you guys had it so bad.'

'Shut up!' She frowned and slapped his arm. 'Go away and call Ma.'

'Ma!' he called out, not budging or taking his eyes off the two, obviously enjoying it all.

Ranvir remembered the time he'd dropped Simi at the gate and wondered if he'd ever come up to her house. Finally, here he was.

Simi tugged at his hand, interrupting his thoughts, and pulled him inside. 'Come in.'

'Yes, come in,' Ayush mimicked, receiving a playful slap from Simi again.

Simi's mother came rushing out of the kitchen, wearing a big, happy smile. Her eyes shone, just like Simi's. 'Hello, Ranvir! So nice to meet you. Simi has been talking about you all morning.'

'All good things, I hope, ' Ranvir said.

'Mostly,' she replied.

'Ma . . . ' Simi interrupted with a groan as Ranvir's lips parted in surprise.

'No, just kidding.' Her mother laughed.

Ranvir relaxed and broke into a smile.

Simi's father joined them on the couch, hardly saying much, except the usual questions, what do you do, and such. He almost seemed a bit nervous. Just like Ranvir.

Simi's mother fawned over him, offering him tea and snacks, while her brother teased him and Simi about their ice cream date.

As they were leaving, Simi's father finally said, 'Come again.'

'Yes, come again!' Ayush added for effect. His father scowled at him.

Simi looked happy as she held on to his hand while waiting for the elevator. 'I think that went well, don't you?'

'I don't know. Did your father like me?'

'Might be better if you talk about cars and cricket the next time you see him.'

'Glad you told me,' Ranvir said with a smirk.

She giggled. 'You're welcome! But I think that "come again" was a sign that he liked you.'

The elevator door opened, and there were already four to five people inside. There was barely any place for the two of them, but they managed to squeeze in.

He pulled her towards him, and she leaned against his chest. He wrapped his arms around her waist and held her tightly. He breathed in her sweet smell and wished he could kiss her.

'I hope it is a good sign,' he whispered in her ear.

She turned around to face him, smiling sweetly. 'Yes,' she whispered back, wrapping her arms around him and they stayed there like there was nowhere else they wanted to be.

* * *

The party was in full swing when they entered Deepa and Abhi's house. Simi recognized a few people from the office.

Deepa rushed to her, smiling, and gave her a hug. 'I'm so happy to see you.' She looked at Ranvir, his arm casually around Simi's shoulder. 'You came together?' she said, her eyes widening with surprise. 'So, you're . . . ?'

'Yes.' Simi broke into a grin.

'That's— I can't wait to tell Abhi!'

As they walked into the party, Champak came towards them. 'Hey, Simi! Great to see you!'

'Good to see you too. How are you?'

'Missing the usual *tête-à-tête* between you and Deepa . . . ' he said, sighing. 'I was hoping you'd say you were missing us.'

She laughed. 'So you're not getting any gossip now?'

'Sadly, no. When are you coming back?'

'Coming back? I like it there.'

'I thought so. But Deepa is miserable, and so am I,' he said, to Simi's utter surprise. For Champak to admit that he was missing anyone was a first. 'And the meetings aren't the same without you any more.'

She couldn't help but smile at the memory of Champak at the morning meets. He meant he had one less person to criticize during those meetings. *Too bad!*

Abhi eyed them as they approached him. 'Why wasn't I the first to know about you two?'

'That's why we're here together,' Ranvir said, smiling cheekily. 'Now, you know.'

Deepa dragged Simi off to meet the others. They met, chatted and laughed with old friends. Soon it was time to exchange rings. Everyone clapped as Deepa slid a ring on to Abhi's finger. Abhi did the same, except the ring was too tight for Deepa.

She frowned. 'Didn't you get my measurements?'

Abhi looked hurt. 'Sorry.' But then he laughed and pulled out another ring. 'Just wanted to give you one last chance if you wanted to back out,' he joked, holding the ring but not slipping it on to her finger.

Deepa gave him a coy smile. 'Don't want to.'

He slid the ring on to her finger amid claps and cheers. After watching the happy couple make it official, everyone turned their attention to the sumptuous food and drinks.

Ranvir and Simi slipped away to the balcony after the delicious meal.

Ranvir put an arm around Simi's waist as they leaned against the railing and watched the beautiful sky. A crescent moon shone in front of them. It was a beautiful night. 'I can't believe we set them up, and now they're engaged.'

'Yeah, we did it!' She wrapped her arm around his waist and leaned into his shoulder. 'Didn't we have a bet?'

'I forgot what it was,' Ranvir said.

She turned to look at him. 'That's not fair!'

He flicked her nose and laughed.

She couldn't take her eyes off him. 'Ranvir . . . '

'Hmmm . . . ?'

'What colour are the walls of your house?'

'My house?' he asked.

'Yeah, what colour are they?'

He looked down into her eyes. 'You want to see?'

'Yes!' She nodded emphatically.

THIRTY-FIVE

Ranvir unlocked the door to his home and welcomed Simi in.

She took a step in, and the first thing she noticed was the Murano couch in the living room, sitting there with such grace and beauty. It could not be missed. He was glad he'd finally purchased it last week.

Simi looked at it and then at him, a confused look crossing her eyes. 'So you did come to Murano to buy a couch!'

For a moment, he didn't understand what she was saying, then suddenly it dawned on him. *The couch!*

He cupped her face in his hands. 'No, I came to see you!' he said, his heart beating so loudly that he could hardly hear himself. 'I didn't even need a couch that day.'

She placed her hands over his and held his gaze.

'I bought this just a few days ago. I figured'—he realized that he was blushing—'you might like to come visit sometimes, and we'd have a place to sit.'

He eyed the rust-coloured beauty that had stolen his heart the day he'd seen it in the showroom. He'd told himself he'd buy it if Simi came back into his life. And here she was.

She walked up to the couch and touched it, her fingers skimming over the soft fabric. He stood there watching her as she sat down and looked up to meet his gaze.

Something in her face changed just then; there was a twitch of those lips. A . . . smile?

The next moment, her eyes grew wide and she flashed him a naughty look. Before he could understand what was happening, she picked a cushion and threw it at him. It hit his face.

He hadn't seen that coming. Then, she sent another one flying at him that almost got him again.

Too late! He shook his head as he saw the next one in her hand. He was next to her in a jiffy throwing himself on the couch and grabbing her hand to stop her.

They tussled over the cushion, her laughter tinkling in the room. It was music to his ears.

'That's for taking so long to come see me,' she said, as she threw the last cushion at him, knocking the breath out of his chest.

He doubled over, feigning injury.

'Are you okay?' Her eyes were suddenly clouded with concern.

He was ready for her this time.

Before she could see it coming, he went for her dupatta. Twisting it around his hand, he pulled her towards him.

She was yanked forward, her nose inches from his, and her eyes wide and clear bottomless pools.

He laughed at her, enjoying every bit of her surprised expression.

She frowned and tugged at her dupatta to claim it back, unfurling it instead, like a translucent sail.

He leaned in and kissed her, pressing his lips to hers.

She moaned as he deepened the kiss, opening her mouth to let him in.

Her hands mapped his hair, his neck, his jaw and then the corners of his lips as if she was touching and feeling him for the first time.

Like she couldn't get enough of him.

A throaty sigh escaped him, and his hands moved against her, roaming across every inch of her until she was squirming and giggling with delight. He lifted her, and in one sweeping move, she was on his lap.

Not expecting it in the least, she smiled at him through hooded eyes and straddled him, her thighs pressed against his. He smothered her with kisses all over her face and ears and the side of her neck until she was moaning with pleasure, arching into him, pressing her body against his, her hips thrusting with longing.

He buried his head in her cleavage, wanting to devour her. She pushed him back on to the couch, and they shifted and adjusted in the narrow space until she was on top of him.

He squeezed her waist and sighed. 'Am I being punished for taking so long to come see you?'

She watched him with suggestive eyes. 'If you want me to.'

With a groan, he lifted her kurta, pulling it off her, while she fumbled with the buttons of his shirt, tugging it off until they were skin to skin.

'I like being made love to rather than being punished,' he heard himself croak with wanting.

It was cramped on the couch as they lay entwined in each other's arms, but hot and sexy nevertheless.

With a shy smile, she ran her fingertips over the muscles of his chest, dipping into their centre. Her lips followed the same path, sucking, kissing. He lay back and let her explore, grunting with pleasure as she kissed her way from his head to his neck and chest and down his body.

'I like being made love to too,' she said when she reached the band of his jeans, her voice husky and bursting with need.

Her words pushed him over the edge. He raised himself above her and soon the words were swept aside as was everything else they were wearing.

* * *

She savoured his feverish kisses. She wanted this. She wanted him. She'd dreamt of this moment so many times.

Her eyes were moist and filled with longing.

'I love you,' he said, cupping her face and pulling her closer.

She shut her eyes and revelled in the words she'd waited to hear for a long time. It felt like everything she'd imagined.

'I love you too,' she said, tears filling up her eyes as he caressed her with such love and gentleness and looked at her as if he couldn't have enough of her.

She could barely wait, when he said, 'Hold on for a sec. I'll get the condom from my drawer.'

When they made love, it was slow and soft at first. Her body tingled with awareness, burning everywhere he touched her, and even where he didn't. It was nothing like she'd ever imagined as he got her warm and wet and ready.

An intense wave took over, and like the opening of floodgates, desire surged through her. She squeezed her eyes shut as he entered her and their bodies melded together. With each thrust, the swells of pleasure grew and grew until it was beyond her, until she shuddered and let out a cry. He groaned and shook, coming with a shudder right after her. Panting, they collapsed against each other like a mush of limp bodies.

'A memorable inauguration for this couch,' he whispered several minutes later, his breath still fast, his arm around her. Tucking a stray lock of hair behind her ear with the other, he looked at her with such devotion that she blushed.

She shivered in the cool air, her nipples pebbling as he pushed off her slightly.

'You're cold,' he said, running his warm tongue over her breasts.

She was grateful for his warmth.

He skimmed his hand over her bare waist and gazed at her, a sudden tear spilling from the corner of his eye. 'I'm so lucky to have you,' he said, his voice breaking.

Her heart squeezed with love. She hugged him to her chest. 'I'm so lucky to have you too.'

They rocked together, chest to chest. Finally, he pulled away and turned to his side, gazing at her with open hunger for more. 'Maybe I could show you the colours of my room.'

'I know I'm going to love them,' she said, with a grin.

He kissed her on the nose. 'I see.'

'Yes.' She wrapped her arms around him, and let out a deep, long sigh of contentment, staring into his eyes with a hope that this night may never end.

Acknowledgements

This is how it all began: set in a co-working space, this was just a seedling of an idea that grew into a story about two widely different characters and their lives, inside and outside the workplace. I discovered these flawed and diverse characters as I was bringing them on to the page. The more I explored and delved into the many facets of relationships—permanent and transient—and their juxtapositions, the more fascinated I became. Thinking back now, I really don't know how the puzzle pieces came together, but I'm incredibly proud of what it turned out to be. And, here we are—a living, breathing book that's in your hands.

Huge thanks to you, dear reader, for picking up this book. I hope you enjoyed reading this book as much as I enjoyed writing it. Thank you for coming along with me on all my book journeys, and if you are new to my stories, I hope you love this story and find something inside that deeply resonates with you.

Roshini Dadlani, my first editor and the person who discovered me. This book would not have been possible without you. From picking the co-working space idea during our very first discussion to all our subsequent interactions, I've really enjoyed working with you.

Priya Gopalan, my darling sister, I'm so deeply grateful for having you in my life. From our shared love for stories and storytelling, the moment we both gushed over this story idea, I knew this was the story I wanted to write. This story owes its shape to all those exciting weekends of discussions and brainstorming. I'm out of words to express how much you being a part of Simi and Ranvir's story means to me.

Thank you for always being close by, Nitya Nair, for those times when I have one of those story dilemmas and need to talk through a problem. You always pull me out of the deepest holes that I manage to dig up for myself.

Sanil Nair, I could not have made Ranvir a financial whiz without your knowledge of start-ups and financial apps. You are a true ninja star!

Thanks, Nicholas Rixon, my second editor-in-charge, for the delightful metaphor that you came up with for this book and my writing: 'It's like a cup of Darjeeling tea. You need a spoonful of tea leaves (second flush), hot water and a kettle. You need to make sure you don't over brew it; four to five minutes max. No sugar. And when you take that first sip, that flavour lifts you up. It's never overpowering, always hits the right spots, and wholly refreshing.' You are as wonderful and refreshing as editors come.

Copy-edits are never fun, but Saloni Mital made it look breezy and effortless. Thanks for making this book shine.

I'm so grateful for the opportunity to work with the amazing team at Penguin. Thank you for believing in me and for all your efforts in bringing this story out into the world.

To my loving family and friends, thanks for supporting me and always cheering me on.

Sanil, Abhi, Nitu, my angels, you are the best! I'm forever grateful for having you by my side.

Last but not least—dear God, thank you!

The Girl with a Secret Crush
(an Excerpt)

Malini peered at her computer screen, then rubbed her eyes, shook her head, and looked closely at the words again. Bestselling author, Vikram Mathur's exact words were: "Tara lay there, unmoving, and Vicky knew it was over."

Malini's hands involuntarily shot up over her gaping mouth. Vikram had killed Tara, a character from his latest book, the cute neighbour who had brought the hero, Vicky, and his college crush together. Malini couldn't believe her eyes. This couldn't be happening to a beloved character like Tara. It caused a feeling of panic in her chest, and the page blurred before her eyes.

She had to tell her boss that this scene was going to tank Vikram's sales. It was a sure-shot disaster. She turned towards her boss, editor-in-chief, Sanghamitra Banerjee's cabin, before she realised that her boss was on a long-deserved vacation to Igatpuri, and unlikely to get back before next week, which meant she had to wait for her return.

Sighing, she shut down the wide screen that the office had provided her for easy proofreading. She hadn't refused the fancy screen, even though, she'd been able to work perfectly well without one, like back in the days when she was a bright-eyed, literature graduate, fresh out of college. She was damn good at what she did, even then, with a smaller screen, a tinier office, and shitty work. But once Vikram's books had started coming in, her work life had changed. She'd read every one of his books ever since he'd started writing. In the last eight years, he'd published fourteen books, and she'd proofread every single one. Even though the pay was bad, and she had never got a promotion, her love for Vikram's books was what kept her at Jayco Publishing for this long—or that's what she told herself. His books were funny, and they could also make her cry.

Malini had always been the quiet sort, lost in her world of books. When her colleagues went out for coffee, she preferred to sit in the park and read a book or go to the movies. She loved movies as much as books. When a new movie came out, she'd go and watch it alone. Then, she'd analyse it to death. She'd wonder why the heroine ran away. Or she'd chuckle at the funny scenes or a clever plot idea that made the story shine. In short, she was in love with stories. All sorts of stories. And especially, Vikram's stories.

She wondered what Vikram did when he wasn't writing. She'd watched all his interviews, and read every blog post he'd written. Sometimes, she thought she had had an overdose of him and his stories, as she could easily visualise his characters and sometimes predict what they would do next, in his books. That's why Tara's dying had come as a shock. She'd never expected it. She had to tell Sanghamitra about this gaffe.

She also wondered when she sat alone, curled up with his books, even earlier ones she'd read a million times, what it would be like if she ever got to meet him. What would she feel? What would she say?

She was the girl with a secret crush on him but how could she ever talk to him? Or even see him. Sanghamitra handled his account, and all these years she'd been the only one who'd met and spoken to him. She sighed again.

Maybe that day would probably never come, she thought idly as she picked up her bag, and locked her drawers. Of what use would it be to think of Vikram when he hardly even knew she existed?

When Malini peeked around her cubicle, the corridor was empty. The entire office was empty. As usual, she had decided to stay back and work late because the peace allowed her to work faster and enjoy the solitude as she drowned in the story she was working on. But it meant locking up the office too, and handing the keys over to the watchman at the gate. She was almost at Sanghamitra's cabin to get the keys, when the phone on Sanghamitra's desk started ringing. The sudden shrill trilling blasted through the silence, startling her.

She put her hands on her chest to calm her nerves. It was strange to hear that phone ring. Nobody ever called on the regular phone anymore. She decided to let it go. Whoever was calling obviously knew the cell phone number to call, or maybe it was a wrong number. She wasn't going to pick it up. The rings stopped, and started again by the time she had picked up the keys from the peg on the wall.

She almost dropped them out of fright. It rang for longer, and all she wanted to do was get out of the office. As suddenly as the ringing had started, it stopped. She had already let herself out of the cabin when it started again. She puffed out a frustrated breath. Who the hell was this annoying caller?

She was almost about to pick the receiver when the ringing stopped. Thank you, she mimed.

She'd just turned around when it started again. Darn! She picked it up. "H—"

"Where the hell is Sanghamitra? Why is her phone switched off?" a voice barked into the phone.

Malini almost dropped the receiver sensing the extreme irritation of the caller—someone who probably knew Sanghamitra well enough to sound so angry. "She's...she's gone to Igatpuri," she mumbled.

"Igatpuri! And who the bloody hell pays her to do that! How can she go without telling me?"

The loudness of his voice struck her dumb. It was a few minutes before she found her voice. "Did you need something, Sir?"

"Yes! I thought you'd fallen asleep. I need Sanghamitra to call me back ASAP. Tell her Vikram Mathur wanted to talk to her urgently."

"Vi . . .Vikram—"

He had cut the call.

Malini stared at the receiver in her hand for a full minute before putting it down.

She couldn't believe she had just spoken to the man himself. The man who sounded nothing like the man of her dreams. The man who kept her awake all night when she held his new book. The man who had the power to make her do anything he wanted. With trembling hands, she put down the receiver, fished out her cell phone from her bag, and dialled her boss's husband. That was the number that Sanghamitra had given her in case of dire emergencies. And this certainly did seem like one.

In two rings, someone picked up, and the next instant Sanghamitra's voice boomed through. "Something urgent?"

Malini told her what Vikram had said.

"God, what do I do with Vikram!" Sanghamitra whined. "Didn't you tell him I was on vacation?"

"Of course, I did."

Sanghamitra exhaled sharply. "I can't believe he needs me every time I want to take a break. Thanks. I'll call him."

When Malini locked up the office, she wasn't thinking of Peepal, her cat, waiting for her at home, or the milk she had to buy on the way because her milkman hadn't turned up for two mornings. She was thinking of spending the rest of her evening curled up with a glass of wine, and her personal copy of one of Vikram's early books, even though he had sounded every bit a high-handed, obnoxious snob. Of course, he had been upset and anxious. She gave him that little excuse to be rude.

By nine p.m. she was already done with dinner, and on her second glass of wine. Peepal rested by her side while she was curled up in bed, engrossed in the climax of

Vikram Mathur's very first book, the one she still loved, the one she'd re-read almost fifty times.

The phone rang out of the blue, making her jump. The half-filled glass in her hand swayed dangerously. She tried to find her phone by the sound of its ring, and then realised it was all the way around the bed, at the far corner of the room. How she hated to be disturbed from her cosy position in bed!

With a grunt, she got up and made it across the room, swaying happily. This had to be her mom telling her about a new boy she had found on shaadi.com. What she needed was a break! A break from feeling terrible about her age, her single status, and the fact that the only living thing she talked to, besides her colleagues at work, was Peepal.

It turned out to be Sanghamitra, a very unlikely caller at this hour, breaking office rules for the first time—no work calls at home. She attributed it to Vikram's call to the office earlier. For once, Malini wasn't annoyed, but excited and feeling light because Vicky from the book was about to enter his girlfriend's balcony. Adrenalin rushed through her as she picked up the call. "Hello?" She let out an involuntary giggle. "Yeah?"

"You're going to meet Vikram," Sanghamitra started off without preamble.

"But he's meeting Tara." Malini smiled, her eyes blurry with intoxication. Now, where the hell had she put her glass?

"What!"

Sanghamitra's sharp tone was like a slap; it ended her silliness even though what she did at home in her own free time was nobody's business. Sanghamitra didn't know how tipsy she was.

"I'm sending you the place and time. Be there tomorrow." And just when Malini was starting to feel so confused that her head spun, Sanghamitra added, "Please!"

As it turned out from what Sanghamitra was blabbering from half way across the country, on the only vacation she had taken in probably all the years since Malini had known her, was that Vikram was having a major writer's block. He wanted to discuss the story problem of his latest book, and he would have nobody but Sanghamitra to discuss it with. And Sanghamitra had tried really hard to convince him that her substitute would be good, probably even better, since in her own words to Malini, "You're the only one who's read all his books. You know his stories like nobody else does. You're the best one to go if I can't."

How could Malini refuse? On top of which, this was turning out to be what she had wanted most of her adult life. It was freaking unbelievable!

Sanghamitra was adamant about wanting her vacation more than anything else. It would be at least two more weeks before she was back, she said. Malini understood how it must have felt to have no time to give to a marriage, no time to have babies, no time to relax.

When she tried to tell Sanghamitra that Vikram had killed a favourite character in his book, Sanghamitra had only one word for her. "Go!" and four more, "Discuss it with him."

Sanghamitra finally hung up with, "And, Malini, please don't let me down."

But suddenly Malini wasn't so sure about this. Her knees wobbled. Maybe it was the effect of the wine. Her stomach churned with anxiety. What if this meeting didn't go well?

The next morning, still nervous, she had to remind herself that meeting Vikram was not the end of the world. She had to stop acting so jittery and behave like a grown-up.

Looking into the mirror, she talked to herself, "Malini Vaidyanathan. Unmarried. Twenty-nine years old. Cat lover. Lives alone. Has a crush on Vikram Mathur. Is meeting him today."

She fidgeted in front of her wardrobe, waffling over what to wear. She didn't have too many clothes, let alone fancy ones. And nothing seemed good enough for meeting Vikram. She touched her hot cheeks and stared into her wardrobe, confused. Finally she settled on a long skirt she'd purchased on a whim a few months back. What better opportunity to inaugurate the lovely powder blue, mulmul material? She topped it with a white tucked-in collared blouse and was happy with the look. A bit girlish, yet one that radiated a good deal of professionalism and poise. There was no one to ask if she looked good after she'd worn it, except for her cat.

"Peepal, do I look nice?"

"Meow."

"Great!"

She twirled around in front of her mirror. The skirt draped around her hips like a dream, and it was very soft. It complemented her honey skin tone, and she hoped it would help with today's test of showing off a confidence she didn't feel. She pinned up her waist length hair into a neat little chignon, put on her kitten heels, which looked cute on her dainty feet, and was off to the rendezvous, trying to keep down the butterflies in her stomach.

She hated to be late. Half-an-hour before the scheduled time, she was at the hotel, The Grand Heron, and looking into the receptionist's warm eyes. Sanghamitra had said he wanted to meet her by the poolside.

"Please wait by the pool, Ma'am! I'll let Mr. Mathur know you're here, when he arrives."

She nodded dazedly, her mind unsettled, her heart beating as if there was a fire alarm going off. She was finally going to meet him!